Addicted to the Drama

Lock Down Publications and Ca$h Presents

Addicted to the Drama

A Novel by *Jamila Mathis*

Lock Down Publications
P.O. Box 1482
Pine Lake, Ga 30072-1482

First Edition November 2017
Printed in the United States of America

Lock Down Publications
Like our page on Facebook: Lock Down Publications @
www.facebook.com/lockdownpublications.ldp
Cover design and layout by: **Dynasty Cover Me**
Book interior design by: **Shawn Walker**
Edited by**: Sunny Giovanni**

Stay Connected with Us!

Text **LOCKDOWN** to 22828 to stay up-to-date with new releases, sneak peaks, contests and more…

Thank you!

Submission Guideline.

Submit the first three chapters of your completed manuscript to ldpsubmissions@gmail.com, subject line: Your book's title. The manuscript must be in a .doc file and sent as an attachment. Document should be in Times New Roman, double spaced and in size 12 font. Also, provide your synopsis and full contact information. If sending multiple submissions, they must each be in a separate email.

Have a story but no way to send it electronically? You can still submit to LDP/Ca$h Presents. Send in the first three chapters, written or typed, of your completed manuscript to:

LDP: Submissions Dept
Po Box 1482
Pine Lake, Ga 30072

DO NOT send original manuscript. Must be a duplicate.

Provide your synopsis and a cover letter containing your full contact information.

Thanks for considering LDP and Ca$h Presents.

Acknowledgements

First I like to thank God for helping me discover my talent in writing and guiding me through this difficult but rewarding journey. I like to thank my family and fiends for their never-ending love and support. I want to give a shout out to my fellow alumni and the current students of Dougherty Comprehensive High School of Albany, Georgia and Savannah State University of Savannah, Georgia. I also want to thank my readers who have been with me since day one during my Cynthia Blue days (Don't worry I'll finish the Bryson Blood Wars Series LOL!). You guys are my everything! I appreciate you giving my books a chance, giving me feedback and encouraging me to keep pushing. I also want to thank my CBC family for giving me a chance even though things didn't quite work out, but hey things happen. Thank you Nyeshia, The Cunning Linguist and Paradise Taylor.

Last but not least I like to thank my beloved C.E.O. Ca$h aka Big Sweetie Who Never Smiles (That's my pet name for him LOL!). Thanks for giving me this opportunity to join LDP. I hope I make you proud and I hope we have a long, flourishing and successful professional relationship and make big things happen in this industry.

Also to my beloved C.O.O., Coffee. Thanks for the kind words and encouragement. Your professionalism, optimism and highly positive attitude have opened my eyes on so many levels. You are one of the very few people I've met who delivers harsh criticism and still be sweet and gentle. It makes it hard to argue LOL!

Thanks Ca$h and Coffee for opening your doors to me and the rest of the LDP family for making me feel welcome and I hope y'all like what I came up with. Enjoy! *hugs and kisses*

Dedication

Reico Lamont Welch
B.K.A.
R.L. Welch

February 22, 1976 – November 19, 2016

I like to dedicate this project to the man who gave me my very first chance in this industry. Thanks Reico for giving my pen a chance under your publishing company G-Princess Publishing and helping me get my foot in the door. No matter how far I travel down this road in my literary journey I'll always carry your wisdom with me.

Chapter 1

Macal was laying in a hotel bed in a deep slumber. In his arms was Lolette, his fiancée's best friend. In the wee hours of the night, he had snuck the lowdown bitch in his room where they had fucked and fucked like there was no tomorrow, and neither one of them felt guilty about their nasty indiscretion.

Their sweat drenched bodies were intertwined with Lolette's juicy right titty in Macal's mouth like a pacifier, with his hand squeezing her lovely onion ass. Lolette's leg was slung over Macal's body causing their dripping wet cum covered genitals to rub against each other.

Still in their fuckfest induced slumber, neither of them heard the door open or the woman step into the room and softly close the door behind her. She moved quietly, like a panther.

The smell of dick, pussy, ass and balls permeated throughout the room, invading her nose. *These dirty ass muthafuckas been doing the most up in this bitch!* Her face balled up as her eyes surveyed the room.

Clothes were scattered all over the floor. Lolette's nasty ass thong was up on top of the TV, and last but not least, the lover's naked bodies were laying on the bed in their disgusting afterglow without a care in the world.

Ignoring the funk, Tylisha took a deep breath and walked over to Macal's side of the bed. She leaned over in his ear and yelled. "Nigga, wake the fuck up! You're busted, muthafucka! You and this trifling bitch!" She snatched their clothes off of the floor and slung them onto their faces.

Macal and Lolette shot straight up, at the same time.

"What the fuck!" His heart pounded hard in his chest.

Lolette didn't give a damn about being caught; the dick had been worth whatever drama they were about to face. *As long as my pussy is satisfied, fuck the rest.*

Tylisha shook her head in disgust. "Macal, nigga, you know this is beyond foul!"

Macal looked up into the face of his baby sister and let out a huge sigh of relief. For a minute, he thought he'd been caught creeping by his fiancée. He was relieved but still hot.

"Girl, what the fuck is wrong with you?" He yawned. "Busting up in here like you on some crazy shit! How in the fuck did you find us and get a key?"

"None of your motherfucking business!" Tylisha replied with rudeness, and then switched to a calm, sarcastic tone. "But since you asked nicely, I'll tell you. While I was at Fallon's bachelorette party— you know, that sweet, beautiful chick you're supposed to be marrying in a few hours?" She then pointed at Lolette and said, "At the party I overheard her two-faced, nasty, hoe ass, so-called BFF over here making plans to sneak away with you."

Lolette was about to say something but Tylisha shut her ass down with the death stare and turned her attention back to her brother. "It took a while but I found the right hotel. How did I get a spare key? All I had to do was give the front desk clerk a bullshit sob story and, well, look at me." Tylisha flashed her sexy smile that lit up her beautiful facial features that her and Macal's deceased mother Belinda passed down to her.

"So, what the hell are you doing here?" Macal asked with a yawn.

Tylisha frowned. *You have got to be the most ignorant nigga in the world.* "I'm here to save your reckless ass."

"From what?"

"Oh, I don't know. How about trying to stop you from making the biggest mistake of your life? Trying to prevent you from fucking up a good thing with a good woman by fucking these nasty ass hoes." Tylisha rolled her eyes and sighed. She loved her big brother dearly, but she didn't get him at all. In the business world Macal is a genius being the owner of one of the most successful investment firms in the country but when it comes to women, the nigga can't find his way out of a paper bag. Even if you gave him a map, a two year old would understand and pointed at a straight shot direction. "I don't know what the fuck I'm going to do with you. Your ass needs a lifetime supply of Thot-Away spray and Hoe Be Gone cream."

Tylisha glanced over at Lolette who was taking her sweet time getting dressed and mumbling under her breath. She ignored it and said, "Psst!" imitating a spray can, and Lolette stomped out of the room all pissed off and slammed the door behind her. "That bitch know better." Tylisha said with a chuckle, and turned her attention back to Macal.

"Can a man enjoy his last night as a single man in peace?" Macal groaned.

"Ditching your own bachelor party at Magic City to fuck some scandalous ass hoe is not part of the itinerary." Tylisha said. "Now let's get you dressed and on the way to the wedding and hope you don't fuck this up like you did all your other relationships."

Macal took offense to Tylisha's last statement. "Wait a fucking minute—"

Tylisha cut him off. "Save the bullshit excuses and get your ass ready, ASAP!"

"Alright, I'll get dressed! Shit!" Macal said with defeat.

Tylisha saw Macal was about to put on his pants and held up her hand like she was a crossing guard. "Hold it! Get your black ass in that shower and wash your ass real good first. The last thing you need to do is come to your own wedding smelling like rotting, crusty ass pussy. You got fifteen minutes so hurry your ass up!" She ordered. She saw how slow Macal was moving and rolled her eyes. "Pick up the pace, nigga! My kids move faster and have more discipline. That's a fucking shame!"

Macal passed Tylisha on his way to the bathroom and commented with sarcasm. "I love you too."

"Very funny," Tylisha replied with a fake smile and gave Macal a bag with fresh clothes, soap, cologne and other hygiene products inside. "Enough small talk. Get your ass in that shower this instant," she demanded.

"Yes ma'am," Macal mocked. "I love you, baby girl."

"Yeah! Yeah! I love your fucked up ass too! Now hurry the fuck up!"

Macal entered the bathroom and closed the door. Tylisha shook her head and whispered to herself, “Sometimes I feel like I’m raising three kids instead of two.”

“I heard that!” Macal yelled in the shower.

“Good!” Tylisha yelled back and sat in a chair, waiting on Macal to come out.

***

Fallon was in the dressing room at the Emory Conference Center Hotel getting ready for her wedding to Macal. Her Aunt Naomi was helping her with her makeup. Her career as a makeup artist came in handy and she traveled all the way from their hometown of Columbus, Georgia to make her only niece’s wedding.

“You look so happy and beautiful, baby.” Naomi said to Fallon while putting the finishing touches on Fallon’s makeup. Fallon’s long, thick, natural jet black hair was braided in goddess cornrows. Her glowing brown skin and perfect size eight figure made her wedding dress flawless.

“Thanks, Aunt Naomi.” Fallon said and kissed her beloved aunt on the cheek. “I’m glad you could make it.”

“Girl, you know good fucking well I’m not missing your big day.”

Fallon then sighed heavily as her mind drifted off to a sad place.

“What’s wrong, baby?”

“I’m good, Aunt Naomi,” Fallon replied. “I just wish that momma was here. That’s all.”

Naomi pulled Fallon into her arms. “I know, baby. I miss her too.” Naomi tried to hold back the tears at the thought of her baby sister Capri, who died when Fallon was five-years old and Naomi took her in and raised her like the child she always wanted. Naomi will forever hate the worthless deadbeat fuck nigga who she holds completely responsible for Capri’s death. The bastard played with her innocent baby sister’s heart and left her when she was six months pregnant like the bitch nigga he was. He was never heard from again and Capri never recovered from the hurt and betrayal.

"Knock! Knock!" Tylisha said as she knocked on the door twice.

"Come in Tylisha," Fallon said.

Tylisha walked in and greeted Fallon with a big hug. "Hey, girl. You look fabulous."

"Thanks, and so do you," Fallon complimented her.

Tylisha turned around to show off her knee length, strapless light blue dress hugging her well-toned curves she managed to keep up after having two babies, her deep peanut colored skin and long medium brown, curly hair flowing in the breeze.

"Thanks for decorating the wedding. I really appreciate it." Fallon said.

"Anytime," Tylisha replied with a smile, and gave Naomi a hug. "Hey, Ms. Potter."

"Hey, baby, great job with the wedding decorations," Naomi said. "Excellent work."

"Well, it's not really work if you love and enjoy what you're doing," Tylisha slightly bragged. She's the best interior decorator in Atlanta, Georgia.

"Hey, Fallon." Lolette entered the dressing room, making herself known in her designated hot pink Maid of Honor dress, putting on her fake ass supportive friend act. "Are you ready to go through with it?"

"Yes, I am Lolette," Fallon answered with glow and hugged her best friend since childhood. "How are you doing today?"

"Better than great," Lolette blushed, not attempting to hide her hoeish afterglow.

During the hug, Fallon noticed the strong cologne scent on Lolette and her skin slightly moistened with sweat. "You must've had a very festive night." She teased. "Who's the lucky man?"

"Wouldn't you like to know," Lolette teased but was serious. She'd love to turn Fallon's life upside down. That was just the kind of foul, backstabbing bitch she was. "After the party, my night was great and orgasmic."

"You don't say."

“Yes, I do say.” Lolette boasted. “He couldn’t take his hands off me for nothing. Not that I wanted him to.” She and Fallon giggled to each other. The fact that Fallon was completely unaware that she was giggling over her best friend fucking her soon to be husband made Lolette all giddy inside.

Naomi and Tylisha glanced at each other. No words were exchanged but they shared the exact same thought. Lolette was a disgusting, heartless bitch. Naomi never liked Lolette and always thought the sneaky little bitch was no good, took advantage of Fallon’s kindness and had a strong feeling she and Macal were fucking. The audacity of her rubbing it in Fallon’s face on the sly made Naomi want to pull out her razor and cut that hoe.

Tylisha couldn’t stand Lolette at all. Not only was she a nasty hoe, but a disloyal hoe at that. That’s much worse in her book. Tylisha hoped one day Macal would grow the fuck up and leave these hoes alone. Lolette in particular. “Let me check on Welton and Ayla. A mother’s work is never done.” Tylisha said and took her leave. Actually, she really didn’t need to check on the kids, because thanks to her parenting they were highly independent for their ages. She just used them as an excuse, because if she spent another minute around Lolette, her ass was gonna itch.

Chapter 2

Nighttime on the other side of town…

"Where the fuck is that nigga at?" Thuy yelled out in pissed off frustration. She paced back and forth in the living room of her boyfriend, Atlanta Braves starting pitcher, Jeromy Fuller's mansion. Thuy was hoping the relationship wouldn't end in a total disaster like the others. In the beginning things were perfect. Jeromy was the perfect romantic, loving gentleman. Then, as usual, somewhere down the line history started repeating itself. The blatant evidence of infidelity, finding out about the affairs, and eventually Thuy either ends the relationship, or she gets tossed out on her ass for the side bitch.

Now Thuy's current relationship with Jeromy started to really go straight to shit when she announced her pregnancy. Thuy was excited about becoming a mother. Jeromy, on the other hand, didn't seem to share the same excitement, causing Thuy's suspicions to strengthen even more. Waking up in the middle of the night to an empty bed and house was making her pisstivity meter go off the charts.

Thuy was tiring herself out from all the pacing and took a seat on the couch to rest. In a futile attempt to calm down she rocked herself back and forth. "If this nigga is out fucking another bitch, that's his motherfucking ass!"

On cue, Jeromy strolled inside the house like everything was cool.

"Well, it's about fucking time your black ass came home! Where the fuck did you run off to?" Thuy greeted Jeromy with venom and stood up on her feet.

Fuck! Her ass is awake! Jeromy was not prepared to deal with Thuy's bullshit bitching interrogations. "Hey, baby, what you doing up? It's four in the morning; you should be sleep." He tried to act all innocent and concerned.

I know damn well this motherfucker didn't just ask me that shit, with his wannabe slick ass! "What am I doing up at four in the morning?" Thuy repeated the question. She rolled up on Jeromy and got in his face. "The question is why in the fuck did I wake up in the middle of the motherfucking night and your black ass ain't nowhere to be found?"

"These pregnant mood swings are something else." Jeromy said with an aggravated sigh. He wished he was back inside that sexy, caramel groupie's pussy instead of dealing with Thuy and the unwanted little bastard growing inside of her. He had to try to put up a good front or else Thuy would use her power to destroy him and he was not gonna be brought down by anyone, especially a bitch.

"These what? Never mind! All I want to know is who is the bitch you fucking?" Thuy was getting angrier by the second.

"Look, Thuy, you need to calm your ass down. I'm not fucking these hoes out here. I can't help it that I have pussy thrown at me all the time. That's the life of a celebrity athlete. You know that. You need to get all that insecure shit out your head because the shit is getting old and tired!" Jeromy demanded.

Thuy couldn't believe the balls on this nigga. Telling her to quit being insecure, get over it and deal with having random hoes jumping all over his dick. Thuy maybe a sucker for love but she ain't going out like no punk. "I wouldn't be so fucking insecure if you didn't have different bitches coming for me, disrespecting me, and throwing their stank sour ass pussies all up in your face!"

"Baby, it's all in your head." Jeromy tried to play it off like he was the rational and reasonable one trying to calm Thuy down like she was the crazy, delusional one.

"I'm going back to bed," Thuy said in a dismissive manner and went back upstairs, into the master bedroom and crawled back into bed.

She tried to go to sleep but felt Jeromy's big, strong hands gently rubbing her back. It felt so relaxing. Jeromy knew exactly what to do to make Thuy completely forget she was pissed off. He leaned over to whisper in her ear, "You know I love you, baby?"

Thuy turned over to face Jeromy. "I want to believe that. I don't know what happened to us. Ever since I told you about the baby you've been distant, acting like you don't want this baby." She expressed her concerns.

"What are you talking about? Of course I want this baby," Jeromy lied through his teeth. "I'll admit the news shocked me, but trust and believe I couldn't be any happier." He pulled Thuy closer into his arms. Thuy's anger towards Jeromy was disappearing. Being in Jeromy's strong, muscular arms was very intoxicating. He was a handsome man with a body to die for— dark chocolate skin and a dick women would slap their momma for.

"Do you love me?" Thuy asked softly.

"Yes, baby. I really do," Jeromy answered with a kiss.

"Good, because I'm excited about this baby. Sure, it wasn't planned, but I always wanted to be a mother." Thuy said. "Jeromy, I love you so much, but I also need you to be supportive and completely be by my side, especially since I'm carrying your child. Also, I need you to be sensitive and care about my feelings."

This bitch is beyond needy! Her ass planned this shit to trap me! "Of course, sweetheart. Anything for you and our baby," Jeromy said and rubbed Thuy's stomach. She was in the middle of her first trimester. "I love you, baby." Jeromy said and kissed Thuy with deep passion.

His kisses got Thuy wet every time. Her panties were getting soaked with the nectar from her arousal. Jeromy reached down and slid off her panties, using his index finger to gently rub on her clit. Her clit was extra sensitive. Even the slightest touch made Thuy lose control.

"Ah!" A moan escaped her lips. She was squirming with anticipation. She wanted the dick and she wanted it now.

Thuy moved Jeromy's hand from between her legs and laid him down on his back. He knew it was about that time Thuy would do his favorite sexual act from her. Thuy yanked Jeromy's pants down and his dick sprung out like a clown popping out of a jack-in-the-box. His thick, eight inch rod looked so delicious. Thuy couldn't wait to dine on it. She grabbed the dick, getting ready to put it in her mouth, when she felt something sticky. She put her hand to her nose to confirm what that slimy residue was. The disgusting, foul smell made her pussy dry up instantly. She used her fingers to give the tip of dick a pinch hard enough to almost pull the skin off.

"Ouch!" Jeromy shrieked in pain. "What the fuc—" He was cut off by multiple slaps in the face by Thuy.

"You nasty motherfucker!" Thuy yelled in Jeromy's face, and gave his face about five more painful slaps, making sure she wiped the foreign pussy residue all over his face. "Your lying, cheating ass didn't even have the fucking common courtesy to wash up after sucking and fucking another bitch!" Thuy jumped out of bed, quickly changed her clothes and packed her overnight bag.

"Woman, what the fuck is your problem?" Jeromy yelled out when he recovered from the dick pinch and slaps, and followed Thuy out of the room, catching up to her as he wiped the pussy juice off his face.

"I smelled the bitch's stank pussy all over your dick, you lying motherfucker!" Thuy ranted as she made her way downstairs and to the front door. "Fuck this shit! I'm out this motherfucker!"

"Thuy, don't leave like this. I can explain." Jeromy tried to come up with a shit filled story but all that came out of his lying ass mouth was stuttering. "I...I...I..."

"*I...I...I...* Nigga, bye!" Thuy mocked Jeromy's pathetic ass stuttering and opened the door.

"Baby, don't leave." Jeromy pleaded. "Please stay. It's too dangerous for you to be out at this time of night by yourself." He said with genuine concern. "Something terrible could happen to you."

"Like you give a fuck!" Thuy scoffed with contempt and stormed out the house and slammed the door behind her.

She's right! I don't give a fuck! Jeromy thought.

Chapter 3

Thuy was in her six bedroom house, sleeping like a baby in her soft queen-sized bed in her master bedroom. Her beauty sleep was interrupted by the ringing of her smartphone. She assumed it was Jeromy, but he was the last person she wanted to talk to. The phone kept ringing and Thuy had no intention of answering, but she knew she had to face him eventually, so she might as well put on her big girl panties and woman the fuck up.

Thuy let out a big yawn and reached over the nightstand to grab the phone. She looked at the caller ID and frowned. "Fuck!" She mumbled with irritation. She stood corrected. *This* was the last person she wanted to talk to. She rolled her eyes and answered the phone. "What the fuck do you want, Tori?" Thuy answered rudely to her half-sister.

"Is that how you greet your big sister?" Tori asked.

Is this bitch serious? "Oh cut the fucking bullshit, bitch! The only time I'm your sister is when your ass want something. Now what the fuck is it?" Thuy didn't have time to entertain fake ass bullshit this early in the motherfucking morning.

"Look, Thuy, you need to let that shit go!" Tori demanded.

Thuy let out a sarcastic chuckle. "This coming from the chick who's always singing the same played out, shitty song about how it's all my fault our daddy went to prison, how it's all my fault you and Jett's bitter, hateful bitch of a momma died, and how it's all my fault Jett ended up a career criminal—"

"Which is why your ass owe us!" Tori cut Thuy off. "Look I need—"

"Bitch, please!" Thuy heard enough and hung up the phone. "If that hoe wants some money from me, her ass better come at me more correct like she got some motherfucking sense! She better ask one of those gullible niggas she duped into giving her those babies for some motherfucking money! That bitch got me fucked up!" She vented to herself.

Thuy hated being treated like an outsider by her father Olson and her half siblings. Despite it all, she was the only one in Olson's bunch to even graduate from high school, let alone earn a B.B.A. in Marketing and a M.B.A. in Sports Management, which helped pave the way for Thuy to build a flourishing Audi dealership and become one of the best sports agents in the country.

"The nerve of that bit—" Thuy's stomach started to turn. She knew what that meant. She covered her mouth and bolted for the bathroom. She lifted the toilet lid and let loose. It seemed like the vomiting would never stop. When she was sure it was completely out her system, Thuy picked herself off the floor and flushed the toilet.

"This morning sickness ain't no fucking joke!" Thuy pulled herself together and turned on the shower. "Soon, it'll all be worth it, little one," she added with a smile and rubbed her stomach.

Thuy entered the shower and let the water hit her body in full blast. It felt great. She grabbed the Moonlight Path shower gel from Bath and Body Works and poured some on her wash rag. She rubbed the shower gel all over her body. The lather and its pleasant scent refreshed her skin. This is just what Thuy needed to start her day.

After her shower, Thuy dried off and did her hygiene ritual. Then, she went inside her walk-in closet and decided to put on a navy blue pantsuit that complimented her size ten curvy body, and slipped on a pair of matching blue stiletto pumps and her jewelry. She wasn't showing yet so she had to enjoy this body while she could. She then went back in the bathroom and applied her makeup, and put her long, jet black hair in a bun. Thuy checked herself out in the mirror to find that her glowing brown skin was flawless.

Thuy grabbed her black designer bag and briefcase, then headed out. She walked downstairs into the kitchen to fix herself a sandwich, but was met with a surprise by her two best friends, Bryn and Vida.

"Surprise!" They cheered.

Thuy was speechless after she saw the spread on the kitchen counter. Sausages, pancakes, biscuits, bacon, cheese eggs, grits and freshly squeezed orange juice. "Bryn! Vida! This is so nice! Y'all didn't have to do all of this for little ole me!" Thuy gave her two day ones from childhood a big group hug.

They fixed their plates and took their seats in the dining room.

"It was our pleasure," Bryn said. "We need to make sure you and our baby are taken care of, and are all nice and comfy."

"Our baby?" Thuy asked with confusion.

"Yes, our baby," Vida said. "You're not just our best friend, you're our sister. You family, girl. That makes this baby family too."

"I appreciate this guys. Me and this baby are hungry like a mug." Thuy said and took a bite out of her bacon.

"We know." Bryn and Vida said.

"Between waking up to Tori's bitching demands and what went down last night, this is just what I need." Thuy turned to Vida and said. "I'm sorry if I woke you up last night with my door slams."

Vida had been living with Thuy a little over five years after she and Bryn drove from Atlanta, Georgia to Charlotte, North Carolina and back to rescue Vida from her abusive boyfriend. Thuy and Bryn helped Vida get her life back on track and now she was a college professor at their alma mater, Clark Atlanta University. She also teaches online classes for Troy University.

"You good. I was already up, grading papers," Vida said. "What went down anyway? I thought you were spending the night with Jeromy."

"Oh shit! What the fuck did that bastard, fuck nigga do now?" Bryn automatically assumed the worst, due to his deep animosity towards Jeromy.

Thuy shook her head and recapped her latest Jeromy drama. "Long story short, he disappeared in the middle of the night. His black ass came home acting like it was no big deal. After I got finished cussing his lying ass out, he tried to fuck his way out of it. I'll keep it one hundred. It almost worked until I grabbed his dick and found traces of stank ass smelling pussy juice all over it."

"Eww!" Bryn and Vida exclaimed in disgust. They couldn't believe this nigga didn't bother to wash his ass before coming home to Thuy after fucking some nasty hoe.

"Nasty motherfucker!" Bryn rolled his eyes with contempt.

"My words exactly," Thuy added.

"What did you do?" Vida asked.

Thuy flashed an evil smile and answered, "I did what any calm, rational woman would do. I pinched the shit out of the tip of his dick and slapped the shit out of him a whole bunch of times. Not to mention I wiped the hoe's pussy juice all over his face." Her answer made everyone laugh and Bryn and Vida gave Thuy congratulatory high fives.

"That'll teach his ass!" Bryn cheered.

"Exactly!" Vida agreed, and when the laughter stopped she got serious. "Real talk, Thuy. Why do you put up with him? He doesn't deserve you."

"I really want this to work." Thuy said. "I'm tired of all the failed relationships and I want this baby to have all the things I didn't have growing up. Starting with a father in his or her life." This conversation was depressing Thuy and she quickly dropped it. "Let's eat this breakfast."

As they were eating, Thuy admired her friends in silence. She was lucky to have them in her life. She could honestly say she didn't know where she'd be without them in her corner to help her cope with the shitty hands life dealt her.

Thuy was also proud of her friends' professional accomplishments. Vida is a well-respected college professor. Even though Bryn is a licensed psychiatrist, he ended up wearing several hats in the entertainment industry. Standup comic, director, producer, filmmaker and writer.

"Thanks for the breakfast. Y'all negros cooked y'all asses off." Thuy got out of her seat and walked over to Bryn and Vida. "Hugs." Thuy hugged them. "Kisses." She kissed them on the cheek. "Goodbye, and clean up this kitchen." Thuy instructed as she was leaving.

"Yes ma'am," Bryn and Vida teased.

Chapter 4

Slurp! Slurp! Slurp!

In Macal's office Lolette was giving Macal oral pleasure as he sat at his desk. Her warm, wet mouth covering his dick sent a shockwave throughout his whole body.

"Oh shit, girl!" Macal moaned. Lolette sucked hard on the dick like she was trying to suck the skin off that motherfucker. "Oh, you can suck a mean dick!"

Lolette mumbled through her hard sucking, using her heavy spit to cover his dick and letting the tip hit her tonsils. Macal reached around to lift up Lolette's dress. He moved her thong to the side and stuck his middle finger inside her slippery wet pussy. He wiggled his finger around to find her G-spot.

Macal located his target and kept his concentration on the spot. Lolette's ass started vibrating, causing her to suck harder and play with the nuts. Lolette was about to cum so she backed her ass back and forth, fucking Macal's middle finger, and picked up the pace until she got her nut.

Boom! Boom! Boom! "Macal! Open this fucking door! We need to talk, right motherfucking now!" Tylisha yelled with authority, banging on the door. She knew what was going on in there because she saw Lolette's car in the parking lot. *Boom! Boom! Boom!* "Open this fucking door, right now! I ain't got all motherfucking day!"

Lolette lifted her head from Macal's lap and said with a laugh, "I guess you need to get that, huh?"

"Macal, answer this motherfucking door!" Tylisha continued to yell and bang on the door.

Macal and Lolette got decent in a hurry and he yelled back, "Coming, Tylisha! You don't have to yell! Shit!" He gave Lolette a kiss and said to her, "And I'll make you do plenty of that tonight."

Lolette blushed and her pussy began to tingle with excitement. Macal gave her ass a squeeze before opening the door. "Tylisha, dear sister! What a pleasant surprise!" He greeted with over the top enthusiasm.

"Awe, you're too kind, sweet, caring brother of mine," Tylisha greeted with a big smile, entering the office and gave Macal a big hug while fighting the urge to vomit at the sight of Lolette's spit and cum covered lips.

"What brings you here?" Macal asked.

"Because I need to talk to you alone," Tylisha said and gave Lolette the evil eye.

Lolette caught the hint and strutted out the door. "I'll see you later Macal," she said with seduction. "I'll meet you at—"

Tylisha slammed the door in Lolette's face before she could finish. Tylisha then turned to Macal and shook her head. "When are you gonna leave these hoes alone? Particularly the one that just left?"

"And when are you gonna stop banging on the door and barging in my fucking office like you the police?" Macal retorted. "I told you about bringing that loud, ghetto hood shut up in here! This is a place of business, in case you forgot! Security could've dragged your ass out of here for that shit!"

Wasn't you getting your dick sucked in this office just now? Tylisha thought. She laughed off Macal's weak ass threat. "Marlon, Carl and Tiger wouldn't dare lay a finger on me. Besides, the office is used to my ghetto hood side. I used to work here, remember?"

After being dumped for a white woman by her ex-husband and father of her children, NBA player Milton Dryer, leaving her and the kids with nothing, Macal moved them into his house. He gave Tylisha a job in public relations in his firm. Her interior decorating business started when one of Macal's client's wives was impressed on the wonderful job she did decorating for one of Macal's office parties. She had Tylisha decorate their summer home. Word got around and the rest was history.

Tylisha motioned for Macal to sit next to her by patting on the available space on the couch next to her, and he followed suit. "Now, Macal, real talk, you're my brother and I love you. I know you are a good man and love Fallon. I don't know where me and my babies would be without you. You're married to a wonderful woman. Don't fuck it up over the likes of her so-called fake, hoe ass best friend. You know we became young orphans because our daddy couldn't keep his pants zipped. I don't want that to be your future. I worry about you."

"Don't worry, baby girl," Macal said, pulling Tylisha into a hug, and kissed her cheek. "I'll be alright," he tried to stop Tylisha from worrying, and changed the subject. "What brings you here?"

"Oh yeah!" Tylisha almost forgot why she stopped by, but now she remembered. "Tonight, I have an important business dinner with a potential client, and I need you to babysit Welton and Ayla."

"I can't, I have plans!" Macal whined.

"Macal, meeting to fuck a nasty, two-faced hoe don't count as plans, so you're on babysitting duty. Deal with it nigga," Tylisha coldly replied.

"You could've had Grandma Doris babysit for you," Macal suggested.

"Well, I didn't ask Grandma Doris. I asked you," Tylisha said with a playful attitude.

"And another thing," Macal continued to complain. "Why can't you at least ask me? Make some type of request? Instead, you just gonna tell me I'm babysitting."

"Because if I ask, or make some type of request, it'll be a possibility you'll say no," Tylisha shot back with a smile.

"And you fucking right I'm gonna say no," Macal said unapologetically. "Because it's the principle, baby sister, dear. Look, I love Welton and Ayla, but I can't babysit tonight. I'm sorry."

"Oh, come on! Please!" Tylisha begged and flashed the sweet, innocent little girl look at Macal.

This girl needs to quit! Macal thought. Tylisha's cute act was not going to work this time. It was time for Macal to put his foot down, lay down the law and stay firm. "Now, Tylisha, you're thirty-years old now. This sweet, cute face, innocent act is not gonna work anymore. It worked when you were a little girl. It may have worked when you were a teenager. In your twenties, I let you get away with it. But not now? You just have to learn that you can't weasel anything you want out of me. I'm sorry, but the answer is gonna have to be no."

Tylisha got off the couch and sighed in defeat. Macal followed suit and hugged Tylisha. "Okay, Macal, I understand. I'll give Grandma Doris a call to see if she's available."

"I'm glad you're taking this well, and good luck with your meeting," Macal said.

"Thanks, Macal." She walked over to the door and opened it. She stuck her head out of the doorway and yelled, "Kids come in!"

Out of nowhere, Welton and Ayla ran in the office and bum-rushed Macal, causing him to fall back on the couch.

"Hi, Uncle Macal!" Ayla cheered with a big smile on her face, looking like a spitting image of her mother.

"Ayla, baby girl! How you doing?" Macal asked.

"Great! We're going to have so much fun tonight!" Ayla cheered with excitement.

"We are?" Macal asked with an unsure tone.

"Yeah, Uncle Macal!" Welton said, who was a visual mixture of both his parents. "What are we doing tonight?"

"Have fun babysitting, Macal," Tylisha smiled in triumph as she walked out the door.

"How's school going?" Macal asked his niece and nephew.

Both Ayla and Welton answered at the same time. "School is going great! First..."

I can't believe she pulled the okie-doke on me! Macal was half listening to the kids' school stories. His mind was on how Tylisha played him like a sucka. Macal felt his smartphone vibrate in his pants pocket and he took it out to answer it. It was a text message from Tylisha.

Tylisha: You should've known better!

Macal: LOL! Yeah, you got me!

Tylisha: LOL! I know. I'll pick up the kids when the business dinner is over.

Macal: Alright, and don't worry, Welton and Ayla are in good hands.

Tylisha: Thanks!
Macal: Anytime!

Chapter 5

Thuy had an easy productive day at work and was on her way to visit her mother Isla and her stepfather Gregory Dawson. They got married when Thuy was in the eleventh grade. Thuy was so happy that her mother found a great man who treated her like a queen. She deserved it after all the drama Thuy's sperm donor and his bitch of a wife Mycha put her through.

Thuy's phone started to ring. She saw the caller ID and smiled. It was her mentor and former employer, Antonio 'Tony' Blanchi. He taught her everything she knew about the business of sports. His parents were Italian immigrants. His deceased wife was a black beauty queen turned social worker, and they had a daughter named Sophia who's a doctor.

Thuy blushed and answered the call. "Hi, Tony!"

"Hi, Thuy. I wanted to check on you to see how you're doing."

"I'm doing great," Thuy replied. "The dealership is doing great and I had only one meeting with a client today."

"How's the baby?" He asked.

"He or she is doing fine. I can't wait until he or she makes their debut so to speak," Thuy giggled, grinning from ear to ear. She was excited about becoming a mother. "Look, let's talk about you. What's up?"

"Everything is great on this end. Sophia is trying to get me to retire again."

Thuy laughed. "Aww, she's your daughter. She wants you to take it easy and enjoy life," she said in a sweet baby tone. "Speaking of which, I need to call her after I visit with momma."

"How is Isla?" Tony asked with joy in his voice. It was no secret that Tony had a huge crush on Isla.

"She's great and still very happily married!" Thuy picked up on Tony's tone.

"Oh!" Tony replied with slight disappointment.

"Oh yeah! I know what you trying to do. You ain't slick Tony," Thuy teased. "Greg is not letting momma go."

"Smart man."

"Don't be sad. There's a woman out there for you. A woman who's beautiful, nice, smart and single!"

"If you say so," Tony said in defeat, "I have another call coming in. I'll talk to you later, okay?"

"Okay, goodbye."

Less than a minute after the call ended, Thuy was getting another call and she answered. "Hello—"

Thuy was cut off by an automated recording. "You have a collect call from an inmate at the Dekalb County correctional facility. State your name: *Jett*." Jett was heard stating his name.

"This nigga," Thuy said with an eye roll. "First Tori and now his ass."

"Will you accept the charges?" The automated message asked.

Thuy was about to hang up but her petty senses started tingling. "Yes, I'll accept."

Jett cut straight to the chase. "Look, Thuy, I need—"

Thuy hung up the phone. "Bwahahaha!" She laughed maniacally as she pulled up in the driveway. She got out of the car, walked to the front door and rang the doorbell. The door opened and there was Greg with a big, handsome smile on his face.

"Hi, Greg!" Thuy greeted and hugged her beloved stepfather.

"Hi, Thuy! You're just in time for dinner," Greg said as he let Thuy inside.

"Anytime. Where's momma?"

"Momma's right here!" Isla made herself known as she walked downstairs and rushed towards her only child.

"Momma!" Thuy cheered with a glow and hugged the slightly older version of herself.

"How's my baby and grandbaby?" Isla asked.

"Grandbaby is great. Baby is a mess," Thuy confessed with a sigh.

"What's wrong, baby?"

"I'll fill you in after dinner."

"Sure, baby," Isla said as she and Thuy went into the kitchen. "Luckily, Greg cooked his specialty tonight."

"You're taking advantage of this retirement, aren't you Greg?" Thuy assumed.

"You got that right, and I'm enjoying every minute of it." Greg took Isla in his arms and planted a big, fat kiss on her. "This woman right here makes retirement even better."

"I do what I can," Isla said, trying to be modest.

The trio fixed their plates and went into the dining room to eat the special meal Greg prepared. It was a chicken alfredo casserole with baked salmon on the side. It was delicious. It was a very unique combination but Greg pulled it off nicely. That's why the meal was his specialty.

"That was a great meal," Thuy complimented. "Greg, you got skills."

"Thanks, and don't worry about cleaning the kitchen," Greg said as he was gathering the plates. "I'll take care of the kitchen so you ladies can talk."

"Are you sure, Greg?" Isla asked.

"It's cool, Isla. Thuy needs you," Greg insisted and kissed Isla on the cheek.

"Alright." Isla then turned to Thuy and said, "We'll talk in my room." Isla headed straight for the master bedroom and Thuy followed suit. When they entered the bedroom, Isla let Thuy inside and she closed the door behind her. The ladies sat on the bed and Isla began to speak. "Alright, baby, what's up?"

All of Thuy's emotions poured out all over the place. She collapsed in her mother's arms and let the tears fall freely down her face. "Oh, momma! Why can't I get it right?"

"Things aren't going well between you and Jeromy?" Isla guessed.

Thuy shook her head. "Things have gotten worse. I don't know what's going on with him. It's the other women and not being able to shake this feeling that he's not happy about the baby, even though his mouth says yes."

"It's gonna be okay, baby. I'm here," Isla assured and kissed Thuy on the forehead. "What do you want from this man, baby?"

Thuy regained her composure and wiped her tears before giving her an answer. “I want this relationship to work. I failed so badly in the past.”

“You should never say things like that. You are a wonderful girl. Don’t let no nigga make you think and feel any different.”

Thuy wasn’t sure if she was even destined for a happily ever after, but she was glad Isla found hers. “Greg is a good guy. He really makes you happy. You deserve it.”

“Fucking right I deserve it!” Isla declared. “After all the shit your sorry ass daddy and that bitch put me through, I think I deserve a happily ever after.”

Thuy let out a soft chuckle. “Can I stay here for the rest of the week? I need to clear my head.”

“You know you don’t even have to ask. You’re my baby and you bought this house.” They busted out laughing at Isla’s statement.

“Good thing I have spare clothes and supplies in one of the guestrooms to tie me over. I just need to call Vida to let her know she’ll have the house to herself for a few days. Oh, and I also need to call Sophia. By the way, her daddy says hello.”

“Aww,” Isla blushed. “Does Tony still think he has a chance?”

“Yep,” Thuy answered, and the ladies laughed.

“If Greg wasn’t in the picture, and if Tony’s ass didn’t flirt so much, he might’ve had a shot,” Isla said with a laugh. “Good thing I cleaned the house today. I’ll get your bath water ready while you make your calls.”

“Thanks, you spoil me.”

“Old habits die hard. Besides, this is nothing. Just wait until the baby is born.”

Thuy left and went into the guestroom where some of her belongings were. She closed the door behind her and laid on the bed. She pulled out her phone to call Vida and Sophia. Neither of them were available, so she left voicemail messages.

Thuy laid in the bed in complete comfort. No matter what type of bullshit life threw her way, she could always count on her momma. She treasured their extremely close relationship and she always felt safe and secure when her momma was around. Isla was definitely a ride or die momma, and she's proved it time and time again, especially during one of the most extremely turbulent times in her life.

1996

Fourteen-year-old Thuy was lying in bed at Grady Memorial Hospital in excruciating pain. Her face was fucked up with bruises and swelling with both of her eyes blackened. Her ribs were cracked and her left arm was fractured. Plus, she had a splitting headache.

"I'm scared, momma," Thuy said to Isla with worry.

"I know, baby. Don't you worry. I'm right here," Isla replied and kissed Thuy's forehead while holding her hand.

Thuy let out a heavy sigh and glanced over at the beautiful light-skinned woman with a Toni Braxton haircut. Her name was Detective Marsha Brinkley who was assigned to the case and ready to take Thuy's statement. Marsha was very compassionate and patient, and Thuy felt like she could trust her, but she was worried about what her mother would think of her after she gave her statement.

"I know what I have to do," Thuy then turned to Isla and said. "I'm scared that you'll hate me."

"Why would you think such a thing?" Isla asked.

"Because it's my own fault that I'm here and you might not believe me," Thuy answered with shame.

"That's not true. Of course, I'll believe you. Where is all of this coming from?" Isla was baffled.

Let's get this over with! Now or never! Thuy thought. "I'm ready to make my statement and I want to press full charges," Thuy said to Marsha.

"You're making the right decision," Marsha assured her.

"She's right, baby," Isla agreed, "that bastard can't get away with this."

Before Thuy began to give her statement she needed double assurance from Isla. "Are you sure you won't be mad at me or hate me? There are some things I'm about to say that I'm not very proud of that went down leading up to this, but I have to get everything out."

"Thuy, I love you. None of this is your fault. Whatever you have to say, I'll understand and I will always be by your side," Isla made it very clear and squeezed Thuy's hand for support.

"Thanks." Thuy turned to Marsha and said, "I'm ready."

"Okay." Marsha took out a tape recorder and pressed play. She then spoke into the microphone. "This is Detective Marsha Brinkley. I'm with the victim, Thuy Ellis and her mother, Isla Ellis who are pressing charges against Levi Parsans." Marsha put the tape recorder on the table next to Thuy. "You may begin your statement, Ms. Ellis."

"It's a very long story," Thuy warned.

"That's okay. Take your time," Marsha insisted.

"Okay, here it goes." Thuy took a deep breath and began to tell her story into the tape recorder. "It all started on my very first week of high school. I was dating a sophomore named Connor Hale. He said he loved me and eventually I slept with him. He was my first and only. Afterwards, Connor distanced himself from me and ended up dumping me a few days later. Not even less than twenty-four hours later he started dating someone else. I was so hurt, but that's not the worst of it. Conner promised me what happened would be between us, but it ended up being all over school and I ended up being labeled a hoe. Other boys would ask me out and after the date they assumed I would give it up, and when I didn't, they'd get pissed and lie about sleeping with me. It was my word against theirs, and of course nobody believed me. Then I met Levi Parsans, who was a junior. We started dating and I thought he was different. He was kind, sweet and he didn't let the rumors scare him away. I was in love. Last night, we were out on another date at the park. We were at the secluded area at the park, making out. He then reached under my dress, trying to take my panties off, and I pushed his hand away. He told me to relax. I told him to stop but he ignored me. Then he started to get very forceful and I got scared. I yelled 'stop it' and slapped him. Levi got angry and punched me in the face. He started

beating me like I was a man. He called me all kinds of sluts, hoes and bitches' excuse the expression. He was mad that I didn't give it up like he heard I did with the others. It turns out he was friends with Connor and he told Levi how great I was and that he should see for himself. The beating didn't stop until my friend Bryn found us. He carried me away and kicked Levi in the balls so we could get a head start to the hospital. Now I'm here."

Marsha turned off the tape recorder. "You're a very brave young lady, Ms. Ellis. I know it wasn't easy to tell your story."

"I'm so proud of you, baby," Isla said and hugged Thuy.

"I'm so sorry, momma. How could I have been so stupid?" Thuy cried.

"None of this is your fault and you're not stupid. I'm glad you told me what was going on. You have nothing to be ashamed of. If anybody should be sorry it should be me. I'm sorry for being so blind and for not protecting you," Isla said with regret. She would've admitted that hearing about her teenage daughter having sex caught her off guard but she had to deal. Right now, her only concern was helping Thuy recover from this nightmare that this sick little fuck put her through.

"It's not your fault, momma," Thuy said and kissed Isla on the cheek.

There was a knock at the door and Isla answered, "Come in."

Thuy's best and only two friends entered the room. Bryn Hawkins, who was an open homosexual, and Vida Townsend.

"Hi, Bryn. Hi, Vida." Thuy greeted them and gave her friends a hug.

"Hey! We dropped by to check up on you," Vida said.

"I'm trying to make it," Thuy said with a yawn. "I did it. I made my statement, explained everything and pressing charges." She informed her.

"That's good," Bryn said.

"Bryn, you're a hero," Isla told him and gave him a hug. "Thanks for saving my baby."

"Anytime, Ms. Ellis. I had to get to her because I had a feeling she was in danger," Bryn explained.

"Thanks for following your gut," Thuy said. "I should've listened to you. You were trying to warn me. I'm sorry I didn't listen."

"It's cool," Bryn responded. "I was determined to get there in time. I had to or else—"

"I would've been raped," Thuy finished. The thought of what could've happened frightened Thuy to the core. "He almost raped me. I could've been raped or killed." Thuy hugged Bryn tightly. "I am so lucky you came when you did. The sad part is there are a lot of girls out there who aren't as fortunate."

"Like me," Vida confessed in a whisper.

"What did you say, Vida?" Isla asked.

"Levi raped me," Vida repeated loud enough for everyone to hear her. She turned to Marsha and said, "Detective Brinkley, I want to press charges too."

"Trust me. It's the right thing to do," Thuy encouraged.

Marsha nodded in agreement. "Alright, Bryn, I have your statement and Vida, I need you to come with me down to the station so we can get your statement."

"Alright," Vida said. She then followed Marsha out the door.

"I'll be in touch," Marsha said to Isla. "Before I leave, there's something you should know, Thuy."

"Yes?" Thuy responded.

"Not only is Bryn a hero, but you are a hero too." Marsha left Thuy with those final words and walked out the door with Vida in tow.

"She's right," Isla said. "Because you had the balls to report that bastard, you paved the way for other girls to have the courage to come forward too."

"Momma."

"Yes, sweetheart?"

"Does daddy know about this, and if so, is he coming?" Thuy asked, hoping her father didn't disappoint her again.

Isla sighed before giving the best answer she could. "He knows and I'll see."

"Thanks," Thuy said, "I love you momma."

"I love you too, baby," Isla said and kissed Thuy on the forehead. "I'll make the call, okay?"

"Okay."

"Let me know if you need anything," Isla said before she left.

When they were left alone, Thuy said to Bryn, "Thanks for being there. I don't know where I'll be without you and Vida."

"You're our friend. We're here for you every step of the way." Bryn paused before asking the hard question. "Has Jett and Tori come to visit you?"

"Of course not," Thuy replied with sarcasm. "They're too busy adding fuel to the rumor fires about their 'other sibling' to give a fuck what happens to me. I don't even know if daddy is gonna show up. I'm guessing my not so beloved stepmother Mycha is still barring him from contacting me. Fucking heartless bitch! All the perks of being an outside kid." Thuy flashed a big, fake ass smile and quickly wiped it away.

Bryn and Vida saw first-hand how it fucked with Thuy being treated like a pariah by her own blood. They tried their best to fill the void her so called half-siblings left in her heart.

"Thuy," Bryn called her.

"Yeah?"

"You still got a brother and sister." Bryn was referring to him and Vida.

"Thanks." Thuy gave Bryn a big hug.

Chapter 6

Tylisha entered *Paulina's*— one of the best restaurants in town. She walked up to the hostess and said, "Hello, I'm here to meet Xavion Goss. Is he here?"

"Yes, he is. Follow me please." The hostess replied.

The place was packed tonight, but surprisingly they didn't have to walk too far before reaching Xavion's table.

The hostess placed the menus on the table. "Here are your menus and your server will arrive shortly."

"Thanks!" Tylisha said and the hostess left. Tylisha took a good look at her potential client and was blown away. He was tall, very muscular, and very handsome with a nice, smooth midnight dark complexion.

"Hello, I'm Xavion Goss," he greeted her with a sexy smile and voice to match as he extended his hand.

What a great smile! "Hello, I'm Tylisha Kilborn-Dryer. It's a pleasure to meet you." She shook his hand. *And strong hands too!*

Xavion pulled out Tylisha's chair for her and she took her seat.

"Thank you!" *Such a gentleman!* "How did you hear about my services?"

Xavion sat down and gave his answer. "From the Sheppard family. I'm a family friend of theirs."

"For real?" Tylisha responded with excitement. "They're my biggest and favorite clients. I had so much fun decorating Ligia and Vaxter's wedding two years ago." Vaxter owns a department store chain that's been in his family for years, and Ligia is a high school principal. Tylisha had never seen a couple so much in love.

"They highly recommended you. You see, I recently bought a new home, and let's just say decorating is not my thing." Xavion explained, blushing in slight embarrassment.

"Well, don't you worry about a thing. Me and my crew will take great care of you." Tylisha assured her potential, sexy client. She pulled out a portfolio from her briefcase and handed it to Xavion.

"Here are some sample layouts for you to look through to give you a general idea of what we have to offer, and a few suggestions."

"Alright, let me see," Xavion said, as he started flipping through the portfolio.

The server came up to the table and greeted them. "Hello, what can I get for you?"

Tylisha placed her order. "I would like a glass of water, shrimp alfredo and a baked potato."

"And you, sir?" The server asked Xavion.

"I'll have the same," Xavion answered.

"I'll be back with your orders," the server assured them.

"Thanks," Tylisha and Xavion said.

When they were left alone, Xavion couldn't take his eyes off Tylisha. Her beauty was magnificent.

She noticed his gaze. "What's wrong? You don't like the layouts?"

"Oh, no! The layouts are great and I would love to work with you, but I'm a little disappointed," Xavion explained.

This shocked Tylisha. "Why?"

"Because you don't remember me."

"Have we met somewhere before?" Tylisha was baffled. She felt kind of silly. Xavion knowing Tylisha but Tylisha not knowing Xavion. If a man that fine ever crossed her path, of course she'd remember him.

"Maybe this will help you out." Xavion dug in his pants pocket to put on his reading glasses. He then blew his cheeks out with air.

Tylisha couldn't believe it. "Enzo?"

Xavion nodded for confirmation and took his glasses off. Xavion lived in Doris' neighborhood. He went to school with Tylisha and was two years older than her. They were on the debate team together.

"Wow! Hey!" Tylisha jumped out of her seat and gave Xavion a big hug. "I haven't seen you since you moved to New Orleans in middle school. How have you been?"

"I've been good."

"Wow, what a small world!" Tylisha calmed down from her enthusiasm and went back to her seat. "When did you move back to Atlanta?"

"I moved back years ago," he answered. "I graduated from Georgia Tech and I'm now the president of AGlobe Loans and Trust Bank."

"How's that working out?"

"Pretty well. How about you?"

"Well, you already know what I do for a living, and business is booming. Grandma Doris is doing great. I have two kids. My son Welton is ten and my daughter Ayla is eight. Macal was nice enough to babysit them on such short notice." Tylisha kept a straight face while giggling on the inside about the boldface lie she just told. She enjoyed her victory over Macal. It was like killing two birds with one stone. Her kids were being supervised and Lolette's thotting plans for tonight are ruined. The way Tylisha saw it, she was doing Macal a favor by keeping him out of trouble and out of Lolette's pussy.

"Your brother still trying to be The Mac?" Xavion guessed. He remembered very well how Macal was with the ladies.

"Worse than ever," Tylisha confessed. "Macal went on to have a successful investment firm and he recently got married."

Xavion's eyes stretched in disbelief when Tylisha used the words Macal and married in the same sentence. "We're talking about your brother Macal, right?"

"Yes." Tylisha confirmed. "He may be a hoe but I love him. He helped me and my babies out of a huge jam that my bastard ex-husband put us in. I'm sure you heard about it."

"Yes, I did. I was being polite," Xavion said with sympathy. "I'm sorry you had to go through that."

"You're so sweet." Tylisha gave him a sexy smile. "What about your love life?"

"I'm divorced but my ex-wife and I are still friends. We have a twelve year old son named Amery," Xavion said.

"That's good that you guys can be cool with no animosity and are able to co-parent," Tylisha commended him. "It's nice to see that type of maturity. Some people have it and some people don't, like Milton for example."

"Yes, it is. By the way, my ex-wife is Ligia," Xavion confessed.

"You mean to tell me your ex-wife and her new husband recommended me to decorate your new house?" Tylisha couldn't believe this shit.

"I told you I was a family friend of theirs," Xavion replied.

"This is a trip, but in a good way." Tylisha had to laugh and Xavion joined in. She had to ask another question. "Didn't their age difference surprise you?"

"Yeah, I'll admit it shocked me that Ligia started dating a dude who was old enough to be our daddy, but hey, as long as Vax treats her and Amery with respect. We good."

"Right! Right!" She understood how Ligia managed to ignore Vaxter's age. He was one good looking, sexy ass dude. "Excuse me, I need to go to the ladies' room."

"I'll be right here, looking through your portfolio," Xavion told her.

Tylisha went into the restroom and found the nearest available stall. As she was using the bathroom she heard someone walk in, or rather stomp in. Tylisha paid it no mind until the woman began to speak in a very familiar voice.

"Hello, Macal, this is Lolette again. I'm still waiting for you at *Paulina's*. Call me as soon as you get this message."

Tylisha giggled to herself and flushed the toilet. She came out of the restroom stall and locked eyes with Lolette. Tylisha then busted out in hysterical laughter.

"What the fuck is so funny?" Lolette hissed at Tylisha, but she didn't respond. She just kept laughing at Lolette and washed her hands. "What's the fucking joke?"

Tylisha turned to Lolette and simply answered, "I'm looking at it." She grabbed a paper towel to dry her hands real quick and threw it in the trash. "Here you are, blowing up your best friend's husband's phone, not even trying to hide your backstabbing, hoeish ways. Let me save you some time. Macal will not be joining you tonight. He's babysitting my babies while I have my business dinner. Besides, you shouldn't feel so special and entitled. You're not the only hoe my brother is fucking," she boasted with an evil smirk.

This bitch set this shit up! Lolette rolled up on Tylisha and pointed her finger in her face, "Look—"

"No, you look!" Tylisha growled and swatted Lolette's finger out of her face like it was an annoying mosquito. Lolette better be lucky that was all she got from Tylisha. "You're a pathetic, two-faced bitch ass hoe that needs to get the fuck out of my brother and his wife's lives."

Lolette was taken aback by Tylisha's demands. "I can't go away just like that. Fallon is my best friend and I love her dearly." She defended herself innocently, but her facial expression told a different story.

This bitch is something else! "You can't even say that bullshit with a straight face." Tylisha pointed out. She could go on and tell Lolette all about herself but she had more important things to tend to. Like her eye candy new client. "You know what? I wasted enough time being in the same vicinity as you. Your scandalous ass will be gone soon. Eventually Macal will toss you on your ass the second he gets bored with you and get another hoe to replace your ass. It's always the same song and dance with you side bitches."

Tylisha brushed past Lolette to leave the restroom. She opened the door to get out when Lolette shot back with, "Didn't somebody give Milton's current wife this same speech?"

Tylisha spun around so fast anybody would've sworn she was Wonder Woman. She thought about punching the shit out of Lolette but she chose to use her words to bring the bitch down instead. "You know what they say. If he'll cheat with you, he'll cheat on you." Tylisha smiled with triumph. "Good day," she concluded and slammed the door behind her to leave Lolette alone in her filthy, disgusting, defeated shame.

Chapter 7

1993

"Macal, can I play your video games?" Seven-year-old Tylisha asked, working her cute, little girl charm on her thirteen-year- old brother.

"Well..." Macal stuttered. When Tylisha flashed that cute, innocent charm it was hard for Macal to say no, but he had plans to beat off to the new Playboy magazine he bought yesterday. "Well... Well..."

All of the sudden, Macal and Tylisha were startled by a loud crashing sound. "You fucking bastard!" Belinda yelled in a drunken rage from their parents' bedroom. Their father Rufus barely had enough time to duck for cover after Belinda threw the bottle of Vodka at him, aiming straight for his head.

"Woman, what the fuck is wrong with you?" Rufus yelled.

"I'm tired of your shit, Rufus! I'm sick of you disrespecting me and our family!" Belinda yelled.

Macal looked over at Tylisha and saw she was tearing up. They hated the explosive marital problems their parents were having right before their very eyes. Macal could deal with it, but Tylisha was a different story. Macal couldn't stand to see his baby sister so upset. He may not be able to stop the fighting but he could at least put a bandage over the immediate problem. He turned to Tylisha and said, "Alright, let's play video games."

"Yay!" Tylisha cheered up instantly.

Macal took Tylisha by the hand and led her upstairs into his room. He set up the game and turned up the volume loud enough to drown out their parents arguing.

"Why do you get a fucking kick out of embarrassing me?" Belinda yelled.

"Belinda, nobody is emb—"

"Cut the fucking shit, nigga!" Belinda cut Rufus off. "I know all about the baby!"

"What baby?" This was news to Rufus.

"Don't you fucking dare act like you don't know what the fuck I'm talking about!" Belinda was beyond pissed. The one thing she hated more than being lied to and cheated on was being made to look like she was crazy.

"Look, I don't know nothing about no baby!" Rufus defended himself.

"Oh, no, well let me refresh your motherfucking memory," Belinda said with sarcasm. "When I was at Kroger's with the kids," Belinda made sure to emphasize that the kids were with her to drive the point home. "Taryn got all up in my face with her usual bullshit and told me she was pregnant with your child!"

"She's lying!" Rufus quickly denied.

"Is she?"

"Yes, she is. Hell, her ass might not even be pregnant. If she is, it ain't mine."

"Did you fuck her?"

"No, I didn't!"

"I will never understand why you got to cheat on me with these bitches and have them all up in my fucking face. You know I had the kids with me. I was so humiliated."

"Damn it!" Rufus sighed. "Baby, I'm so sorry."

"Like fuck you are," Belinda scoffed. "What the fuck is wrong with me? I'm not woman enough for you? I'm ugly as hell? I'm not fucking you right?" Rufus just stood there in complete silence and that annoyed the fuck out of Belinda because she was actually expecting Rufus to answer these questions. "Well, nigga, what the fuck is it?"

"Just calm down."

"Like hell I will!" Belinda snapped. She slightly stumbled over to Rufus, breathing her loud lemon Vodka scented breath in his face. "Since you don't know how to keep your dick in your motherfucking pants, I should go out and fuck the first nigga who even winks at me," she taunted him with an evil smirk.

"Hold up!" That struck a nerve with Rufus. He might not had been the faithful husband Belinda deserved, but the thought of her even giving another man the time of day drove him insane.

"Hold up nothing!" Belinda continued to taunt him. "As a matter of fact, I might not let him strap up. Just let him cum deep inside me. He'll probably have a bigger dick and fuck me better than you ever did!"

"You better slow your motherfucking roll!" Rufus' blood was boiling over and Belinda knew it.

"Wait a minute. I have a better idea. Maybe I should throw a party. The number of bitches you fucked around on me with, I'll invite twice as many niggas and have them run a train up in here. Oh, and feel free to watch and take notes." Belinda teased.

"Shut the fuck up!" Rufus yelled with disgust.

"Aw, what's wrong? You can dish it out but you can't take it? Bad tasting medicine, huh?" Belinda replied with a giggle. "Well, that's too motherfucking bad! I been tasting this foul, nasty ass medicine for over thirteen motherfucking years, and your weak, pathetic, punk ass can't even taste a drop on the tip of your tongue for two seconds! Weak ass little bitch nigga!"

"Look, I know you're upset, but don't fucking play with me like that!"

"It looks like I finally got your attention." Belinda walked over to take a seat on the bed. She gave herself a moment to calm down and decided to handle the latest Taryn situation rationally. "Rufus, I'm going to ask you once and I want the truth. Is there any chance at all that the baby is yours?"

"No, of course not," Rufus answered and took a seat next to Belinda.

"Okay." Belinda sighed with relief. "I'm exhausted. I'm going to bed." She turned to Rufus and asked, "Will you lay with me?"

"Anything for you, baby."

The two took off their shoes and laid on the bed.

Belinda snuggled in Rufus' arms with complete comfort and gave him a kiss. "I love you so much."

"I love you too, baby." Rufus said and started stroking Belinda's hair.

"You and the kids mean the world to me. I don't want to lose our family." Belinda said with worry.

"You won't." Rufus assured her. "Always remember that no matter what, I love you, and our family means everything to me."

"Really?"

"Yes, baby, I promise."

"Since we're making promises, I have one to make."

"What's that?" Rufus asked with curiosity.

"I'm going to cut back on the drinking. I don't want to go further down this path."

"That's very good to hear," Rufus said happily and kissed Belinda. "Goodnight, baby."

"Goodnight to you too." Belinda fell fast asleep in Rufus' arms.

Rufus held Belinda for a few more minutes before climbing out of bed and quietly exiting the room. He made sure the kids were still playing video games and made a mental note to tell them to turn the volume down on his way back to bed. Rufus crept downstairs and found the cordless phone in the living room. He went to the patio and closed the door behind them before making the call.

"Hello," Taryn answered on the first ring.

"We need to talk," Rufus cut straight to the chase.

"About what, baby?" Taryn asked with seduction.

"About you getting that abortion." He stood firm.

"And I told you I ain't getting one!"

"Look, that shit you pulled today wasn't cute!" Rufus argued in a hushed voice. "Stay the fuck away from my wife and kids!"

"We wouldn't be having these problems if you would keep your fucking promises. Namely, dumping that drunk, needy bitch and marrying me!" Taryn snapped.

"Look—"

"No, you look, nigga! I'm sick of this shit! I'm keeping our baby and that's final. There's nothing you can do or say to change my motherfucking mind!"

Taryn had unintentionally gave Rufus an idea to get rid of the little problem inside her womb. "How about this? If you get the abortion, I'll get a divorce and we'll get married."

"Really?" Taryn asked with hope in her voice.

"Yes, really," Rufus said in a charming voice. "You know I love you, baby. You know we can't raise any eyebrows and I don't want you to get hurt by the backlash." He was laying it on thick.

"I understand. It's so much to think about."

"You love me, don't you?"

"Yes, I do."

"I know it looks like I'm asking a lot from you." Rufus said with loving tenderness. "I understand you need to think about this and I don't wanna to pressure you. Don't you worry. Once we get married, we can have as many kids as you want."

"That sounds wonderful!" Taryn cheered. "I'll do it."

"Are you sure, baby?" Rufus asked with concern.

"Yes, I'm sure. I'll go first thing Monday morning. Will you be there with me for support?"

"Of course, baby, I know this is gonna be very difficult for you."

"Thanks Rufus. I love you."

"I love you too, Taryn."

When the call ended, Rufus congratulated himself. "That was too easy!" He felt like he dodged a huge bullet. Little did he know, the outcome of what he had just done would affect him and his family for the rest of their lives.

"Uncle Macal? What game do you want to play next?" Welton asked.

Macal lost track, thinking about his conversation with Tylisha earlier when she mentioned the deaths of their beloved mother and bastard father. "I'm sorry, nephew. We can play whatever you want."

"Tekken it is." Welton said and he setup the game.

While they were playing video games in the game room, Fallon was helping Ayla with her school project in the living room. Fallon was able to use her experience as a freelance photographer to pick out the perfect pictures in the magazine to make the collage. Actually helping Ayla was a great distraction for Fallon to take her mind off her internal worries.

"Alright, we need to add three more pictures and we'll be all set," Fallon said as she was cutting the pictures out of a magazine.

"Thanks for helping me with my school project, Aunt Fallon," Ayla said, as she started gluing the pictures on the poster.

"Anytime, baby." The doorbell rang and Fallon asked, "Who is it?"

"Tylisha," she answered.

"Your momma's here," Fallon said to Ayla. "Alright, I'm coming." She left the table to answer the door. "Hey, Tylisha, how was your business dinner?" Fallon greeted her with a hug, letting Tylisha inside.

"Hey, girl, it was quite interesting," Tylisha answered.

"I thought I heard your voice in here," Macal said as he appeared in the living room with Welton in tow.

"Hey, Macal," Tylisha greeted and hugged Macal.

"Hey, momma!" Welton and Ayla cheered and hugged Tylisha.

"Hey, babies. Did you have fun with Uncle Macal and Aunt Fallon?" Tylisha asked.

"Yes, momma. We ate pizza, watched cartoons and Aunt Fallon helped me with my school project," Ayla recapped.

"And me and Uncle Macal were playing Tekken," Welton added. He then whispered to Tylisha, "I beat him five straight times."

"Yeah! Yeah! Yeah! You got lucky," Macal tried to play it off.

"Awe, don't be a sore loser!" Tylisha teased.

"Yeah!" Fallon agreed with a chuckle.

"You guys are right. Good game, Welton," Macal congratulated as he and Welton bumped fists.

"See, baby, I told you babysitting could be fun," Fallon said to Macal, and walked over to kiss him.

"Okay, I admit it. I had a good time," Macal confessed.

"Ayla, go with your brother in the game room and you can finish up your school project there," Tylisha instructed her.

"Yes, momma," Ayla said. She gathered her things and followed Welton back in the game room.

"So, Tylisha, how was your business dinner? You said it was interesting," Fallon said. "By the way, thanks for decorating the house. It looks beautiful."

"It sure does," Macal agreed.

"Anytime. Glad to do it," Tylisha said. "Oh, about the dinner. That reminds me. Macal, guess who my new client is? You'll never believe who it is."

"Who?"

"Enzo."

"Are you talking about that short, big faced kid with the glasses who was on your debate team in middle school, who also lived in Grandma Doris' neighborhood?" Macal refreshed his memory.

"That's him," Tylisha confirmed. "He moved back to Atlanta to go to Georgia Tech and decided to stay."

"This world is too small," Macal said.

"You can say that again," Fallon agreed. The doorbell rang again and Fallon answered it. It was Lolette, who was obviously pissed off. "Hi, Lolette. What's the problem? You seem upset." Fallon showed deep concern while letting Lolette in the house. "Your date didn't go well?"

"Worse than that, the punk ass fuck nigga stood me up!" Lolette sounded distressed and took a seat in the living room.

Macal was shitting bricks while Tylisha tried to figure out what the fuck Lolette was trying to pull.

"I'm sorry to hear that," Fallon said and hugged her friend. "Maybe he had a good excuse."

This is too easy! Lolette thought in amazement about how well her plan was working out. She managed to keep up her innocent, hurt victim act and continued her performance. "Not really, but come to find out his bitch of a baby sister sabotaged our date," she hissed. "The meddling little bitch! No wonder her husband left her ratchet, ghetto ass!"

"That's low down and dirty. How did she manage to sabotage you?"

Let me get the fuck outta here before I stomp this trifling hoe to the ground! "Welton! Ayla! Get your things! We're out of here!" Tylisha hated using her kids but it was the only way to cancel the Lolette Bates Show.

"Yes, momma!" Welton and Ayla called out and headed straight for the living room to meet their mother.

"Tylisha's right. It's getting late," Fallon said.

"Are ya'll ready? Ya'll got everything?" Tylisha asked her children.

"Yes, momma," Welton and Ayla answered.

"Alright, say goodbye to everybody," Tylisha instructed while opening the door.

As they were walking out the door, Welton and Ayla said their goodbyes. "Bye, Uncle Macal. Bye, Aunt Fallon. Bye, Miss Lole—"

Tylisha shut the door, cutting them off. She raised her babies to respect adults and she didn't want them to break the habit, but Lolette was one adult that didn't deserve any respect.

"It's been a long day," Fallon said. "Call you tomorrow?"

"Thanks girl," Lolette said as she got out of her seat. "I'll be okay. I got some photos to develop at home tonight." Along with Fallon, Lolette was also a freelance photographer.

"Are you sure?"

"Yeah! I'll be alright. I know if I don't hear from that nigga soon, he can kiss this ass and pussy goodbye," Lolette said with confidence and glanced quickly at Macal to make him sweat.

"That's telling him," Fallon encouraged. "Goodnight."

"Goodnight," Lolette said and let herself out.

"Well, baby, it's just me and you," Macal said.

"Yes, we are all alone." Fallon locked the door. "I'm gonna take a quick shower and turn in."

"Okay, baby."

When Fallon was out of sight, Macal took his phone out of his pocket and sent Lolette a text.

Macal: What the fuck was that bullshit you pulled?!

Lolette: Well your ass stood me up and ignored my calls. I don't play that fuck shit from anyone. I don't give a fuck how good the dick is!

Macal: That was too close. You can't be reckless like that!

Lolette: Don't worry baby! I'll be good!

Macal: Good!

Lolette: How are you going to make it up to me?

Macal: I'll swing by your place before I head to the office.

Lolette: Okay baby.

Macal: Alright bye and have it wet for me.

Lolette: LOL! Always! * blush*

Chapter 8

"Why do the cute and sexy ones always have to turn out to be complete fucked up psychos?" Thuy mumbled to herself as she was reading *Restraining Order* by Ca$h and Coffee on her tablet. She was sitting in the waiting room at the doctor's office. "That Choppa is one crazy ass nigga. Oh, Julz darling! You were way in over your head." Thuy knew she couldn't talk. She and Vida knew first-hand what women will put up with in the name of love and great dick.

"Nigga, why the fuck you ain't here?"

Thuy was startled by the outburst, almost dropping her tablet. She looked around to see where the disturbance was coming from and she discovered a barely legal-aged looking girl with her pregnant belly, looking like it was about to pop, yelling on her phone.

"Your motherfucking ass knew what time my appointment was!" The young woman was breathing heavily in frustration, listening to the caller. "You had something important to do? Nigga, I'm pregnant with your baby! You should be here with me! Your ass is probably fucking some ratchet, hoe ass bitch! Listen, you better get your motherfucking ass over here, ASAP or—" The young woman took the phone off her ear and looked at it funny. "I know his ass didn't just hang up on me!"

The nurse entered the waiting room and called out, "Kelly Sewell!"

"Right here!" The young woman answered and followed the nurse.

Everyone in the waiting room was in disbelief about what they just witnessed. All except Thuy. Even though Thuy and Kelly were in different stages and walks of life, they were both in the same boat. Pregnant by unfaithful and unsupportive men.

"Hey, baby," Jeromy greeted her with a big, charming smile, walking over to Thuy.

Thuy was caught completely off guard. It'd been two weeks and she still wasn't ready to face Jeromy. "What the hell are you doing here?" Thuy asked Jeromy quietly. Unlike Kelly, Thuy actually mind having an audience witness her personal matters, if it could be avoided. Thuy has been known to act an ass no matter where she was, if pushed.

"I wanted to be here for you and our baby," Jeromy answered. He had a plan to get back on Thuy's good side and he knew her well enough to know her weaknesses.

"Aww, you remembered my doctor's appointment," Thuy said with a smile. "That's sweet but that don't change what happened."

"Baby, let's not talk about that now," Jeromy said.

"I actually agree," Thuy said, but she agreed for a different reason. Jeromy didn't want to discuss it at all and Thuy didn't want to discuss it in a room full of witnesses.

"Thuy Ellis!" The nurse called out.

"Here!" Thuy answered.

"The doctor is ready for you."

"Thanks."

Thuy and Jeromy followed the nurse into the exam room, and a tall, slender, dark chocolate skinned woman greeted them. "Thuy, it's great to see you again."

"Thanks, you too, Dr. Caldwell," Thuy returned and shook her hand. "This is the father, Jeromy Fuller."

"Nice to meet you, Mr. Fuller. I took my kids to the game last week; you were great," Dr. Caldwell complimented him.

"Thanks, but the great one is my woman right here, who I plan on making my wife," Jeromy said and pulled a stunned Thuy into a quick kiss.

"Let's get on with the exam," Dr. Caldwell said and gave Thuy a hospital gown. "Alright, here's the gown and make yourself comfortable on the exam table. I'll be right back."

"Thanks, Dr. Caldwell," Thuy said.

Dr. Caldwell took her leave. Thuy noticed Jeromy was still in the exam room and gave him a crazy look.

"What?" Jeromy asked.

"Can you step out please, so I can change?" Thuy requested.

"Oh, come on! I've seen you naked before. That's why we're here," Jeromy joked.

"Good point, but this is a doctor's office, not a bedroom," Thuy shot back.

"Touché," Jeromy said. "I'll turn around."

"Deal," Thuy compromised.

Jeromy turned around and Thuy started to change into the hospital gown provided.

She placed her clothes on the chair in the corner and hopped on the exam table, waiting on Dr. Caldwell to return. "Alright, you can turn around now."

"Are you okay, baby?" Jeromy asked with concern.

"I'll be fine," Thuy said and squeezed Jeromy's hand for support. "Thanks for being here."

"I'm always here for you, baby," Jeromy said.

"Alright, I'm back," Dr. Caldwell announced when she entered the exam room. "How are you feeling, Thuy?"

"Okay I guess," Thuy answered. "A little morning sickness, but other than that I'm okay."

"That morning sickness is something else," Dr. Caldwell sympathized. "Let's start the exam, shall we?"

"Let's," Thuy replied.

Dr. Caldwell started off with the usual. Checking for blood pressure, heartbeat and temperature. Then there was the pelvic exam. Last but not least was the ultrasound. Thuy and Jeromy looked at the screen, watching their baby move around.

Thuy was filled with pride and joy. "Aww, look at there, there's our baby."

"I think I saw the hand move," Jeromy said. "I think he or she is trying to wave at us."

"Boy, you silly," Thuy laughed.

"Everything seems to be fine," Dr. Caldwell said. "I just have to print out the sonogram and you'll be all set." Dr. Caldwell pressed the button on the computer to print out the sonogram. When the sonogram was printed, she handed it to Thuy. "There you are. The first of many beautiful baby pictures."

"Thanks, Dr. Caldwell," Thuy said.

"I'll leave you two alone. Make sure you sign out before you leave," Dr. Caldwell said before she left.

"Our baby," Jeromy said.

"Yeah, our baby." Thuy's mood changed when she remembered the reason why she and Jeromy hadn't spoken to each other until today. "Jeromy, do you want this family?"

"Of course I do. Why would you ask such a thing?" He asked in disbelief.

"Because of the other women," Thuy voiced her concerns. "You not being excited about the baby."

"What are you talking about? I love you and our baby," Jeromy insisted.

"But we still need to talk about what went down at your house."

"Baby, it was nothing," Jeromy said before spitting out the first lie that popped into his head. "One of my teammates had an emergency and called us over to his house. Afterwards, we had a few drinks and one of them brought some girls over, and one of them must've taken advantage of my drunken state. I'm sorry, baby."

Thuy didn't know what to think. She wanted to believe Jeromy but the story sounded completely far-fetched. "Jeromy, I want to believe you and forgive you but—"

"Then do, baby," Jeromy said in a deep sexy voice. "Tell me you believe me and forgive me."

"Oh but Jeromy—" Thuy struggled to say, but Jeromy's hands slowly caressing her body was making it very difficult for her to concentrate and think logically.

"Shh! Tell me you believe me and forgive me," Jeromy softly commanded and planted a gentle kiss on Thuy's lips.

He planted a few more kisses on Thuy until she said the words, "Yes, I believe you and forgive you."

Without breaking the kiss, Jeromy lifted up Thuy's hospital gown to expose her bare ass. Jeromy quickly unzipped his pants and pulled out his dick. He stuck his tongue further down Thuy's throat as he jammed his dick deep inside her.

He fucked Thuy at high speed and used his deep kiss to silence her moans. Thuy's pussy was getting wetter by the second. She didn't want the pleasure to stop. She savored every vigorous stroke.

"Ah!" Thuy moaned through the kiss.

"Oh shit!" Jeromy grunted. His dick was being covered with Thuy's juices as her pussy gripped his pleasure tool for dear life. "Oh baby, you're super wet!" Jeromy punished the pussy for one more minute before shooting his load deep inside her.

The impromptu quickie left Thuy and Jeromy winded. Between their heavy breathing Jeromy helped Thuy off the exam table.

"Wow, that was amazing!" Thuy said with glow and kissed Jeromy.

Jeromy pulled Thuy into another kiss and grabbed a handful of her ass. "And there'll be plenty more where that came from when we get home."

"Oh really?" Thuy blushed. "Well, let me get dressed and check out so we can go home."

"I'll meet you outside. I need to use the bathroom."

"Alright."

Jeromy left the exam room and walked down the hall to find the restroom. He went inside and, luckily for him, no one was there. He pulled out his phone and dialed a number.

"Hello!" A woman's voice answered.

"I got your message, Onya. Does this mean you took care of that?" Jeromy assumed.

"Yes, I did it. I got the abortion."

"Good girl."

"Now, when are you going to give me that five hundred thousand dollars?"

Jeromy hung up the phone. "Never, you dumb hoe!" He growled and walked out of the restroom to take Thuy home for round two.

Chapter 9

Fallon was in the shower, lost in her thoughts. She had a very tough life, and her relationship history wasn't any better. She never, in a million years, imagined a man like Macal would give her the time of day, let alone want to marry her. She loved Macal with all her heart, body and soul, and desperately wanted this marriage to work. She just couldn't shake this disturbing feeling she'd been carrying inside her.

"Surprise!" Macal interrupted Fallon's thoughts by entering the shower with her.

Fallon turned around and saw her sexy, tall, muscular, handsome husband in front of her. The water in the shower made Macal's smooth, milk chocolate skin glistened like the sun. The sight of his body mesmerized Fallon. Every inch of his body, down to the thick and curved nine inches he was packing between his legs.

Macal noticed her stare and pulled Fallon into a deep kiss. Fallon was turned on by his rough passion. Her pussy juices poured freely down her legs.

When the kiss broke, Fallon even shocked herself with her next few words. "Why did you buy a box of condoms?" That question literally came out of nowhere, but somehow the question managed to escape her lips. Fallon did her damnest to hold that shit in, but she couldn't hold it in a minute longer.

"What are you talking about?" Macal was dumbfounded.

Fallon jumped out of the shower with Macal on her heels. She grabbed her purse where she kept the receipt. She took it out and handed it to Macal. He examined the receipt and saw the condoms listed. "I found the receipt in the trunk two weeks ago while I was gathering my equipment. The receipt was from when you took your second car to go grocery shopping," Fallon reminded him.

Oh shit! Macal had to come up with a lie, and quick. "Oh, now I remember. Some teenage boy needed to buy some condoms. He couldn't afford them so I offered to buy them for him."

Fallon sighed with relief. "What a kind and generous thing to do. I'm sorry for jumping to conclusions." She jumped into Macal's arms and kissed him.

"Baby, you have nothing to worry about. I love you."

"I love you too. You mean the world to me."

"Now, can we dry off so I can make love to my beautiful wife?" Macal requested.

"Yes, we can make love, my husband," Fallon blushed.

Macal went into the closet in the bathroom and grabbed two bath towels. He gave Fallon one of them and they dried off their bodies. After disposing of the towels, Fallon climbed into bed and laid flat on her back to give Macal a terrific view of her naked glory.

The sight of Fallon's sexy, well-toned body made Macal's dick rock hard. He climbed on the bed and positioned himself between her thighs. He spread her thighs apart and dove headfirst into her pussy. He licked all over her clit and made sure he kept his focus.

"Ah!" Fallon moaned and squirmed. Her squirming made Macal laugh while still having his face buried in her wet, slippery pleasure cave. "What's so funny?" Fallon managed to ask between moans.

"You're squirming," Macal said with muffled laughter as he whipped the clit with his tongue.

"It's so good! I can't help it, baby!"

"Mmmm! You taste delicious!"

"Oh yeah! Oh shit! Right there!" Fallon screamed as she came all over Macal's long tongue.

After licking all the tasty residue from Fallon's orgasm, Macal lifted his head, gasping for air. "Oh, you good and ready," he said while rubbing her pussy.

"Yes, baby! I want it now!" Fallon begged.

Macal pounced on Fallon like a ferocious lion ready to devour its unsuspecting prey. He stuck his tongue in Fallon's mouth and forced his dick deep inside her pussy without warning. He lifted both of her legs up in the air and placed them on his shoulders. He pinned her down with his body so she couldn't make any types of movements. All she could do was take the dick. Fallon loved Macal's rough handling of her. His aggressive sex made her pussy cream. Macal roughly pumped in and out of her wetness, making her clit throb and her pussy muscles tighten.

Macal stuffed one of Fallon's titties in his mouth and sucked hard on the nipple. Fallon's pleasure-filled moans motivated Macal to stroke her pussy harder. "Shit, this pussy is good!" Macal grunted.

"Ah!" Fallon couldn't form actual words. The dick was that good to her. She knew she'd be sore in the morning but she didn't care. The pleasure Macal unleashed on her was worth a sore pussy any day.

Macal let out an intense growl as he filled Fallon's pussy up with his hot seed. He collapsed on his back and pulled Fallon into his arms.

"Macal," Fallon was the first to speak.

"Yes, Fallon," Macal responded.

"Will you promise to stand by me no matter what?"

"Of course, baby."

"Are you sure?"

"Yes, I'm sure."

"Sure you're sure?"

"Yes, baby, I'm sure." Macal kissed Fallon and gave her ass a light tap. "Now, let's go to sleep. Tomorrow is a new day."

Chapter 10

Thuy, Vida and Bryn were spending the day volunteering at the Restart Project Women's Center. Actually, they were not just volunteers; they were board members. The board members of this foundation preferred to be more hands-on and involved. Bryn and his longtime friend, surrogate mother, mentor, and business partner, Ambrosia Jackson, were the founders. Bryn suggested to Ambrosia to make Thuy and Vida board members due to their kindness, generosity and their experiences with difficult crises women go through.

Thuy proposed to the board to add a library and a computer room to the women's center in order to help women and their children gain access to resources in regards to finding employment, education, advancement, leisure, and etcetera. The library and computer room was freshly painted. The next step was to move in the furniture and get everything organized.

A couple of delivery men carrying boxes with the word *books* written on them in big letters, walked over to Bryn and Vida who were putting together a bookshelf.

"Excuse me, where do you want us to put these boxes?" One of the delivery men asked.

"The donated books! Great! Sit them over there and she'll sort them out. Thanks." Bryn instructed, pointing in Thuy's direction, who was sitting at a table, sorting out magazines.

"Anytime," the delivery man said and followed the directions.

After the moving men took their leave, Bryn and Vida walked over to Thuy's table to check on her. "Everything is coming along nicely," Vida commented.

"It wasn't easy, but happy to do it," Thuy said.

"This was a great idea, Thuy. You did an amazing job putting this whole thing together," Bryn said.

"Thanks, but I only suggested adding a library and computer room. I didn't pull this off all by myself. Everybody did their part." Thuy started opening the boxes.

"But you, my dear, got the ball rolling," Vida said.

"Thanks, but I feel like I'm being lazy though." Thuy stopped opening boxes. "You guys are doing all the hard, manual, back-breaking labor while my happy, black ass is just sitting here sorting through shit, looking all cute."

"We've been over this, Miss Missy. You're taking it easy until the baby is born," Bryn reminded her.

Thuy looked at Bryn like he was crazy. "Boy, I'm pregnant, not an invalid. I can do some work around here. It's not like I'm showing." Deep down Thuy loved the special treatment and gave in with a smile. "But if you insist."

"Hello, children," Ambrosia greeted them as she made her entrance. Ambrosia was a hard-working woman. Building her own production company and channel—the A-Jack Network—that Bryn is under. Despite a childhood of abuse and neglect, Ambrosia managed to graduate from high school and college with honors, and climb all the way to the top. She started the Restart Project Foundation because she wanted to use her experiences to help women and make a difference.

"Hello, Ambrosia," Thuy, Bryn and Vida greeted her simultaneously.

"Everything seems to be coming along nicely," Ambrosia said after taking a quick glance at the library. She saw the glass window and peeked into the room where a few volunteers Vida recruited from the university were setting up cubicles. "That's where the computers are going to be, right?"

"Right," Thuy answered.

"Which is why I stopped by. We still need to figure out which computers and printers to order. I brought the catalog for you guys to take a look at." Ambrosia handed Thuy the catalog with Bryn and Vida looking over her shoulder.

"We'll get right on it. Are we still within budget?" Thuy asked.

"That's the other reason I stopped by. Thanks to your client, Douglas Harris, we have a huge increase in our budget."

"Oh yeah! He's very generous. With his help, we'll be able to finish the library's add-on in no time."

"Excuse me, I need to speak to a Thuy Ellis." Everyone turned around to see who the voice belonged to, and there stood a beautiful, caramel-skinned woman with a worried *what the fuck am I gonna do* look on her face.

Thuy got out of her seat and walked over to the woman. "I'm Thuy Ellis. May I help you?"

"Yes, I heard this was a place for women to go for help, no matter the problem. Somebody recommended you," the woman explained.

"You came to the right place. All of our surrogate buddies seem to be unavailable right now, but I can still help. Let's go into one of the rooms and we can talk more." Thuy turned to Vida and asked, "Vida, can you take over for me at the table until I get back?"

"Sure," Vida said.

"Thanks." Thuy turned her attention back to the woman. "Alright, follow me."

The woman followed Thuy out of the library and down the hall. They found an empty room and the ladies went inside. Thuy closed the door behind them and the ladies took their seats.

"What seems to be the problem?"

It wasn't easy but the woman managed to hold back the tears. "I feel like such a fool. I've been used and thrown away like garbage." The woman held her head down in shame.

Thuy's heart went out to this troubled woman. She lifted the woman's head up and flashed a warming smile to silently let her know she was not alone and she could trust her. "What happened?"

The woman took a deep breath and started to tell her story. "I fell in love with this guy. He said he loved me and everything was great until I found out I was pregnant."

"He didn't want the baby and dumped you?" Thuy guessed. She has seen this play out one too many times. Women think they've found the perfect man and the second they end up pregnant he reveals himself to be nothing more than a deceitful, deadbeat, bitch nigga.

The woman confirmed with a nod. "He ordered me to get an abortion because he had a girlfriend, which I didn't know until I told him about the baby."

That bastard! "That's when he confessed to you?"

"Right," she confirmed. "He also told me she was pregnant with his baby too. He promised to pay me five hundred thousand dollars after I got the abortion. I went through with it and called to let him know. When I mentioned the money, he hung up on me. Now he's not returning my calls."

That motherfucker! Thuy withheld her anger towards the fuck nigga. Her focus was showing support for this beautiful young woman who was left damaged and broken. She held the woman's hand for comfort. "I'm so sorry that happened to you. I know it feels like it now, but this is not the end of the world. One day this will pass and life after this will be very bright."

"Thanks for not judging me," the woman said with a weak smile.

"We're not here to judge. We're here to help, heal and support." Thuy assured her. She reached into her pants pocket for her wallet and pulled out one of her spare business cards and handed it to the woman. "Here's my number. Feel free to call me anytime, Miss... Oh, I'm sorry, I didn't even catch your name."

The woman let out a little chuckle. "It's okay. My name is Onya Hanks."

Chapter 11

1992

In the park, Macal was enjoying a game of two on two basketball with his friends. They weren't really playing, just showing off their moves.

"Macal, check this out!" Lewis yelled and ran to the basket to make a dunk.

"That was smooth," Macal said with a nod. "Real smooth." He repeated with a yawn and stretch before snatching the ball from Lewis. Macal then ran towards the basket in lightning speed and did an over the top, nasty dunk. "Yes! Fucking yes! Can't fuck with it! Can't fuck with it!" Macal gloated while beating his chest.

"Macal, why you got to always be a show off?" Joe complained.

"Because I'm that nigga!" Macal replied with cockiness.

Roscoe grabbed the ball from Macal's hand and started to dribble. He was about to make his shot when a short, big faced boy with glasses bumped into him, almost knocking him down. Roscoe managed to maintain his balance. He then turned around with venom in his eyes and yelled, "Hey, watch it you little—"

"Hey, cool it. It was an accident." Macal got in between the boys to try to diffuse the situation. Roscoe was known to be an asshole and a hothead, and those two traits did not mix very well. "He's alright. He goes to my sister's school and lives in my grandmomma's neighborhood." He turned to the boy and asked with concern, "You alright, Enzo?"

"Yes, Macal," Enzo said with relief.

"Alright, you hurry home and you be careful, okay?"

"Thanks, Macal, I will."

When Enzo left, the boys continued their game, or showing off session until three beautiful girls walking by, distracted them. Roscoe had his eye on the brown-skinned cutie with the baby face and adult body.

"Oh shit! Look at there!" Roscoe couldn't take his eyes off her brown skin. "She's finer than a motherfucker!" Roscoe then started yelling like a fool to get her attention. "Hey! Hey, girl! Come over here!"

Brown Skin looked at Roscoe like he was crazy, rolled her eyes and continued to walk with her friends.

That pissed him off. "Well, fuck you, bitch!"

Macal shook his head at his friend's ignorance. "Oh yeah, Roscoe! That's really gonna get you some play."

"Man, fuck that stuck up hoe!" Roscoe dismissed.

"Aww, look at you trying to front," Joe teased.

"Obviously, somebody needs to school you clowns on how to get women," Macal said like he was a teacher talking to his students.

"Oh, teach us, oh wise one," Lewis teased with sarcasm.

"I can show you better than I can teach you. Roscoe you just made this lesson a whole lot easier for me to demonstrate," Macal boasted.

"How?" Roscoe asked with no emotion in his voice.

"Watch and learn," Macal said and walked towards the girls who were sitting on a bench talking. Macal never had any problems in the girl department. He had the looks, the brains, the body, the charm and he watched Rufus. That was the only advantage Macal had in having a compulsive cheater for a father.

He approached Brown Skin and began to speak. "Excuse me, I don't mean to bother you, but I came over here to apologize for my friend's behavior. He don't have any good sense."

"Obviously not," Brown Skin responded and gave Roscoe a quick death stare.

"Some guys see a beautiful girl such as yourself and don't know how to act and end up saying or doing something stupid. I mean, you are very beautiful," Macal said with a smile.

"Thanks," Brown Skin said with a blush. Her friends giggled.

"My name is Macal, and yours?" He introduced himself as he held out his hand.

"Chelsea," she replied with a smile and shook his hand. What strong hands! She thought.

"Well, it was nice to meet you, Chelsea. I better get going. I hope to see you again."

"Me too," Chelsea said.

Macal made his way back to the basketball court. His number one rule when it came to picking up girls was to never ask for the number during the first meeting. Let her volunteer the number or ask her for it the next time you see her. In between time, she'll have you on her mind. Macal glanced over his shoulder and saw Chelsea and her friends smiling and waving at him. His ego was on autopilot.

"You see. That's how it's done. You saw how I got them all smiling and shit!" Macal bragged when he reached his friends, but their attention was elsewhere and he noticed. "What's up?"

"Macal, isn't that your dad's car pulling up in that house across the street?" Joe asked.

Everybody's eyes were on the 1992 jet black Ford Mustang.

"No, I don't think so," Macal tried to lie to himself, but deep down he knew better.

"It looks like it," Roscoe said.

When the car parked, a man got out and it was clearly Rufus.

"That is him."

Macal stood there with his blood boiling when he saw Rufus knocking on the door, and a woman wearing nothing but a towel answered. He gave her a big kiss and went inside.

The display made Macal sick to his stomach. "I got to go. Catch y'all later."

"Alright, bye," was all his friends could say. They felt so bad and embarrassed for him.

Macal was very heated during the walk home. This wasn't the first time his father humiliated him with his infidelities in front of his friends. Macal wondered why his mother doesn't just leave his nasty ass. She was a sweet and beautiful woman who deserved so much better. Didn't Rufus know Belinda's drinking was the result of his fucking around? Did he even care? Those questions flooded Macal's head all the way home.

He was about five houses down when he heard a woman yell, "Bitch, where the fuck he at?"

Shit that bitch is back! Macal thought. He definitely knew who that voice belonged to. It was Taryn's scandalous, hoe ass starting shit with his momma Belinda again. Macal made a run for it to the front yard and found Belinda and Taryn in each other's faces with Tylisha directly behind Belinda. Belinda had a Colt 45 forty ounce in her hand, which was half full. Belinda was kind of tipsy but not quite drunk yet.

"Bitch, I'm not leaving until I see my man!" Taryn refused to budge.

"Get the fuck off my property, hoe!" Belinda yelled in Taryn's face, breathing her strong malt liquor breath all on her.

"I'm not going anywhere, you drunk bitch!"

Macal wished his mother was sober during this confrontation. Her being under the influence was making this display even more humiliating.

"Oh, you mean my husband!" Belinda corrected her and took another swig of her forty. "I don't know where the fuck he is, so your stank ass better stay the—"

"Liar!" Taryn screamed and slapped the shit out of Belinda. The slap left a stinging feeling on the side of Belinda's face. Taryn was about to say something else but decided against it and flashed a victorious smile. "You know what? I'll find him myself. You just go ahead and finish off that forty, you pathetic bitch!"

Taryn turned around to walk away. Something came over Belinda fast. She took the forty ounce bottle she had in her hand and hit Taryn over the head with it so hard she fell down the steps. She was now covered with broken glass and left over malt liquor. "You bitch you!" Belinda screamed, pouncing on Tyran like a panther and started beating her ass.

Macal saw Tylisha standing on the porch in shock. He ran over to her and grabbed her by the hand. "Let's go in the house. You don't need to see this."

Macal led Tylisha in the house and in her room. He sat Tylisha on the bed and saw the tears in her eyes. "I'm scared, Macal."

"Scared of what, baby girl?"

"She's hurting mommy."

Macal took a quick peek out the window and saw Belinda with her hands around Taryn's neck and then she gave her face a punch. Macal laughed on the inside at the fact that Taryn couldn't fight. Who gets their ass beat by somebody who's intoxicated? "I think momma will be just fine." He took a seat next to Tylisha. "There's nothing to be scared of. Momma will be just fine. I know what will make you feel better."

"You gonna do it!" Tylisha dried her tears and cheered like the hyper little girl she was.

"Yes," Macal said with a laugh. He busted out with Biz Markie's Just a Friend. Tylisha got a kick out of Macal singing off key and ridiculous, and she laughed like she was being tickled.

"Macal!" The sound of Tylisha's voice snapped him out of his private reminiscing moment as she walked into his office and found him at his desk.

"Hey, Tylisha," he responded. "What's up?"

Tylisha went straight to the point. "I need you to pick up the kids from school today, because I'm going over to Enzo's house to check out the layout before my crew gets started."

"Alright, cool. I'll be there," Macal agreed with no argument.

"Thanks." Tylisha was about to leave when she realized something was off. She turned around and walked back over to Macal. "Hold the fuck up! That shit was too easy! What the hell is wrong with you?"

"Nothing, I'm good," Macal unconvincingly replied.

"And you know I'm not buying that bullshit, right?" Tylisha walked over to the couch and patted the seat beside her. "Now, bring your ass over here and spill the motherfucking tea."

"Really, I'm good." He made his way towards the couch and took a seat next to her. "I was just thinking about momma."

Tylisha hugged him and kissed him on the cheek. “I know. I miss momma too.”

“It’s more than that. It’s my fault she died in the first place,” Macal confessed.

Tylisha shook her head. She knew Macal was carrying this guilt inside him. Her heart ached for her big brother. “Macal, that wasn’t your fault. You were only thirteen. You had no clue the accident would happen. I know. I was there.”

“Tylisha, I should’ve kept my mouth shut,” Macal insisted with guilty shame. “If I did she’d still be alive and with us.”

“Come here.” Tylisha pulled Macal into her arms and rocked him like a baby. “It’s not your fault. I know how much you loved momma. Not a day goes by that I wish she was here. My heart aches for her too. We loved her and she loved us with everything she had to give. Always remember that, okay?”

Macal nodded. “For the record, I’m thankful to have a big brother like you to look after me and my babies.”

Macal escaped Tylisha’s loving embrace and regained his composure. “I do what I can. I’m also glad to have a baby sister like you to keep me in line.”

“Yeah, but it’s a tough ass job.” Tylisha sighed and the Kilborn siblings shared a laugh. “You remember what you used to do for me whenever I was upset, or to take our minds off momma and daddy’s drama, or just playing around for no reason?”

“I was just thinking about that,” Macal answered with a smile. “Our song.”

“Yeah. Our song,” Tylisha said and all of the sudden she started singing. “You! You got what I need, but you say he’s just a friend. And you say he’s just a friend.”

Macal joined in and played the song on his phone. “Oh baby you...” Macal and Tylisha were singing along to the record before it was time for Tylisha to meet with Enzo.

Chapter 12

Tylisha enjoyed the drive to Enzo's house in her brand new gray Mercedes she picked up last week. When she reached her destination, she parked in the driveway and stepped out of the car. As she was walking towards the front door she admired the house in awe.

"Nice house," she uttered and rang the doorbell.

Enzo flung the door open wide with a sexy smile on his face. "Why, hello, beautiful," he greeted her.

Keep it professional, girl! Tylisha had to remind herself. She had to admit, Enzo had come a long way. She shook his hand, returning his greeting. "Hello, Mr. Goss, I'm here to check out the layout of the house before my crew gets started."

"Right this way." Enzo led Tylisha in the house and closed the door behind him. "By the way, you don't have to be so formal with me. Call me Enzo."

"Of course," Tylisha blushed. She looked around the house. It was very nice and spacious, but it was also very empty. "Wow, you weren't kidding. There's nothing here. Where and how you living?"

"I've been living in a pre-furnished condo since my divorce," Enzo answered. "Once I get all settled in here, I'll sell it. Let's start the tour." Enzo grabbed Tylisha by the hand and led the way. She was blown away by the house. She was sure to have fun decorating it.

When they arrived upstairs, Enzo and Tylisha took a peek in one of the rooms.

"This will be Amery's room during his stays," he informed her.

Tylisha nodded and followed Enzo into the master bedroom.

"Here's my room."

Tylisha looked around with amazement. She walked into the master bathroom and fell in love instantly. She loved the marble luxury tub and the matching marble sink. She almost had a heart attack when she took a gander at the design of the walk-in shower. She joined Enzo back in the bedroom. "The layout of this house is perfect. Trust and believe you'll love the finished product. I'm coming up with ideas about this bedroom alone."

"So am I." Enzo implied while visually checking out every inch of Tylisha's body.

Tylisha was fighting the urge to reach under her skirt to take her thong off and let Enzo take her pussy. She had to keep reminding herself that she was a professional businesswoman, not a hoe.

"Come and check out the view."

Tylisha walked over to the window and couldn't believe how beautiful the view was. "This is an excellent view of the pool and the backyard. Simply beautiful."

"Yes, it is." Enzo used his hand to turn Tylisha's head to face him and gazed deep into her eyes. "And so are you."

"Thanks for the compliment," Tylisha giggled like a school girl. "Let's go back downstairs so we can discuss the details and schedule."

Tylisha turned around to exit the room with Enzo's eyes glued to her plentiful backside. *Mmmm, so luscious and juicy!* Enzo's lustful thoughts took over.

Tylisha reached the doorway and out of nowhere she spun around and said, "Don't think I didn't know you was staring at my ass."

"Can't blame a man for enjoying the gorgeous view," Enzo replied unapologetically, as he approached Tylisha.

This is one bold nigga! Tylisha thought as she was creaming in her thong. "Don't start something you can't finish." She shot back.

"Baby, when I start something, I never stop." He winked.

Look at him! "Oh really?"

"Really." Enzo eyed Tylisha's briefcase she had over her shoulder along with some kind of designer handbag. "That's a lot of stuff for you to be carrying."

"It's only my briefcase and handbag."

"I got it." Enzo grabbed the briefcase off Tylisha's shoulder.

"If you insist," Tylisha said with gratitude.

"My pleasure, but something is still not right," Enzo said.

"What's that?" Tylisha asked curiously.

"This!" Enzo scooped Tylisha up in his arms with surprise and she let out a loud scream.

"Boy, put me down!" Tylisha laughed. *Shit, he's strong and smells great!*

"We don't want your feet hurting, do we?"

"Boy, you are a mess," Tylisha laughed.

Enzo carried her all the way downstairs and went into the kitchen. He put her down and handed her the briefcase.

Tylisha placed the briefcase on the counter top and pulled out a folder. "Let's go over these designs, and just so you know," she turned to face Enzo to drive the point home, "I don't mix business with pleasure."

"Wise rule to live by, but you know I'm not going to be your client forever," Enzo pointed out.

"You got me there."

Enzo was a very charming and sexy man. He's not exactly a stranger, but Tylisha only knew Enzo the boy, not Enzo the man. Maybe she should've checked this guy out.

"How about this? When the job is done, I'll go out with you. Deal?" She proposed.

"Deal," Enzo accepted. "Alright, let's get a move on. The sooner this house gets set-up, the sooner I can collect."

They laughed.

Chapter 13

Thuy was hard at work in her office at her dealership where she also did her sports agent work. As a result, her dealership was booming. The customers and employees loved getting the chance of running across one of Thuy's famous clients that came to see her and occasionally bought a car. Thuy took pride in being able to provide for herself and her mother so she could retire early.

Her phone rang and she answered. "Thuy's Audis. Thuy Ellis speaking, how may I help you?"

"Hey, Thuy," Thuy's big cousin Samuel Ellis, Jr. greeted her. He was a world famous racecar driver. He and his father Sam, Sr. were the reasons Thuy took an interest in cars and sports. Sam was also her very first client. When Thuy branched off on her own, Tony let her take Sam with her. He went by 'SamIAm' when he drove.

"Hey, Sam! How you doing?"

"Great, I'm getting ready for the race this afternoon in Los Angeles. Thanks again for my latest endorsement. You're the best sports agent, baby cousin in the world," Sam boasted.

"Aww, you're just saying that because it's completely true," Thuy bragged.

They laughed. Thuy and Sam talked for over an hour. Sam was the closest thing Thuy had to a loving sibling. She always treasured their relationship. Their deep conversation was interrupted by a beep.

"Thuy, I think you have a beep," Sam said.

The beep was heard again. "I'll take this and call you right back," Thuy told him.

"Alright, cool."

Thuy clicked over to the caller on hold and greeted them. "Thuy's Audis. Thuy Ellis speaking. How may I help you?"

"Thuy, this is your father."

Fuck! Why the fuck did I click over! Thuy rolled her eyes and braced herself for her sperm donor's bitching.

"I heard about you still treating Jett and Tori terribly and I don't like it. What you need to do is stop being all bitter like your mother and get over—"

Olson made a huge mistake by speaking negatively about Thuy's mother. That's a big no-no in her book. She had to end this call before her mood got completely fucked up. "I'm sorry, I can't chat right now. I have something more important to tend to." She hung up the phone without guilt.

Olson had her really fucked up. He never once put Thuy first. No matter what the circumstances were. All he cared about was kissing his bitch wife and real kids' asses and expected Thuy to suck that shit up and accept the crumbs. Even during her ordeal with Levi, his ass still couldn't grow a pair and support her.

1996

"Where the fuck is that deadbeat ass nigga?" Isla paced, waiting for Olson to show up. She didn't care how he treated her but he was not going to mistreat her baby. Not if she had anything to say about it. "Fuck it! I'm calling his ass again!" She was about to find the nearest pay phone when she saw Olson heading her way. He looked aggravated but Isla didn't give a shit. "Well it's about fucking time your punk ass showed up!"

"Woman, what the fuck do you want?" Olson asked rudely. "I paid your ass last week!"

That's a deadbeat daddy for you, Isla thought with disgust. "What I want is for you to finally grow some balls and be by your daughter's side. You know she's in the hospital."

"Yeah, I know and she'll be okay," Olson dismissed. "Now, if you'll excuse me."

Isla pulled Olson's arm, preventing him from walking away. "Your ass ain't going nowhere until you see my baby. She's been asking for you. She needs your support and protection. You're not shutting her out and disappointing her this time."

"I don't have time for this bullshit, and quit motherfucking calling me! It pisses off my wife and kids!" Olson snatched his arm away from Isla's grasp and walked off in a huff.

That did it for Isla. "Nigga, fuck you and your bitter, stuck up bitch of a wife and bad ass, fucked up 'real kids'!" She yelled back and went back into Thuy's room.

Isla knew Thuy and Bryn overheard everything by the look of disappointment on Thuy's face and the shocked expression on Bryn's face. "I'm sorry you guys had to hear that." Isla said with regret. "Bryn, do you need a ride home?" She offered.

"Ms. Ellis, look out!" Bryn yelled and pointed behind Isla.

Isla turned around and was met with a punch to the face by Olson. He then jacked her up and screamed in her face, "Bitch, don't you ever talk about my wife and kids like that! Do you understand me?" Olson threw her to the ground and kicked her three times. He pulled her off the ground and gave her face another punch.

"Ah! Help! Stop, Olson, please!" Isla yelled.

"You ungrateful, money grubbing bitch! Know your fucking place!" Olson yelled and punched Isla again.

Bryn tried to pull Olson off Isla, but Olson yanked Bryn off him and threw him hard enough for him to hit his head on the dresser and slip into unconsciousness.

"Let go of my momma!" Thuy yelled.

Olson turned around and yelled at Thuy with intense hatred, "Shut the fuck up!"

Thuy couldn't believe how her own father spoke to her, especially in her condition. Bryn was knocked out on the floor and Olson continued to savagely beat Isla. Thuy found the button to call the nurse and pressed it frantically.

In no time the staff came in. It took four of them to pull Olson off Isla and drag him away. When Olson was gone, a nurse tended to Isla while a staff member carried out a still unconscious Bryn, heading for the emergency room.

"Are you alright ma'am?" The nurse asked Isla.

"I think so," Isla said, trying to breathe.

The nurse visually examined Isla's bruises. She was almost as badly beaten as Thuy. "This doesn't look good," the nurse said. "We need to examine you right away."

"Alright," Isla agreed.

"Momma, I'm sorry!" Thuy cried out.

"Thuy, you have nothing to be sorry about," Isla said. "If anybody hurts you, you make them accountable like you did with Levi. Now I'm about to follow your example." She turned to the nurse and said, "I want to report this."

The nurse nodded in agreement. "We'll make the call for you and when the police arrive we'll be able to collect evidence."

"Thanks," Isla said with gratitude before being led to the examination room.

Thuy was in disbelief about what had just transpired in her hospital room. Her father beat her mother up, knocked out her best friend and yelled at her with contempt. Her own father couldn't even stand by her side during an extremely turbulent time in her life. It was official. Thuy had seen and heard enough. Her father and siblings didn't give a fuck about her at all. In return, she decided to not to give a fuck about them either.

"He has his fucking nerve!" Thuy's sperm donor got her so upset she forgot to call Sam back. She dialed the number and he answered on the first ring. "I'm back, Sam. What were we talking about?" Thuy was clearly aggravated.

"Olson, Jett or Tori?" Sam guessed.

"It was the sperm donor. What tipped you off?"

"You always sound annoyed, aggravated and pissed the fuck off right after you talk to them. What was it about this time?"

"Oh, his deadbeat ass bitching about how bad I'm treating Tori and Jett, and I need to stop being bitter like my mother."

"Oh shit! How bad did you cuss his ass out?"

"I rushed him off the phone and hung up on him."

"You're getting soft." Sam would've beaten the breaks off Olson's ass. He was so lucky Sam was visiting his father out of town that day at the hospital. If he or his father saw him lay one finger on his favorite aunt, his father's baby sister, a five year prison sentence would've been the least of Olson's problems.

"I wasn't in the mood today, that's what it was. He had the nerve to call to tell me that I'm wrong for the way I'm treating Jett and Tori. Where the fuck was all this bitching when they were terrorizing the fuck out of me growing up." Thuy found this whole shit fucked up. Those motherfuckers were the ones who were mistreating her, and because she made it in life, they thought she owed them something because they share the same blood? Get motherfucking real! They really had her fucked up!

"Yeah, it's fucked up," Sam agreed.

"Thanks for sticking with me for all these years," Thuy said with gratitude.

"That's what family is all about, right?"

"Would you mind teaching my sperm donor and his 'real children' that?"

"Baby girl, I'm a racecar driver, not a miracle worker," Sam replied with a serious tone, and they let out a loud, hysterical laugh.

"Thanks for calling me. I'll talk to you later, and good luck in the race."

"Thanks, and bye."

"Bye."

Thuy started checking her email when she heard a knock at the door. "Come in." Thuy heard the door open and close and she looked up and was surprised to see Jeromy's face. "Jeromy? This is a pleasant surprise! What's the occasion?"

"I wanted to stop by and take my favorite girl out to lunch." Jeromy was working overtime keeping Thuy happy. Now, if he could only get rid of the problem that's growing in Thuy's belly. Then, he'll be free from being tied down, and his wallet will be safe and sound.

"That will be great. Let me get my purse and we'll be on our way." Thuy turned off her computer and grabbed her black Brahmin handbag. She grabbed the phone on her desk and called the manager. "Leslie, I'm stepping out for a while."

"Yes, Ms. Ellis," Leslie replied.

"Alright, let's go," Thuy said with a smile. Her smartphone rang and she dug in her handbag. She found the phone and saw it was Onya calling. "I'm sorry, baby, I have to take this real quick."

"Take your time, baby." *Hurry up, you bitch!*

"Hello," Thuy answered. "Hey, Onya! What's up?"

The mentioning of Onya's name set alarms in Jeromy's head. He remained quiet so he could pay close attention to the conversation. Even though he could only hear Thuy's end, he had no choice but to make due.

"How are things going for you? Still no word from him? Just calm down, and don't let him get to you, or else he wins. I'll call you tonight. Alright, goodbye."

"Who was that on the phone?" Jeromy casually asked, trying to hide his suspicions.

"She's a woman I met at the center. She's going through a difficult time," Thuy answered and put the phone back in her handbag.

"How difficult of a time?" He asked with innocent curiosity to try to gather information.

"Long story short, she's going through a horrible breakup and she's trying to put her life back together." Thuy placed a gentle kiss on Jeromy's lips. "Let's go."

Thuy locked up her office and she and Jeromy headed out, arm and arm, looking like a couple in love. In actuality, Thuy was in love with her head in the clouds. Jeromy's mind was somewhere else. He didn't want to jump to conclusions and confront Onya. That would give him away. It could only be a coincidence, but he had to be sure. He had to figure out an inconspicuous way to check this shit out. He could be wrong. After all, that dumb, hoe ass bitch couldn't be that stupid and seek out Thuy and slither her way into her circle in order to get to Jeromy. Or could she? Jeromy had to come up with a fool-proof plan to find out what the fuck was going on, and quick.

Chapter 14

The kids were in school and Tylisha didn't have any appointments on this day, so she decided to use this time to check on her grandmother Doris and see how she was adjusting to the retirement village she insisted on moving into.

"This is a very nice place," Tylisha said. She and Doris were drinking coffee in the living room, watching Maury. Tylisha loved the show and was surprised when she learned that Doris watched it too.

"This is a very nice place," Grandma Doris agreed.

The show was almost over. It was time for the final paternity test. Maury took the results out of the envelope and read, "When it comes to three year old Amy. Vino: You are not the father!" After the results were revealed, the usual happened. Vino dancing on stage like a damn fool. The woman, Vallie, running offstage all the way to the back, all humiliated, crying her eyes out in shame.

"That's a shame! That girl had all of those men and ain't got a clue who the baby daddy is." Doris shook her head. "How many men did her little skank ass bring on the show? Five? Six?"

"Eight," Tylisha corrected. "Oh, I keep track," They laughed. "This is a very nice place," Tylisha complimented again and took a sip of her coffee.

The place looked better than the house Doris sold. Doris sure knew how to put a house together. That's how Tylisha took interest in decorating. Doris taught her everything she knew.

"How Macal pulled this off, I'll never know."

Macal and the moving men he hired cleared out Doris' house and moved everything into her new home in record time.

"That boy is a hard and fast worker." Grandma Doris took a sip of her coffee.

"Yes he is," Tylisha said. "I worry about him sometimes."

"Is he still fucking that little slut-tramp-bitch who's posing as Fallon's friend?" Doris asked with the look of disgust on her face.

That question took Tylisha by surprise. "How did you know?"

"Girl, I know every nook and cranny about you babies, inside and out. I'm forever inside your heads." Doris let out a chuckle when she flashed back to all the times Macal had different girls at the house during his high school days. She also remembered the occasional drag out showdowns in the front yard. Those girls fought like grown ass men.

"I've been trying to tell him to leave her and these women alone, but he won't listen. He's just gonna do him," Tylisha said with disappointment.

"That's a grown ass man. You can't control a grown ass man."

"Tell me about it," Tylisha agreed. "Why do they do it? Why do men cheat? I mean, they can have an amazing woman at home but they still do it. Why, Grandma Doris? Why?" Tylisha had been wondering that all her life. From watching her daddy fuck around on her momma to Macal's exploits and trying to talk some sense inro him. Last but not least, her marriage to Milton who ended up shitting on her.

"Baby girl, women have been asking themselves that since the beginning of time," Doris replied. "All I can say is this. Men cheat because they want to. You can be the most beautiful, prefect woman in the world. You can love that man unconditionally and do everything that puts a smile on his face every single day. At the end of the day, it doesn't matter. That man is gonna do whatever the fuck he wanna do. It's up to us, as women, to decide whether to put up with it or not."

Tylisha thought back to all the bullshit she put up with during her marriage. The lies, the cheating, groupies and side bitches coming at her with disrespect. She put up with Milton's shit only to be tossed out on her ass with empty pockets and two babies on her hip.

"I was a fool," Tylisha said with shame. "Why did I stay? I knew it wasn't getting any better, but I still stayed and he ended up leaving me with nothing."

Doris pulled Tylisha into an embrace and kissed her on the forehead. "You're not a fool, baby girl. You were just a woman in love who wanted to make it work and last. That doesn't make you a fool."

"I thought I would never end up like momma. She put up with so much from daddy and it killed her."

It took a long time for Doris to forgive Rufus for bringing so much pain and suffering into her only child's life. She hated that man with a passion, especially after Belinda's drinking problem grew worse. "Yes, it did," Doris said.

"You know Macal still blames himself for what happened to momma?"

That poor baby! Doris felt her grandson's pain. "No! No! He shouldn't! It wasn't his fault. He was just a baby himself." Doris let out a huge sigh. "That boy is carrying so much weight inside of him and, unfortunately, he carried it into his marriage. Fallon is a good girl and I know Macal loves her, but that marriage is doomed!"

"I'm afraid you're right," Tylisha sadly agreed.

"As far as your momma goes, she had a big heart. She loved you and your brother with everything she had to give. She loved hard. That's what y'all picked up from her," Doris said with admiration. Then a strange feeling came over her. A haunting feeling really. "You know I shouldn't talk. Sometimes I blame myself for your momma's death."

Is she serious? Tylisha couldn't believe this. "You? Why?"

"You know your granddaddy died when your momma was fourteen, right?"

"Right." Tylisha and Macal never knew the details of their grandfather's death. In fact, Belinda never really talked about him at all. "How did he die?"

"He was beaten to death by a group of men who were relatives of the young girl he was fucking. She was two years older than your momma at the time," Doris confessed.

Tylisha's eyes widened with shock at this discovery. She thought Doris would be the last woman who would ever put up with an unfaithful man.

Doris knew she stunned Tylisha but continued her story. "Yeah! All her life, your momma watched me put up with your granddaddy's shit, and I took him back every time. Even after I caught him in bed with another woman so many times I lost count at twelve. He had secret kids he thought I didn't know nothing about. Many times I passed by strange kids who were a little too happy to see your granddaddy and them and they momma looking at me like I was worse than Satan. I guess they blamed me for the reason they daddy wasn't around. If only I had set a better example for your momma and was strong enough to walk out, and stop tolerating the bullshit, maybe she'd still be alive."

Tylisha had no idea Doris felt this way. She was the strongest person she knew. What she saw now was the vulnerability she rarely showed. The last time Tylisha saw this side of Doris was when Belinda died. Tylisha wanted her to know it was okay to be vulnerable sometimes. "It's okay." Tylisha rubbed her back and kissed her on the cheek. "I'm sorry, Grandma Doris."

"I'm okay, baby," Doris said. "Thanks, baby. The past can be tragic and painful, but we can't wallow in it forever. If we do, it'll eat us up alive and our future will be doomed."

Chapter 15

"So, we're going with these computers and these two printers," Thuy said as she pointed out the selections in the catalog with Bryn, Vida and Ambrosia hovering over her.

"Sounds good to me," Ambrosia said.

Thuy brought her laptop with her to the center and went on the catalog's website to place the order. "How many computers are we ordering?" She asked.

"Ten," Ambrosia answered.

"Ten it is then. It's all settled. Now, time to place the order." Thuy searched for the computers and printers and made the selections. She used the foundation's credit card to make the purchase, and made sure to forward a copy of the invoice to Ambrosia and Bryn's email addresses. "It's done. Now let's get back to work."

"Hey, Thuy," Jeromy's voice called out as he made his surprise entrance.

Nobody expected to see Jeromy here. His presence caught everybody completely off guard.

"Jeromy, what are you doing here?" Thuy asked.

"I wanted to help my baby out and volunteer my services," Jeromy answered with a genuine straight face and pulled Thuy into a passionate kiss. "Hey, Vida! Hey, Bryn!"

"Hi!" Vida and Bryn greeted him dryly. They couldn't stand Jeromy's trifling ass, but for Thuy they tried to be polite.

"It's good that you're here because we need an extra person to help clean the bathrooms," Ambrosia said. Assigning Jeromy to bathroom duty tickled Bryn.

"I'm your guy." Jeromy perfected his fake front very well. Being in this building with a bunch of whining, bitter, crybaby bitches made his ass and nuts itch and he definitely didn't want to waste his time cleaning piss and shit-filled toilets, and with an occasional bloody ass tampons and pads inside.

The whole thing was demeaning to Jeromy, but volunteering at the center was the only idea he could think of in order to find out for sure if that was the same Onya who approached Thuy. He figured if Thuy and Onya met at the center and Thuy was gullible enough to let Onya into her life so easily, chances were Onya would come back to the center to see Thuy. Jeromy had to stick it out to wait and see.

Everyone was off doing their assignments. Thuy was at the table doing the sorting and Bryn and Vida were putting together a bookshelf.

"That bastard is up to something," Bryn whispered to Vida.

Vida stopped what she was doing because Bryn's accusation puzzled her. "What makes you say that?"

"All this time Thuy has been a part of the Restart Project, and now he's taking an interest and wants to be involved. Get motherfucking real," Bryn explained his suspicions. "I'm not buying that shit for a second."

Vida had to admit that it was strange that Jeromy was all of the sudden taking an interest in the foundation, but what was his plan? It didn't make any sense. On the other hand, Bryn has always been very good at reading people. "You could be right. He is trying to stay on Thuy's good side, but what would he have to gain by helping out around here? What's his motive?"

"I don't know, but this shit doesn't sit right with me." Bryn stuck with his suspicions.

"If he is up to no good, it'll come to light eventually," Vida said.

"Hey, Thuy!" Onya greeted her as she approached Thuy's table where she was working.

"Hey, Onya!" Thuy returned with a smile, and gave Onya a big hug. "Nice to see you again. You seem to be in great spirits." She noted Onya's pleasant demeanor.

"I'm taking it one day at a time. I started taking your advice and not letting him get to me."

"That's good. Good for you. Let me introduce you to some people." Thuy looked around for Bryn and Vida and found them.

She signaled for Onya to follow her. “Everybody, this is Onya. Onya, these are my two best friends since childhood, Bryn and Vida. Bryn and Ambrosia Jackson started this foundation, and Bryn brought me and Vida into the fold. We’re all here to help.”

“Thank you so much,” Onya said. “It’s very nice to meet you guys.”

“The pleasure is ours,” Vida said.

“Anytime,” Bryn said.

Jeromy came up behind Thuy and wrapped his arms around her.

“Hey, baby,” Thuy said with a kiss.

“I decided to take a break and see my baby, and my future baby.” Jeromy rubbed Thuy’s stomach.

“You’re a sweetie,” Thuy giggled. “Where are my manners? Jeromy, this is Onya. Onya, this is my boyfriend, Jeromy. We’re expecting our first child.”

“Nice to meet you,” Onya greeted him.

“You too,” Jeromy returned, flashing that perfect, handsome smile that made women’s panties soaking wet. He turned to Thuy and said, “I better get back.”

“Alright, baby,” Thuy replied, and Jeromy took his leave.

“Excuse me, but did you mention that you were expecting?” Onya asked.

“Yes, I’m four months pregnant,” Thuy said with satisfaction and fulfillment. She couldn’t wait until her bundle of joy arrived. Then, she thought about Onya and how she was tricked into terminating her pregnancy. Thuy didn’t want Onya to feel some type of way. “Oh, I’m sorry. I hope I didn’t make you feel uncomfortable.”

“It’s cool. I’ll be alright,” Onya assured her.

An idea suddenly popped into Thuy’s head. “I need to give you a tour. Do you have time?”

“Oh, I have all the time in the world,” Onya said with slight cheer. “What’s going on in here?” Onya wanted to know about the construction and setting up everybody was doing.

"This is where we're setting up the library and the connecting computer room," Thuy explained. "Alright, let's get on with the tour. If you'll follow me please."

The ladies left the future library and walked down the hall. Thuy began the tour and started describing every room in the center in detail as they passed by and took a peek inside.

During the tour, Onya received a text message. She wanted to ignore it because she wanted to give Thuy her full attention, and she already knew who it was. Onya went ahead and checked the message to get it over with. She made sure to do it on the sly so Thuy wouldn't notice. She took a peek at the message and she was right about who the sender was.

Jeromy: Bitch, get your ass the fuck out of here, now!

Onya: Free country, nigga!

Jeromy: I mean it!

Onya: Why should I? You didn't give me the money you promised me after you made me kill our baby. You want me to leave! Pay the fuck up!

Jeromy: You ain't getting a dime, hoe!

Onya: In that case, I'll make myself very comfy, right here next to your future baby momma, waiting on the perfect opportunity to tell her everything. Like for starters, reveal to her the true identity of the bitch ass, fuck nigga who bribed me into getting an abortion and reneged on our deal.

Jeromy: Bitch, I ain't the one to fuck with! Don't motherfucking push me!

Onya: *Push* Come with it, motherfucker!

Chapter 16

Fallon had a successful day at work. Her assignment today was taking school pictures for a middle school yearbook. Afterwards, she stopped by Wal-Mart to pick up her medication. Since Macal was going to have a late night at the office, Fallon decided to call Lolette and invite her for a girls' night out. She would've invited Tylisha too, but she took the kids on a weekend vacation to Myrtle Beach, South Carolina, and they left that morning.

When Fallon entered the house, she plopped down onto the couch and made the call. It took longer than expected for Lolette to answer, but Fallon paid it no mind.

"Hey, Lolette," Fallon greeted her.

"Hey...Fallon!" Lolette moaned with no shame. She was enjoying the fire head Macal was giving her.

When he heard Fallon's name mentioned, Macal's head shot up quickly, but Lolette used her legs to pull him back down to her hot, steamy center. Since he couldn't move, all he could do was beat up the clit with his tongue and hope Lolette didn't say anything stupid.

"I called because I wanted to know if you had any plans tonight?" Fallon asked.

"No...I...don't," Lolette moaned and started to shake from her intense orgasm. "What's up?"

"Is everything okay?" Fallon wanted to know why Lolette was sounding so strange.

"I'm...fine!" Lolette let out another orgasmic moan. The fact that Fallon had absolutely no clue who was sucking the shit out of her pussy made it all the sweeter. "What did you want to do?"

"Macal is having a late night at the office. I was hoping me and you could have a girls' night out. We can do dinner, a movie and have a few drinks at the club," Fallon suggested.

"That sounds great!" *Especially if her ass is paying!* "We can watch that Tupac movie, All Eyez on Me."

"I did a quick search and the next showing is in three hours at the Atlantic Station," Fallon informed her.

"Alright, see you there. Bye!"

"Bye!"

After the call ended, Lolette released Macal from her grip. "You can come out now!" She teased.

Macal took a moment to catch his breath. "That was too close!"

"Oh hush! You enjoyed it!" Lolette laughed.

"That's beside the fucking point!" Macal loved Fallon with all his heart. He also loved his unlimited access to easy pussy, and Lolette's was his favorite. Still, she needed to be more cautious. "I'm serious, Lolette! Fallon can never find out!"

How cute! He thinks his wife is perfect! "I understand," Lolette replied with a straight face. She wondered what Macal would think if he knew what she knew about his nice, sweet wife. It sure was very tempting to share all the details with him, but now was not the time.

"Good," Macal said with relief. "Since Fallon is not expecting me until late." He pulled Lolette into his arms and stuck his tongue deep in her mouth and grabbed her ass. "Let me know when you get back from your night out. I want some more of that good pussy you got."

Macal licked his lips at the sexy, gorgeous piece of ass he had at his disposal. Five foot, five inches tall. Creamy cocoa coating. Huge ass and titties with a small waist and a beautiful face. Let's not forget the hazel eyes and long, naturally curly, off black, thick hair. What man wouldn't want to fuck the shit out of the woman all the time? A fact Lolette, herself, knows all too well.

"Of course," Lolette said and reached down to squeeze hard on Macal's magic stick. "Well, since I got somewhere to be in a few hours." Lolette climbed back on the bed. She got on all fours and arched her back. She used her hands to spread her ass cheeks apart to give Macal a terrific view of her dripping wet goodness. "This needs attention."

The sight made Macal's dick rock hard. He gently stroked his tool and positioned himself behind Lolette. "Oh, I agree baby because—"

"Less talking! More fucking!" Lolette cut him off.

"Great motto to live by," Macal said before sliding his dick inside Lolette's pussy and went to work.

Chapter 17

Onya was sitting in the living room of her house, watching TV with the volume up loud. One of her favorite movies of all time— *A Few Good Men*— was playing. She giggled to herself, thinking about how Jeromy tried to bully her into disappearing and accept the fact that he wasn't going to pay her off like he promised.

It wasn't even about the money. It was the principle. That bastard lied to her about everything, played with her heart, used her, and threw her away like she wasn't shit. Onya wasn't even a baseball fan. She had no clue he was a celebrity, let alone had a girlfriend. A pregnant girlfriend at that. After the fuck nigga hung up on her, Onya did some research to find out who the girlfriend was. How convenient the center was down the street from her favorite beauty supply store.

What an arrogant bastard he turned out to be. Thuy was too good for him. Onya felt guilty about not telling Thuy the whole story. She was so nice to her. How would she react if she knew the truth? But she needed to know, and if Jeromy didn't pay her, she was going to keep her word and tell Thuy everything. Whatever happened, happened.

Boom! Boom! Boom!

"What the hell?" The loud banging on the door startled Onya.

Boom! Boom! Boom! Onya got off the couch to see who the fuck was this banging on her door like they didn't have any damn sense. "Coming! Coming!"

Onya unlocked the door. She barely was able to crack the door open when it swung open and Jeromy barged through the doorway, almost knocking Onya down, slammed the door behind him and locked it.

"What the fuck are you trying to pull?" He yelled at the top of his lungs.

"What are you talking about?" Onya tried to play dumb, walking backwards into the living room, nice and easy with Jeromy following her.

"Bitch, don't fucking play with me!" Jeromy meant business. "I'm going to say this shit one motherfucking time! Stay the fuck away from Thuy and the center!" He demanded.

Onya looked at Jeromy up and down like he lost his damn mind. "Nigga, you can't tell me what to motherfucking do! I'm a grown ass woman! Thuy is a good woman and needs to know what a trifling ass nigga you are, and I'm gonna tell her!"

"No, you won't!" Jeromy shouted. He was not gonna bend for the likes of Onya. As far as he was concerned, the only thing women like her were good for was a nut. She wasn't worth wasting five cents on, let alone five hundred thousand dollars, but he had to get her to get rid of the baby. He had an image to protect. He couldn't stand Thuy's ass either, but she made him look good in the public eye.

"Oh yes, I will, unless you give me my money!" Onya stood firm.

"And I told your ass I ain't paying you shit, hoe!" Jeromy yelled in her face.

"Then I'm telling Thuy," Onya threatened again.

Jeromy paused and took a good look at Onya. Her tank top and booty shorts were clinging to her body. He had to admit she was very beautiful and sexy.

"I know what you want." Jeromy pushed Onya on the couch. He unzipped his pants and whipped his dick out. "You want this dick, don't you?" He stroked his dick as he was trying to hypnotize her.

Onya scoffed with nonchalance. "No thanks, I already had that. What I want is either my money, or you to get the fuck out my house!" Onya was dead ass serious. She was not in the mood.

Jeromy kept stroking his dick, trying to entice her, but to no avail.

She had enough of this nigga's foolishness. Her focus was on the movie. Not Jeromy's community dick. "You ain't showing me nothing new, nigga! Now get your ass out so I can finish enjoying my movie." She dismissed him.

That crushed Jeromy's ego like a can on I-75. He had to fuck her and now! He pounced on top of her and kissed her passionately.

She tried to squirm and get away, but he knew just what to do to make her give into him. He rubbed the back of her neck, and she got horny and wet instantly.

Onya's pussy began to tighten with anticipation. She was at his mercy. Jeromy slid her shorts and panties off and forced his dick deep inside her throbbing pussy. He spread her legs open and put them over his shoulders, and pounded her pussy like a jackhammer.

The loud TV drowned out Onya's pleasure-filled screams. Her sweet, natural juices gave the dick a slippery wet coating. The pussy felt so good and warm around Jeromy's dick that he had to fight off the urge to nut quick and hold out for about fifteen more minutes.

Onya's seventh orgasm made her pussy muscles squeeze the life out of Jeromy's dick. He had no choice but to bust a huge fat nut deep inside her now extra creamy pussy. "Ahh!" He grunted dramatically. He never busted a nut that huge before. It left him very winded. He laid on top of Onya and they remained motionless with his now limp dick still inside her.

Once his strength came back, Jeromy climbed off of Onya. He started getting dressed and she followed suit.

Maybe he came to his senses. Onya thought. *He might even apologize!* "That was great!" She said with glow.

"I know it was," Jeromy boasted and kissed Onya. He then switched on the charm. "It's agreed. You're going to stay away from the center and Thuy, and not say anything, right?"

"Sure." Onya agreed with a smile. "After you give me my money." She definitely didn't forget about the arrangement.

The mere mention of the agreement made Jeromy's charming nature disappear. His plan failed miserably and he was beyond pissed, and wanted Onya to know it. Jeromy looked deep in her eyes and responded as cold as ice, "Fuck you! Oh, wait, I just did!"

His words left Onya stunned, confused and hurt. She felt stupid for letting him get over on her again.

"And now that I fucked you like the worthless piece of shit, two dollar hoe that you are for the very last time, I'm gonna be on my way out that door forever to enjoy my life. I suggest you get one too. What kind of life, I don't give a fuck. Just as long as Thuy and the center ain't a part of it. So long, Dumb Ratchet Thot With Great Pussy!"

That did it for Onya. Jeromy was not going to get away with making a fucking fool out of her again. Not this time. "You know what! Go! Get out! Get your trifling, no good, nasty, black ass out of my house!" Onya yelled as Jeromy started to walk towards the door. "I don't need you or your money!" Onya continued to rant and rave, following Jeromy out the door.

He let himself out, letting her hate-filled outbursts fall on deaf ears.

"And you know what else? You don't deserve a real woman like Thuy! That's why I'm gonna go ahead and call her right motherfucking now and tell her everything! Fuck the consequences!" Onya slammed the door.

She took a brief moment to recover from her tirade before going back into the living room to find her phone. She looked down and found it on the coffee table. She was about to grab the phone when she felt a hand forcibly turn her around, and *pow*! Jeromy backhanded her so hard she fell on the floor.

Jeromy pulled her off the floor and screamed in her face, "You fucking bitch!" Hhe then punched her in the face.

"Help!" Onya yelled.

Whap!

"Somebody, please help me!"

"Shut the fuck up, bitch!" He screamed. He punched her in the face and threw her on the floor like a ragdoll.

"Help!" Onya continued to scream with her mouth now filled with blood. She tried to get up but Jeromy kicked her back down. "Stop! Please!"

Jeromy laughed at Onya's begging. He pulled her off the floor by her hair and started screaming in her face. "Go ahead, bitch! Yell! Scream! Here! I'll scream with you! *Ah somebody help*!(I know that's what I was going for LOL) *Please*! *Somebody, help me, please*!" He mocked her.

Jeromy gave Onya's face another punch and threw her back onto the floor. He leaped on top of her and gave both sides of her face stinging fire-filled backhands. He wrapped his hands around Onya's neck and started choking her until she passed out. He knew she was still alive because he could hear her loud snoring.

Jeromy got up on his feet, fixed his clothes and regained his composure. He looked down at Onya's beaten and bruised body. "That'll teach you to stay in a hoe's place and not fuck with a real man!" He then leaned back and hocked the biggest loogie he could muster up on her face. He casually walked out of the house cool, calm and collected like nothing happened. He hopped into his car and drove home feeling triumphant and free.

Chapter 18

"Macal is still blaming himself for his mother's death?" Fallon refreshed Tylisha's drink while the ladies took their seats in the living room. Macal's guilt about Belinda's death always puzzled Fallon. She knew about Rufus' infidelities, Belinda's alcoholism, and the accident, but she still hadn't gotten Macal to open up to her about his guilt.

"Yes, he is!" Tylisha sighed and took a sip of her drink.

"I don't understand why," Fallon said and sipped her own drink. "I knew he and his mother were very close but he shouldn't feel guilty. The accident wasn't his fault. He was only a child."

"I know." Tylisha shook her head. "Me and Grandma Doris tried to tell him, but he still feels like it's his fault."

"I try not to press the issue," Fallon said, "I just try to be there for comfort and be a listening ear. Hopefully, one day he'll be able to open up to me about this."

"That's all we can do. At the end of the day, we have to be patient, supportive and comforting."

The doorbell rang and Fallon asked, "Who is it?"

"Lolette!"

Tylisha rolled her eyes. She was hoping to enjoy a relaxing evening of drinking with Fallon while the kids were in the game room. Macal couldn't join them because he had a business dinner. Now her evening was ruined because she gotta be in the same room as this two-faced, nasty ass bitch.

"Coming!" Fallon got out of her seat to answer the door and hugged her best friend. "Hey girl! What's up?"

"I'm good! Just wanted to drop by." Lolette entered the house and gave Tylisha the fakest, friendly greeting she could muster up. "Hey, Tylisha, girl!"

Tylisha flashed a fake ass smile and waved.

"Join us." Fallon offered Lolette a seat in the living room. "We're having drinks. I'll fix you one, Lolette. Tylisha, do you need a refill?"

"That would be great!" Tylisha answered. "Good thing I'm spending the night here."

"That reminds me. Do the kids need anything?" Fallon asked Tylisha.

"I'll check." Tylisha was happy to have an excuse to leave the living room because she didn't want to spend a minute alone with Lolette. Not because she was intimidated by her. Never that. No, actually, Tylisha didn't want to risk Lolette making her choke her to sleep.

After Tylisha checked on the kids and Fallon refreshed the drinks, the women lounged around in the living room, chatting away.

"I'm home, everybody," Macal announced as he walked through the front door.

"Hi, Macal," the women greeted him.

"Baby, how was your business dinner?" Fallon asked.

"It was great. Closed the deal like always. My new client and his wife were amazing," Macal answered.

"Congratulations, honey!" Fallon rushed over to give Macal a congratulatory smooch and was taken aback. Macal had a weird taste in his mouth and a strong, unpleasant scent on his breath. "Eww, what is that fishy smell and taste? Nasty!" She exclaimed with disgust.

Not again! Tylisha thought.

What the fuck! Lolette internally screamed with anger and jealousy.

"Sorry, baby, I had fish for dinner," Macal uttered the first lie that popped into his head.

"Oh okay," Fallon accepted.

Quick on his feet! I give him that! Tylisha thought.

"Tylisha, you and the kids are spending the night, right?" Macal asked.

"That's correct," Tylisha confirmed. "The kids are settled in their rooms and in the bed."

"That's good. Fallon, can you fix me a drink?" Macal requested.

"Sure. Anything in particular?" Fallon asked.

"Surprise me," he said and smacked Fallon on the ass, making her giggle. "I'm gonna jump in the shower real quick and I'll be right back."

"And remember to brush those teeth and gargle." Fallon referred to Macal's stank, fish mouth.

Macal laughed and gave Fallon a salute. "Roger that." Then, he went on his way.

Fallon went to the bar to fix Macal a glass of Hennessy with two ice cubes. She tried to take her mind off the weird smell, but couldn't. She didn't want to assume the worst, but with her history it was easier said than done. She took Macal's drink into the living room; waiting on him to come back. She took her seat and was completely silent.

Tylisha and Lolette picked up on Fallon's mood and Lolette was the first to speak on it. "What's wrong, Fallon?"

"It's probably nothing," Fallon tried to shake it off.

"Come on, Fallon. If it was nothing you wouldn't be all upset. Now what is it?" Tylisha asked.

"Alright, but Tylisha are you sure you want to hear this, because it has to do with Macal," Fallon warned her.

"This is not about me. This is about you. What's up?" Tylisha insisted.

Fallon went on to express her worries. "Like I said before, it's probably nothing. Yes, Macal was at a business dinner and explained the smell, but it smelled more like pussy than fish."

"What?" Lolette blurted out in disbelief like she wanted to tear some shit up. Tylisha noticed and was laughing on the inside.

"Yes," Fallon confirmed. "I know he said it was because of the fish he ate, but I also smelled perfume on him," she added.

Tylisha knew Macal was a cheater, but due to strong family ties she had to keep quiet. She knew it was fucked up and Fallon didn't deserve it. She hoped Macal would change his ways and leave those hoes alone before it was too late. On the other hand, it was fun watching Lolette agonize on the sly about another bitch on Macal's dick. Serves the fake, backstabbing hoe right.

"Well, he had dinner with a client and his wife was there. Maybe he hugged her," Tylisha tried to ease Fallon's suspicions.

Fallon nodded like that could be an acceptable explanation. "Whoever the wife was has very horrible taste. That perfume I smelled was awful and cheap as fuck!" Fallon shivered with disgust and the women burst out with uncontrollable laughter to lighten up the mood.

"Well, there you have it," Tylisha said. "Fallon, my brother loves you, that's all that matters." She then turned to Lolette. "Isn't that right, Lolette?"

"Yes, he does," Lolette agreed and nodded her head, trying to keep her cool.

Tylisha was getting a kick out of this. She slowly gave Lolette a big, evil grin in order to gloat.

"You guys are right." Fallon decided to drop the subject and her suspicions. "I must be tripping."

"Are you ladies talking about me?" Macal came back fully refreshed from his shower.

"Oh, baby, here's your drink." Fallon handed Macal his drink.

He took a sip and kissed Fallon. "Thanks, baby."

"Anytime." Fallon gave Macal another kiss and savored the minty scent and flavor. "Now, that's better! Minty fresh!"

"I best be going now." Lolette wanted to get out of the house and fast.

"Goodnight, Lolette," Fallon said.

"Goodnight," Lolette said, and let herself out of the house.

"I ran your bath water for you," Macal said to Fallon.

"You big sweetie." Fallon gave Macal a quick kiss on the lips. "Someone is getting lucky tonight," she implied seductively.

"Oh really?" Macal got the hint and his dick jumped for joy.

"Not too lucky," Tylisha said and turned on the TV. "And keep the noise down. My babies are fast asleep, and I don't want to hear that nasty shit all night!"

"Tylisha, you are a mess!" Fallon laughed and Macal joined in. "Goodnight!" They said.

"Goodnight, you crazy kids," Tylisha said. Macal and Fallon walked arm and arm up the stairs and into their bedroom. When they were out of sight, Tylisha took a peek out the window to see if Lolette was outside. Just as Tylisha guessed, her pathetic, thot ass was still standing outside, wondering what the fuck was going on with Macal. The correct thought would be, who was Macal fucking? Tylisha pulled out her phone to send a quick text.

Lolette was about to get into her car when she got a text notification. She took the phone out of her purse to check the message and wished she hadn't.

Tylisha: I said it once and I'll say it again. You're not the only hoe my brother is fucking! Goodnight and sweet dreams, you pathetic, filthy bitch!

Lolette turned around to face the house and there was Tylisha standing in the window, looking all cocky. She mouth the word 'goodnight' while waving bye-bye in a taunting manner, and topped it off by flashing her middle finger.

"Fuck that bitch!" Lolette was heated and hopped in her car, slammed the door and took off in the night like a bat out of hell. She didn't know what the fuck was going on, but she'd be damned if another bitch was going to have her dick!

Chapter 19

"So, what do you think? Do you like it?" Tylisha presented Enzo's fully decorated house.

Enzo inspected every inch of the house with Tylisha on his heels. They reached the last room of the house which was his bedroom, and gave his opinion. "I don't like it. I love it!" He cheered. "This is perfect!" Enzo pulled Tylisha into his arms and spun her around like she was a little girl. "Thanks, baby girl!"

"Happy to do it! Happy to do it!" Tylisha giggled as Enzo put her down.

"Thanks for helping me out with the move. I really appreciate it," Enzo said and gave Tylisha the check. Her payment policy was half before the job was started and the other half when the job was done. If they want to pay it all beforehand that was fine with her.

"Anything for an old friend." Tylisha put the check in her handbag.

"I seem to remember a little deal we made," Enzo said.

"What little deal?" Tylisha played dumb to playfully torture him.

"Oh, we're playing games now?"

"What games, darling?"

"Oh, really?" Enzo decided to play along. "I remember a certain smart, beautiful, full of life, and forgive me for saying, very sexy interior decorator who I've known since childhood, turned me down for a date because I was her client."

"She did?" Tylisha was playing the game down to the max.

"Yes she did, so I made a deal with her, because I'm a man who doesn't stop 'til he gets what he wants."

"And what deal was that, may I ask?"

"The deal was when the job was done, she'd go out with me." He recapped.

"You don't say."

"I do say. By the way, if you haven't noticed Tylisha, the job is done." Enzo gave a serious, cut the bullshit look.

Tylisha looked around the room at her flawless, completed handiwork. "It is, isn't it?"

"Yes, it is."

"Since I'm a woman of my word, I guess I gotta go through with my end of the bargain, huh?" She said in defeat like she was being coerced into doing something unpleasant.

"Gee, you didn't have to say it like that." Enzo sounded like he was offended and crushed.

"Aww, you're so sensitive," Tylisha teased.

"You still a trip." Enzo laughed and he and Tylisha made their way back downstairs, into the living room and took a seat on the couch.

"I know, but seriously. I have two babies to think about, and their father put me through a world of shit. I'm trying to be careful," Tylisha expressed her concerns about giving another man a chance. They were two things she doesn't play about. Her family and her heart.

"Trust me. I understand," Enzo said, "I'm in the same boat."

"Ligia is not a bitch and is a good parent," Tylisha corrected him.

"True, but I feel what you saying. All I'm asking for is a chance." Enzo pulled Tylisha into his arms, gently caressing her face. "If I miss that's cool, but at least let me have a chance to shoot."

Enzo's touch and charming swagger mesmerized Tylisha. She had no choice but to give in, but she was still Tylisha. She couldn't let him have all the control. "Baby steps?" She proposed.

"Deal."

Tylisha got off the couch heading for the door with Enzo by her side. "I need to stop somewhere for a bite to eat before my next appointment. It'll sure be nice if a certain smooth, sweet, handsome, and sexy man whose house I just decorated, would join me and probably make suggestions?" She implied with her sexy charm.

"I'm sure he would." Enzo opened the door for Tylisha. "After you, sweet young lady."

"Why, thank you, charming young gentleman." Tylisha grinned from ear to ear and they were on their way to not only a lunch outing but the start of a brand new chapter in their lives.

Chapter 20

It was a great beautiful, sunny day at SunTrust Park. The Atlanta Braves were playing the Oakland A's. Thuy, Vida and Bryn were at the game with their prefect seats. Jeromy was at his place on the pitcher's mound. He took a deep breath and pitched a curveball at the Oakland A batter, causing him to strike out.

"Yay! That's my baby!" Thuy jumped up and down out of her seat cheering. "Way to go, baby! You pitching that ball!"

When the cheering calmed down Thuy pulled out her phone to call Onya, and she didn't get an answer. "Shit! She's still not answering."

"Who?" Vida asked.

"You remember that woman I met at the center, Onya?" Thuy reminded her.

"Yeah. What's up?" Bryn asked.

"It's been two weeks and she hasn't been back to the center, and hasn't returned my calls or text messages. I'm starting to get worried," Thuy explained.

"Maybe she's working, or had some sort of family emergency," Vida said.

"I'm not so sure." Thuy shook her head. "I have a gut feeling that something is wrong."

"Look, Thuy, obviously this is troubling you. If it'll make you feel better, just pay her a visit after the game," Bryn suggested.

"That's a good idea. I'll call her one more time, and if she doesn't answer I'll go over there."

As the game continued with the Oakland A's taking the field, Thuy pulled out the phone and tried to call Onya again, and she still didn't get an answer. "Shit! Still no answer! I guess I'll be going to her house after the game."

The bases were loaded and all Marcus Brooks had to do was hit a homerun and the Braves would win the game. The crowd grew silent, waiting on Marcus to take a swing. The Oakland A pitcher threw a high-powered pitch. Marcus took a hard swing and knocked the ball out of the park, literally. Guaranteed homerun! The game was over! The Braves won!

"Yay! We won!" Thuy and the rest of the crowd cheered in victory as the Braves team celebrated on the field in triumph.

"Congratulations, baby!" Thuy cheered and kissed Jeromy in the parking lot where the team and their loved ones were gathered.

"Thanks, Thuy," Jeromy said.

Out of nowhere, Marcus announced, "Hey, you guys! Party at my house!"

Everybody cheered and was all set to go to Marcus' victory party.

Thuy, on the other hand, had something very important to take care of first before going off to have a good time. "I'll meet y'all there. I got to make a stop real quick," she said to Jeromy, Bryn and Vida.

"Baby, where are you going?" Jeromy asked.

"I'm going to Onya's house real quick," she answered. "I think something is wrong and I want to make sure she's alright."

Shit! This was a monkey wrench Jeromy didn't need right now. For the past two weeks he's been feeling great. Ever since Onya learned her lesson, life's been terrific, for the most part. Now, Thuy was about to ruin everything. "You are? But—"

"Don't worry. I won't be long," Thuy said and hopped in her car. "I'll pay her a quick visit and I'll come to the party afterwards."

"But—"

"I'll be there as soon as I can!" And just like that, she was gone.

Jeromy was left standing there dumbfounded, wondering how in the fuck he was going to get out of this one. His only hope was that he fucked Onya up bad enough for her to keep her mouth shut. Then again, maybe not.

Thuy drove to Onya's house with her head filled with all sorts of thoughts. She didn't get it. When she last spoke to Onya she was doing fine. She was putting her life back together and not letting that fuck nigga get to her. What could've happened?

Thuy found the house and parked in the driveway behind Onya's car. She walked to the front door and started knocking. "Hello, Onya! It's me, Thuy, from the center." She knocked on the door again. "Onya, I know you're there. I see your car parked in the driveway. I want to see if you're okay. I'm worried." When Onya didn't answer, Thuy knocked on the door again. "Onya, it's okay. I'm your friend. I want to help. You don't have to be scared. I got you. I'm here for you." Thuy knocked on the door again and gave Onya one full minute to answer. When she didn't get an answer, Thuy gave up... for now. "Okay, I'll go, but you should know that I'll keep coming back until you answer. Goodbye... for now."

Thuy turned around, all set to walk away and leave. She didn't make it past the front porch when she heard Onya's voice. "Thuy, wait!"

Works every time! Thuy stopped dead in her tracks and turned around. "Finally!" She rushed to the door and was blown away at the sight of Onya's bruised face, and this was after two weeks of healing. Her face was no longer swollen. She had a black eye and a busted lip. Her ribs were healed completely. Her left cheek still had a bruise. "Oh my God! What happened?"

"Come inside. Hurry," Onya whispered in a panic.

Thuy hurried inside and closed the door behind her. Thuy wrapped her arms around Onya tight. She knew something was wrong. She didn't want to be right, but unfortunately she was. She led Onya into the living room and on the couch, nice and easy before taking her seat.

"Onya, what the hell happened, and don't even think about feeding me any of those bullshit, old-school cover up stories. They don't work with me."

Onya was too frightened and ashamed to say anything. She felt like she deserved everything Jeromy did to her.

"Did he do this?" Thuy guessed.

Onya nodded. "He came here. He got tired of me calling him about the money. I threatened to tell his girlfriend everything if he didn't give me the money. I still don't understand what happened. One minute we were arguing and the next minute we ended up...

Ended up... I didn't want to at first, or plan on it. I really didn't, but he started being nice and sweet to me like he used to. I thought he still loved me and was going to pay me but—"

"I understand." Thuy spared Onya the embarrassment of admitting that she was seduced and ended up fucking this poor excuse of a man. "Go on. Afterwards, he broke his promise to you again?"

Onya nodded slowly. "Yeah, and he taunted me about using me like the worthless, piece of shit, two dollar hoe that I am. Those were his exact words to me. I was so angry and hurt. As he was walking out the door, I went off and threatened to tell his girlfriend everything, right then and there, and that's when he beat me up. He choked me to sleep after nearly beating me to death. When I woke up, I found out that he also spit in my face. Oh, Thuy I'm so ashamed and embarrassed. I feel so nasty and disgusting!" Onya couldn't hold back the tears anymore. She broke down and cried like a baby.

Thuy wanted to track this monster down and break her foot all the way up in his ass. For now, all she could do was pull Onya in her arms and let her cry. "It's okay. I'm here. This is what we're gonna do. We're going to the police station and file a report."

"No! I can't!" Onya exclaimed in a panic. She didn't want Jeromy to come after her again. "He's a rich celebrity. No one will believe me! I don't want my business out there on the street."

"I understand all of that, but you can't let him get away with this. You can at least put a restraining order out on him." Thuy suggested.

"I don't know. It might not be a good idea."

"I know it's a difficult decision to make. Will you at least think about it and call me tomorrow to let me know where your head is at?" Thuy tried to compromise.

Onya honestly didn't know what to do. She was so confused. It's not like she disobeyed Jeromy. Thuy came to her. Not the other way around. "Alright, I'll think about it and call you tomorrow."

"Okay." Thuy accepted. "Remember, I'm only a phone call away."

"Thanks, Thuy." Onya said with a hopeful smile.

The ladies said their goodbyes and Onya walked Thuy out. Onya sat back on the couch, thinking about her what her next move was going to be. Should she tell Thuy or keep her mouth shut? Should she press charges and, or, file the restraining order? What would Jeromy do if he found out that she spilled the beans? She continued to ponder until her phone rang. She looked down, and speak of the devil. It was Jeromy. She wanted to ignore the call but she knew that would do her no good. He would just keep on calling until she answered. Plus, he knew where she lived and she didn't want to make him angry enough to come over and beat her ass again.

"What the fuck do you want? Another round?" Onya answered the phone with hate and anger.

"No, baby girl. I want to apologize." Jeromy said in a sweet voice.

Onya wasn't buying that bullshit he was talking. "Apologize for what? Lying to me? Making a fool out of me? Tricking me into getting an abortion? Using me? Beating my ass? Spitting in my face after chocking me to sleep? Save your fake ass apologies for somebody who gives a fuck, because first thing tomorrow, I'm telling Thuy and the police every motherfucking thing, nigga!" Onya just made up her mind at that very moment.

"No, don't do that, baby." Jeromy begged. "I'll give you the money I owe you."

"I heard that bullshit before." Onya snapped.

"No, baby girl. I'm serious. If I give you the money, will you promise me that you will not press charges and never associate with Thuy in any way, shape or form, and never step one foot in the center again?" Jeromy pleaded. "I'm sorry, baby girl. I don't know what came over me. I didn't mean to hurt you. Please!"

Onya wasn't sure. Jeromy sounded sincere and remorseful. This time she didn't mention anything about the money. He was the one who brought it up and offered to pay her. What the hell? She would see what he was talking about. "Okay."

"Alright, you got a pen and paper?" Jeromy asked.

Onya found a notepad and a pencil on the table and grabbed them. “Yeah.”

“Okay, here’s where I want you to meet me to get the money. Write this down.”

“I’m listening.” Onya said, getting ready to write down the information.

“Meet me at the corner of Pine and Elm Street in the parking lot where they just closed that elementary school.”

“Got it.” Onya wrote down the directions. “What time do you want me to meet you?”

“8:30AM tomorrow.”

“Okay, see you then.”

“Bet.”

The call ended and Onya went into the bathroom to take a much needed relaxing bubble bath, while Jeromy casually walked away from Onya’s living room window. He walked down two blocks and saw a black van pull up beside him and stop. The door opened and he went inside. Three men were in the van, and Jeromy said to them, “Everything is all set.”

Chapter 21

"Are you sure I made enough peanut butter fingers?" Naomi asked Fallon. She was visiting for a week. They were preparing for a barbeque at the Kilborn house. Naomi and Fallon were setting the table and preparing the food.

"I think so, Aunt Naomi," Fallon said as she checked out the spread of food. "Let's see, we have the potato salad, baked beans, and Tylisha is bringing her Red Velvet cake. Grandma Doris is bringing her macaroni and cheese."

"This barbeque is going to make me join Weight Watchers," Naomi joked and Fallon laughed. "How are things with you and Macal?"

"Everything is great," Fallon answered with a smile. "Macal, my career and Lolette."

Naomi rolled her eyes at the mention of Lolette's name.

Fallon saw her. "Aunt Naomi, I know you don't care for her, but trust me, she's a good friend to me."

"Is she?" Naomi commented with doubt. "That girl is trouble; always has been. Remember how she sucked you into her shit!"

"She was in a bad place and needed my support. It was the least I could do. She was there for me first."

Fallon tried so hard, for so long to suppress that horrible incident. That memory brought her so much pain and heartache; she tried to pretend that it never happened. She could never tell Macal. What would he think?

Naomi shook her head. She hated Lolette for using Fallon's weaknesses and insecurities for her own selfish gain. She couldn't hate Macal. He didn't know who he's dealing with. "Oh baby, your momma had that same sweet, loyal nature. It was a blessing and a curse." Naomi pulled Fallon into a protective hug. "Fallon, I love you, baby. I just want you to be careful."

"And I am," Fallon insisted.

The two started setting the table.

"How are your treatments?" Naomi asked out of the blue. It was a difficult question to ask, but she had to make sure that Fallon was taking care of herself.

Fallon wasn't expecting to talk about this particular subject, but understood her aunt's concern. "I'm going to my therapist and taking my medication."

"You still haven't told Macal?" Naomi guessed.

"Aunt Naomi, I will tell him when the time is right."

"Fallon, you can't hide a thing like this from your husband."

"I know, but he wouldn't understand."

"Yes, he will, just sit him down and explain everything, and I do mean everything." Naomi sighed and continued to try to plead with her niece. "You're in a good place. I don't want you to get hurt."

"And I won't."

Macal and company burst through the door with different types of supplies; edible and inedible. Fallon and Naomi instantly dropped the subject. "We're here! And how's my beautiful wife?" Macal gave Fallon a quick kiss on the cheek.

"Great, we are finished setting the table," Fallon said.

"Hi, Aunt Naomi." Macal gave Naomi a hug.

"Hi, Macal. Hi ,Tylisha." Naomi hugged Tylisha.

"Hi, Miss Naomi," Tylisha greeted her with the kids right behind her.

"Come here, little sweetie pies." Naomi widened her arms for a big group hug and the kids bum-rushed her. "Y'all doing good in school?"

"Yes, ma'am," Welton and Ayla answered.

"Where's my favorite girl?" Naomi looked around for Doris and walked over to her to get her hug in. "Hey, Doris."

"Hey, Naomi. Enjoying your visit?" Doris asked.

"Yes, I am, and I can't wait to eat this macaroni and cheese," Naomi said while helping Doris put it on the counter.

"Between me and you, I made it just for you," Doris whispered to Naomi.

"Momma, can we watch the living room TV?" Welton asked Tylisha.

"Sure, knock yourselves out," Tylisha said.

The kids made their way into the living room, turned on the TV and started to channel surf.

"Okay guys! Let's fire up the grill!" Macal said to his friends.

"Everything you need is on the patio. I seasoned the meat and it's in the cooler," Fallon informed him.

"Thanks, baby." Macal and his friends went to the patio to get started on the grill.

"While the guys are on the grill, let's get started on these drinks," Tylisha suggested and pulled out the blender, Don Julio tequila, and all the ingredients needed to make her famous frozen margaritas.

"Aunt Naomi, Tylisha's frozen margaritas are off the chain," Fallon said.

"Oh, I gotta try this. Margaritas are my weakness." Naomi turned to Doris and added, "Good thing social media wasn't around in our day."

"You heard me!" Doris agreed with a laugh and high fived Naomi.

Tylisha leaned over to Fallon and whispered, "I think Macal and I played too much rap music around her."

Fallon giggled and whispered back, "I'm guilty of the same thing," and pointed her head towards Naomi.

"Hey, everybody!" Lolette let herself in the house through the patio doors, making a grand entrance. It caused all the ladies, with the exception of Fallon, to scoff and roll their eyes. "What's going on?"

Fallon was surprised to see Lolette. "Hey, Lolette! I wasn't expecting to see you today."

"Really?" Lolette responded with guilt, like she didn't mean to intrude.

"We're having a barbeque, but hey, the more the merrier." Fallon welcomed and hugged her.

"Yeah! Let's eat!" Lolette cheered as she and Fallon went into the kitchen.

"The food is not ready yet, but the frozen margaritas are."

Naomi gave Lolette a glass without saying a word.

"Aw, thanks, Aunt Naomi!" Lolette said with over the top gratitude and gave Naomi a big hug like they were very close relatives.

I know this little immoral whore didn't just call me Aunt Naomi, with her filthy hands all over me! Naomi thought with disgust.

Lolette entered the living room where the kids were watching TV. She took a seat in a chair, found the remote control and started changing the channel. "Oh, sorry kids, I need the TV!"

Welton and Ayla were watching one of their favorite movies—*Toy Story 3*—and were very disappointed. They were obviously upset, but because Lolette was an adult, they didn't argue. "Okay, Miss Lolette," Ayla said with sadness, trying not to cry.

Welton didn't want to see his baby sister cry. He took her by the hand and had an idea to cheer her up. "Let's go to the game room and finish watching the movie."

"Okay, Welton." Ayla perked up instantly and the two left.

That did it for Tylisha. Lolette crossed the line this time. Nobody hurts her babies' feelings and gets away with it. "Excuse me," Tylisha said.

The ladies, including Fallon, knew it was on and that Tylisha was one hundred percent justified.

Tylisha rolled up on Lolette and got in her face. "Look bit—" Tylisha was all set to tear Lolette a new asshole but was side tracked by the breaking news story on the Channel 2 Action News. "What the hell?"

"Something about a woman found dead on the corner of Pine and Elm Street," Lolette explained.

By the looks of the news report, it was the craziest, wildest shit Tylisha has ever seen. "What in the world?" Tylisha snatched the remote control out of Lolette's hand to turn up the volume. Lolette got an attitude but Tylisha ignored it. Unbeknownst to her, this news report saved Lolette's life.

Soon, everybody stopped what they were doing to gather around the TV to listen to the reporter. "The police were stunned to find the body of Onya Hanks. Her car was in the parking lot of what used to be Ferguson Elementary School."

"Ferguson Elementary School? Macal, didn't you and Tylisha attend that school?" Fallon asked and walked over to Macal to wrap herself in his arms.

"Yes, we did," Macal answered, and Tylisha nodded.

Everybody continued to listen to the reporter in silence. "The police are baffled by the brutal murder of this twenty-seven-year-old woman. It appears as if she was lured to this location and was ambushed."

"Who would do such a thing?" Naomi asked.

"That poor, beautiful girl and her family," Doris said with sympathy.

"I hope they catch that bastard, or bastards!" Macal hissed with anger.

"It looks like the victim was dragged out of the car and shot over fifteen times, and her throat was slashed. Foul play is highly suspected." Thuy, Bryn and Vida's eyes were glued to the TV in Jeromy's living room, watching the news report about Onya. They couldn't believe their eyes or their ears.

Jeromy entered the room and glanced at the TV. He found the remote control in a chair so he could turn off the TV. "The victim's car was parked at this secluded, abandoned elem—"

"You don't need to see that, baby," Jeromy said to Thuy.

"Jeromy is right," Bryn never, in a million years, thought those words would ever escape his lips.

"This is all my fault," Thuy spoke, feeling numb.

"Thuy, don't do that to yourself," Vida said. "There was nothing you could've done."

"When I saw her all bruised and beaten up like that, I should've taken her to the police station right then and there. She was so shaken up and terrified. That bastard put her through tons of shit. The humiliation she felt really hit home for me." The tears started to fall down Thuy's face when thinking about Onya in that condition. It took her right back to what Connor and Levi did to her. No woman deserves to be treated like that, ever. "He did it!"

"Look, you did everything you could to help her," Jeromy said. He walked over to Thuy with a box of Kleenex.

Thuy took some out of the box and dried her tears.

"Besides, you don't know if it was him or not."

"That's right, maybe she was a random target. It's a crazy, dangerous world out there," Bryn said.

Thuy was completely drained. She couldn't believe that Onya was dead. She couldn't help but feel guilty about the murder. "I'm going to take a long, hot bath and turn in for the night. Goodnight all," Thuy said with exhaustion.

"We'll be going, and remember to call us anytime you need us," Bryn said as he and Vida gave Thuy a group hug.

"Bye, Thuy. Bye, Jeromy!" Vida said as she and Bryn walked out the door.

Jeromy closed it behind them. He then took a seat next to Thuy, pulled her into his arms and let her get comfortable.

"Thanks for being here," she said.

"Anytime."

The couple laid in each other's arms in silence for a few moments. During their quiet, intimate moment the two rubbed Thuy's barely showing pregnant belly. Thuy was getting sleepy and was mentally drained. She got off the couch to make her way upstairs.

The doorbell rang, and since she was already up, she went ahead and answered the door. "I'll get it." Thuy opened the door and three men were on the other side. "Hello! May I help you, gentlemen?"

"We're here to talk to Jeromy about some business," one of the men answered.

Thuy turned to face Jeromy who was still lying in the couch. "Uh… Jeromy, these men need to talk to you about some business."

Jeromy climbed off the couch to go to the door and saw the three men. "Hi, guys! This is a surprise."

"I'll leave you guys alone. Goodnight, baby." Thuy kissed Jeromy.

"Goodnight, baby," Jeromy said. He made sure Thuy was out of sight before turning his attention to his surprise, unwelcomed guests. "What the fuck are y'all doing here?" He hissed.

"We did the job. We're here to collect," one of the men said.

I guess stiffing them is not going to work! "Meet me three blocks down in twenty minutes, and don't ever bring y'all asses around here again!" Jeromy rudely demanded.

"Keep your word and we won't!" One of the men shot back.

"Fine." Jeromy looked up the stairs where Thuy was probably soaking in the bathtub. Suddenly, an idea popped into his head. "After I pay you, be on standby. I might have another job for you."

Chapter 22

"Alright, close your eyes," Fallon instructed Tylisha, so she could apply her eye makeup. Fallon was helping her get ready for her big date with Enzo in Tylisha's designated guestroom.

Tylisha and the kids were spending the night at Macal's house because she didn't want Enzo to know where she lived just yet. Tylisha was glad Macal had to work late so she could slip out without having to deal with Macal's unnecessary, overprotective, crazy ass.

"This ain't Aunt Naomi's handiwork, but the few pointers I picked up is gonna have to do," Fallon said.

"I appreciate it, Fallon. I'm sure it's going to look great," Tylisha returned.

"Where are you and Enzo going tonight?"

"I don't know. He wouldn't tell me. To be honest, I'm a little nervous."

"Why would you be nervous?" Fallon applied the foundation. "Enzo is not exactly a stranger."

"I know but this is my first date since my divorce. I'm very rusty on the dating scene." Tylisha worried.

"Don't you worry about a thing. Just relax and have a good time," Fallon encouraged her. "And the kids are in excellent hands."

"Thank you so much for letting us spend the night here."

"Tylisha, you know damn well this house is practically you and the kids' second home."

"It should be. I decorated it."

They laughed.

"Now, stop worrying and let me finish your makeup so you can look all beautiful and sexy for your date tonight." Fallon tried to figure out what lipstick to use.

"Date? Who in here is going out on a date?" Macal asked. He appeared in the room out of nowhere.

"Me," Tylisha answered unapologetically.

"You're going out on a what?" Macal acted like he didn't hear Tylisha right.

"Nigga, your ass heard me! I'm going out on a date!"

"With who?"

"None of your damn business!"

Fallon covered her mouth, giggling at Macal and Tylisha's banter. It tickled her. Fallon admired their brother-sister relationship. Fallon always wanted to have a brother or sister she could have these special moments with growing up and in present time.

"But since you asked nicely, it's only Enzo. He asked me out after I finished decorating his house and I accepted."

"Where is he taking you? Are you going back to his house afterwards?" Macal interrogated.

"Boy, take your nosy ass on somewhere," Tylisha dismissed him.

"His ass better not try anything. I know that much," Macal said and walked away.

"Let's get you ready," Fallon said.

"The one time his ass had to come home early." Tylisha shook her head and the ladies laughed as Fallon put the finishing touches on Tylisha's makeup.

Fallon and Macal were cuddled on the couch watching TV. Tylisha was all ready to go. Her hair was partially pinned up. Her makeup was flawless. She was wearing a form-fitting, sparkling, low-cut purple dress with matching peek toe stiletto pumps, topped off with a diamond jewelry set.

"Fallon, how do I look?" Tylisha asked.

"You look beautiful," Fallon complimented her.

"That dress is too revealing," Macal scolded her.

"Nigga, nobody asked you shit," Tylisha shot back.

"Come on, Macal, my hot pink dress you love so much is more revealing than that," Fallon defended her.

"That's different. It gave me a preview of what I was going to get later on." He said with lust, and grabbed Fallon's ass. "And that's why Tylisha needs to go upstairs and change clothes this instant. No nigga needs to be previewing nothing about my baby sister."

"What the fuck ever, Macal," Tylisha said. "Enzo will be here any minute. I need to check on the kids and do a final look-over. If Enzo comes before I get back, let him in and make him feel welcome. Macal, try to act like you got some sense," she said, and went to check on the kids.

Tylisha found the kids in Welton's guestroom. He was watching TV while Ayla was playing a game on her tablet. "Alright kids, give me my hugs and kisses before I head out."

Welton and Ayla rushed over to hug Tylisha and kissed her on the check.

"Are you having another business dinner?" Welton asked.

"No, I'm having dinner with a friend," Tylisha slightly bended the truth.

"Oooh, mommy has a date," Ayla guessed cheerfully.

Tylisha was completely taken aback. "Girl, what you know about dating?"

"You're extra pretty tonight. When a lady is extra pretty, that means she's going out on a date," Ayla explained.

This girl is too much like me! Tylisha couldn't do anything but shake her head and laugh. "To be honest, yes, I'm going out on a date. Me and this guy used to go to school together when we were kids."

"Is he a nice guy?" Welton asked.

"Yes, he is," Tylisha answered.

"Is he cute?" Ayla asked.

"Yes, he's very cute," Tylisha blushed.

"What does he do for a living?" Welton asked.

"What kind of car does he drive?" Ayla asked.

"Alright, you clowns need to stop with all these questions," Tylisha eighty-six-ed the interrogation. "Y'all are worse than your uncle."

"Mommy, why is he picking you up here instead of our house?" Ayla asked.

"When are we going to meet him?" Welton asked.

These kids of mine! "I'm only answering these last two questions and that's it." Tylisha said. "Ayla, when you're older, you'll understand why my date is meeting me here. Always remember to keep your eyes open when it comes to boys. And Welton, as far as you guys meeting him, I have to make sure that we're compatible first."

"What does compatible mean?" Ayla asked.

Tylisha tried to find a way to explain the word compatible in a way an eight-year old would understand. "Let's put it this way. You remember when Uncle Macal introduced us to Aunt Fallon?"

"Yes," Ayla answered and Welton nodded.

Tylisha continued, "The reason Uncle Macal introduced us to Aunt Fallon, because they got along very well and they liked each other very much. When my date and I get to that point, I'll let you meet him. Does that make sense?"

Ayla and Welton nodded. They gave Tylisha a final hug and kiss on the cheek before going to her room to do a final touch-up on her appearance.

Macal and Fallon continued to lay in each other's arms, quietly watching TV. When the doorbell rang, Fallon was about to get up to answer the door but Macal stopped her. "That's okay, baby, I got it."

"Be nice!" Fallon knew what Macal was up to.

"Don't worry, I will." Macal walked over to answer the door and was shocked at Enzo's adult appearance. He really came a long way.

"Hello! I'm here to pick up Tylisha," Enzo said with confidence.

"You're Enzo?" *What confidence!* Macal was impressed. This wasn't the shy, short, dorky, big faced kid with glasses anymore.

"Macal, is that you?" Enzo asked. "What's up? It's been too long!" He and Macal shook hands.

"I've been great and yourself?" Macal let Enzo in the house and led him into the living room.

"Can't complain. I heard you got married."

"Yes, I did, to the most beautiful woman in the world." Macal walked over to Fallon and gave her a kiss before making the introduction. "This is my wife Fallon."

"Nice to meet you," Fallon greeted him and shook Enzo's hand.

"Hi, I'm Xavion Goss, but everybody calls me Enzo."

"Tylisha should be here any minute."

The doorbell rang again.

"Who is it?" Fallon asked.

"Lolette!"

"Come in! The door is open!"

Lolette let herself in. "Hey, girl! Hey, Macal!" Lolette stopped dead in her tracks when she saw Enzo. "And who do we have here?"

"Hi! I'm Xavion Goss, better known as Enzo. I'm a childhood friend of Macal and Tylisha."

"What brings a handsome, sexy man like you into these parts?" Lolette put on her hoe hat and took a seat a little too close to Enzo.

"I'm here to pick up Tylisha. We have a date tonight," Enzo answered.

"Really?" The thought of any man giving Tylisha the time of day had Lolette on pause. "Boy, you are a trooper. You know she has two kids, right?"

"I'm aware," Enzo confirmed. "It's cool. I have a son myself."

"Is that silver Bentley outside yours?"

"Yes, it is. I picked it up today."

Macal took a peek out the window to check out the car. "Shit, that car is sharp! I need to step my game up!"

"Yes, it is!" Lolette agreed and focused her attention back to Enzo. "You know, anytime you wanna—"

"Tylisha!" Fallon was the first to acknowledge Tylisha's presence.

Enzo walked over to Tylisha and gave her an innocent peck on the cheek. "Wow! You're beautiful and breathtaking!"

"Thanks, and you clean-up nice yourself," Tylisha giggled. Enzo kept it simple by wearing a pair of black slacks and a white buttoned down dress shirt. "Y'all don't wait up for me." Tylisha hugged Macal and Fallon. “Bye, you guys!” She turned to Lolette and put on her friendly face. “Hey, Lolette! Girl, come here!” Tylisha pulled Lolette into a hug and hissed in a whisper in her ear while giving her ponytail a slight tug. “Bitch, don’t motherfucking try me! I ain’t the one, hoe!”

Tylisha walked over to Enzo and took her place on his arm. “Shall we?”

“Let’s,” Enzo replied.

“Don’t forget your curfew is at midnight!” Macal yelled as the couple was walking out the door.

“Boy, hush!” Tylisha laughed him off and closed the door behind them.

Chapter 23

Tylisha wasn't gonna let the likes of Lolette ruin her night, but still she felt like she needed to apologize to Enzo. "I'm sorry about Lolette's behavior. It was inappropriate."

"It's cool," Enzo said and made a left turn. "I think I handled it pretty well."

"A sexy man like you should be used to that type of attention," Tylisha teased.

"Aww, I'm flattered," Enzo blushed. "She's Fallon's friend, right?"

"Yeah," Tylisha responded with an eye roll.

"Macal's fucking her, isn't he?" Enzo guessed.

Tylisha's eyes widened with surprise at Enzo's correct hypothesis. "How did you know?"

"Come on, Tylisha. I'm a man. I know these things. A man knows another man's mind."

That makes perfect sense! Tylisha thought. "Gotcha."

"Not to mention, Macal's eyes turned green when she was all up on me," Enzo added.

"I see." Then it dawned on Tylisha that she had no clue where she was going. "Enzo, where are we going?"

"It's a surprise. Trust me. You'll have fun. I promise."

"Alright."

Tylisha and Enzo enjoyed the ride until they reached the Ramada Plaza Hotel. Enzo gave the valet his keys. "Here you go," he said as he and Tylisha entered the hotel and walked through the lobby.

They found a door with a sign labeled *PlayDate* and went inside. Enzo gave the doorman a twenty dollar bill and the couple walked further into the room. It was a party filled with people playing games— board games, card games and video games. Any game you could think of. The next room had a dance floor. The music was playing with a well-stocked bar and buffet table.

"What kind of party is this?" Tylisha asked.

"This is PlayDate," Enzo answered. "They have this every weekend. You can play games, dance, eat, drink, and listen to music; the works."

"I was not expecting anything like this. I am officially surprised. So Enzo, what game should we play?"

"Uh...Beautiful queens make the first choice," he insisted.

"Why, thank you," Tylisha blushed. "Let's see. Let's play Rock'em Sock'em Robot."

"Excellent choice."

The two walked over to the table where the game was set-up.

Tylisha started the count. "Okay one, two, three. GO!"

The game started. Enzo put up a good fight but Tylisha won.

"I won! Yay!"

"Alright, you got me. Let me get a chance to get even." Enzo said.

"Alright, fair is fair" Tylisha started the count again. "Okay one, two, three. GO!" The game started again and Tylisha won again. "Yes! I win again!"

"Damn, girl! You're good at this!"

"Macal had this game and taught me how to play. What do you want to play next?"

"Let's play Sorry," Enzo suggested.

"Oh man, I used to love that game. But before we get started, let's get something to eat and a beer," Tylisha said.

"Good idea."

Tylisha and Enzo went to the buffet table to fix their plates and grabbed a bottle of water and a Heineken. They went back to the table to set up the game. They started playing and snacking on their food.

"So, how am I doing?" Tylisha asked.

"With what?" Enzo asked.

"With dating? I haven't been out on a date since my divorce."

"You seem to be having fun so I think you're doing okay so far. I'll admit, it was hard for me to get out there too, but I got the hang of it. Even though I still haven't met the one. You feel me?"

"Gotcha. How's Amery?"

"He's doing great. He has a recital coming up," Enzo volunteered.

"Really? What instrument does he play?"

"None. He's a singer," Enzo corrected her. "I recorded his last performance. You wanna see?"

"Sure," Tylisha said.

Enzo pulled his phone out of his pocket and played the video for her. It showed a cute adolescent version of Enzo with the exception of the gray eyes he inherited from his mother, singing *All My Life* by K-Ci and JoJo. The boy's voice was strong and powerful.

"Damn! That boy can blow!"

"Can he!" Enzo agreed with fatherly pride. "He gets his musical talents from Ligia's family. I know that for a fact. If me or anybody in my family tried to sing or play an instrument, our assess would've been run out of town with pitchforks and torches."

They laughed.

"Ligia is an amazing singer, plus Vax used to be in a band, which explains how he and Amery bonded."

"Vax used to be in a band?" This was news to Tylisha.

"Yeah, back in the day. He was a jazz musician. The band was huge. Won four Grammys. He played the saxophone and sang on occasion," Enzo explained. "When his mom died, he quit the band and took over the family business."

"What did Amery pick up from you, besides your looks?" Tylisha asked curiously.

Enzo blushed. "I think he picked up my friendly personality. What about your kids?"

"Both of my kids love sports. Welton reads a lot. Ayla loves art. She and Fallon have that in common. Whenever I see my babies interact, they remind me of Macal and me when we were kids," Tylisha said.

"How's your grandmother's new living arrangement?"

"She loves it and is having the time of her life. How are your parents?"

"Parents are great and still happily married."

"That's good." Tylisha looked at the board game and smiled. "Uh oh! One more move and I win the game!"

"Awe come on! You're killing me!" Enzo made his move on the board.

Tylisha made her move and cheered, "I win again!"

"This just isn't my night." Enzo shook his head.

"Aww, don't be a sore loser," Tylisha teased. "Let's play a game together. It'll be like our debate tournaments all over again."

"Okay," Enzo said as he and Tylisha walked around to see the next game to play.

All of the sudden, a couple approached them and asked, "Hey, we need a team to play spades with us. Y'all down?"

"We're there!" Tylisha and Enzo accepted.

Enzo and Tylisha joined the couple in a game of Spades. They won five out of eight times. Afterwards, they played Poker, Connect Four, Uno, Hungry Hippos, Chess and watched a Pac-man tournament. Enzo did well in all the games except Chess. For some reason, he couldn't beat Tylisha in it.

Over the loud speaker, the DJ was heard making an announcement. "To all you beautiful, sexy luscious, ladies here tonight, the Hula Hoop contest will be starting in ten minutes. If interested, sign up with me at the Hula Hoop area. Better hurry! Spaces are limited! First prize: one thousand dollars. Second prize: five hundred dollars. Third prize: two hundred and fifty dollars."

"You should enter, Tylisha," Enzo suggested.

Is this nigga crazy! "Do you know how long it's been since I even touched a Hula Hoop?"

"Baby girl, get over there! You got this!"

What the hell! "Alright, I'll enter just for fun." Tylisha walked over to the Hula Hoop area and found the DJ. "Sign me up."

"You're in luck. You're the very last entry," the DJ said.

Tylisha grabbed the very last Hula Hoop and took off her shoes, waiting on the DJ to start the contest.

"Ladies and gentlemen, the Hula Hoop contest has started. First prize: one thousand dollars. Second prize: five hundred dollars.

Third prize: two hundred and fifty dollars. Remember ladies, the last one standing is the winner. Ready! Set! Go!"

The ladies started Hula Hooping. Tylisha surprised herself. She looked like a professional out there, using her waist to keep the Hula Hoop steady. The way she rocked her hips had all the dudes looking. Enzo was starting to regret the suggestion he made. He felt some type of way with all these men ogling Tylisha, but at the same time, he was enjoying the show. The way Tylisha's curves mesmerized him. All that ass bouncing everywhere and those succulent titties trying to pop out. When the last woman stopped it was just Tylisha. Obviously, the DJ was enjoying the Tylisha Show because he let it go on for three more minutes before stopping the contest.

"First place goes to the young, sexy shawdy in the sparkling purple!" The DJ announced and gave Tylisha the check.

"Thank you," Tylisha said.

"Congratulations!" Enzo said and pulled Tylisha in a hug.

She put her shoes back on. "Thanks. How was the view?" Tylisha knew Enzo and all the men were enjoying her dancing curves.

"Amazing," Enzo confessed.

Tylisha placed a kiss on Enzo's lips. "That's for keeping it one hundred. Let's dance."

"Let's."

"I had a great time tonight," Tylisha said in total bliss.

Enzo held her hand and walked her to Macal's front door.

"I felt like a kid again."

"Me too," Enzo said.

The two looked up at the night's star-filled sky along with the glowing moon shining on them.

"Now, ain't you glad you went out with me?"

"Yes, I am!" She said. "We should do this again some time."

"Yes, we should." Enzo leaned in to give Tylisha a kiss on the cheek. He wanted to do more but he was certain Macal was watching them through the window, and Enzo didn't want any trouble. "I'll text you when I get home."

"Okay, goodnight."

"Goodnight."

Tylisha entered the house and closed the door. She turned on the lights and was shocked to see Macal sitting on the couch.

"Do you have any idea what time it is, young lady?"

"Boy, shut up! Nobody's stud'n your ass!" Tylisha dismissed him and went upstairs to her room with Macal right behind her.

"Where did he take you? I want details!" Macal demanded.

Tylisha took her heels off and rolled her eyes at him. "Since you asked nicely. Enzo took me to the Ramada Plaza Hotel."

Hearing the word hotel made Macal go ballistic. "He took you where? Why the fuck is that nigga taking my baby sister to a hotel for?"

"Nigga, calm your ass down!" Tylisha tried to calm him. "There was a party being held there. They have this PlayDate thing every weekend where you can play games, dance, eat, drink, and listen to music."

Macal was relieved. This was his baby sister. A bastard mistreated, used and threw her away before. He refused to stand idly by and let it happen again. Deep down Tylisha knew Macal's heart was in the right place. "Alright what games did y'all play?"

"We played Sorry, Spades, chess, Monopoly, Rock'em Sock'em Robot—"

"They had Rock'em Sock'em Robot?" Macal interrupted with excitement.

"Yeah."

"That takes me back." He smiled, thinking about the happier moments from his childhood. "Enzo didn't beat you, did he?"

"Nope."

"I taught you well." Macal and Tylisha bumped fists.

"You know it. They also had a Hula Hoop contest and I won first prize! One thousand George Washingtons!" Tylisha bragged and waved the check around in victory.

"Congratulations!"

"Trust me. You'll like it. You'll feel like a kid again, but still have that adult appeal," Tylisha said.

"I might need to check that out. Enzo didn't try anything, did he?" Macal asked, wanting to know if he had to stomp a nigga.

"He was a perfect gentleman," Tylisha assured him.

"Good, because I don't wanna bust a nigga's head open," Macal said.

"Yes, sir." Tylisha responded with fake obedience. "Did you really wait up for me?"

"Hell yeah!" Macal pulled Tylisha into a protective embrace. "You my baby sister. You're a beautiful, priceless diamond that needs to be protected, looked after and treated with care." He kissed her on the forehead. "I love you, baby girl. You mean everything to me."

Macal's words touched Tylisha deeply. "That's so beautiful." She kissed him on the cheek and added, "You mean the world to me too. I love your crazy, fucked up ass too." The siblings laughed. "They also had video games at PlayDate. Enzo and I watched a Pac-Man tournament."

That gave Macal an idea. "Are you sleepy?"

"Nope," Tylisha answered.

"Me neither."

"Pac-Man?"

"And Super Mario Bros?"

"Let's go."

And the Kilborn brother and sister duo headed to the game room to play video games until they fell asleep.

Chapter 24

Thuy's eyes were glued to the TV at Jeromy's house. Onya's murder was all she could think about, and watching the latest news report about it didn't help matters. "The police are still baffled about the bizarre, brutal murder of Onya Hanks. The overkill and how it had been executed, it was indeed personal and a set-up."

Jeromy walked into the living room and found Thuy sitting on the couch, watching the news report about Onya again. He walked over to take a seat next to Thuy and turned off the TV. "You shouldn't be looking at that, baby."

"I know, but I should've done more for Onya," Thuy said with guilt.

"Baby, it's not your fault, and don't stress yourself over this." He wrapped his arms around her and rubbed her belly. "It's not good for you or the baby. Remember the doctor told you to relax."

"I'll try."

"I think I can help."

"How?" she asked.

"Lay back and get comfortable."

Thuy followed his directions.

Jeromy took off her shoes and started rubbing her feet.

"Something told me to get a pedicure," Thuy said. "Good thing I listened," she giggled. The foot massage felt so good. Thuy felt like she was in heaven. "Ahh! Oooh!" She loudly moaned.

Suddenly, Thuy felt a warm, wet sensation around her toes. She looked down and saw her foot in Jeromy's mouth. That man loved her feet. He used all of her toes as pacifiers and made sure they received equal attention.

"Oh! Oh shit!" Thuy moaned and started to cream in her panties.

Jeromy knew her body inside and out. He sucked with intensity until she let out a big moan and took her foot out of his mouth.

"You taste so sweet," Jeromy said.

"Thanks! I needed that!" she returned with satisfaction.

"I got practice, but when I get back, prepare yourself for an amazing dick down." Jeromy grabbed his bag.

"Yes, baby. I feel so much better after this, as well as being able to help out with the case."

"What do you mean?" Jeromy asked.

"Oh, I went to the police station this morning to give them all the information I could about Onya," Thuy explained.

"You don't say."

"It may not be much, but it's better than nothing."

"Right."

"I'm about to take a nap. Have a good practice." Thuy kissed Jeromy goodbye.

"Thanks, baby." Jeromy said as he walked out the door. "That bitch is going to be the death of me," he mumbled under his breath, and pulled out his phone to make the call.

"Hello," the caller greeted him.

"I need to meet with y'all about a potential assignment in the future."

Chapter 25

1992

"This is the life." Doris was relaxing in front of the TV after a long day at work. She was enjoying the peace and quiet while Belinda took the kids out for a day of merriment.

Belinda and the kids moved in three weeks prior, after the brawl with Taryn in her front yard. The clincher was Rufus adding insult to injury by coming home with lipstick, perfume and hickies all over him, literally seconds after the fight. Belinda couldn't deal with Rufus' shit for another minute, so she took the kids and moved out. She hadn't spoken to Rufus since, and she hadn't tasted not one drop of alcohol.

"Rest and relaxation at last," Doris said and flipped through the channels. When she came across Murder She Wrote, she stopped and started watching the program. Doris' peaceful alone time was interrupted by a knock at the door. She was officially pissed off. She knew it wasn't Belinda because she had a key. The knocking continued and Doris decided to go ahead and answer it. She opened the door and it was the last person she wanted to see. Rufus. "May I help you?" She asked with an attitude.

"I'm here to see my wife and kids," he answered.

"They ain't here."

"Where are they?"

"I don't know."

"Do you know when they'll be back?" Rufus was getting frustrated. He brushed past Doris and started looking around.

"Uh... I don't recall inviting your ass into my house," Doris said and closed the door.

"Doris, where's my family?" Rufus asked. "I know they're staying here."

"I don't know where they are, and even if I did, I wouldn't tell your ass. Now, if you'll excuse me." Doris dismissed him, showing Rufus the door.

"You can't keep me away from my kids!" Rufus yelled.

Doris looked around for who in the fuck Rufus was supposed to be yelling at like he was fucking crazy. "Boy, I know your black ass ain't yelling at me in my motherfucking house!" Doris yelled back.

"Look, whatever—"

"And this nigga said whatever to me too?"

Rufus tried to calm down and tried to be more reasonable. "Look, this has gone on long enough. It's time for Belinda and the kids to come home."

Doris scoffed. "I'm surprised you remember you had a wife and kids with all that fucking around you've been doing on my baby."

"You don't know what you're talking about."

"Oh I don't," Doris said. "I know my baby came here with my grandbabies in tears after getting into another fight with another one of your whores. She's fed up!"

"They're lying."

"You gotta be shitting me," Doris replied. She was surprised that men still used those lines in the 1990s.

Then, she heard a car pull up and looked out the window. Belinda and the kids were walking towards the front door with stuffed animals, wearing t-shirts from Six Flags. Also, there was a handsome man walking with them who seemed to be very infatuated with Belinda.

"Well! Well! Well!"

"What?"

"They're back. Looks like they went to Six Flags," Doris answered.

Belinda opened the door and let everybody inside. "Thank you so much for treating us, Willis. Hey, momma!"

"Belinda, baby!" Doris hugged her beloved daughter. "Hello, Willis."

"Hello, Mrs. Blair." Willis greeted her politely and gave Doris a hug.

"You kids had fun today?" Doris asked Macal and Tylisha.

"Yes, Grandma Doris. We went to Six Flags and rode on every ride in the park!" Tylisha exclaimed with excitement.

"Look what I won!" Macal showed off his huge stuffed version of Bugs Bunny.

"That's good, baby," Doris said.

"Willis, thanks for teaching me how to play that game," Macal said, and gave Willis a high five.

"Anytime sport," Willis returned.

"Thanks for the teddy bear, Mr. Willis. It's cute," Tylisha said.

Rufus stood there in disbelief about what the fuck he was witnessing. This motherfucker was all over his wife and kids like they were a family. He had to put a stop to this shit right now. "Wait a minute. Who the fuck are you?"

"I'm Willis. I went to school with Belinda and we ran into each other at the gate. Who are you?" Willis politely asked.

"I'm her husband!" Rufus rudely answered.

"Rufus, isn't it?" Willis asked for confirmation.

Doris had a feeling this could get ugly and didn't want her grandchildren to be witnesses. "Kids, let's get out of here and y'all can tell me about your day at Six Flags." She suggested, and led the kids out of the room.

"I had so much fun!" Tylisha said.

"Me too," Macal said.

"What the fuck are you doing with my wife?" Rufus asked Willis.

"We're just friends. We ran into each other and he offered to treat us. No big deal," Belinda brushed it off. She turned to Willis and said, "Thanks, I had a great time."

"Anytime. A woman like you deserves way more than what you're getting," Willis hinted.

Rufus caught on to his tone and didn't like it one fucking bit. He wanted his feelings to be known. "You got exactly one minute to get the fuck out of here and I'm actually counting!"

Willis put his hands up in surrender. "Look, I don't want any trouble. I'll leave. Goodbye, Belinda, and say goodbye to the kids for me."

"Alright, goodnight and thanks again," Belinda said as she let Willis out. When he left, she turned around to see the face of the

man she didn't want to have anything to do with. "What are you doing here?"

"So, you bringing random niggas around my kids now?" Rufus accused.

Belinda had to laugh. Apparently, Rufus forgot why she moved out. "I know damn well you're not trying to imply that I'm being unfaithful. He's an old friend; completely innocent. Can't say that about you and Taryn."

"I told you I was sorry about the fight. I had no idea she'd come to the house," Rufus tried to defend himself.

"But she did!" Belinda yelled. "She did come over! Starting her usual bullshit and having me fighting in broad daylight in front of our children and neighbors. And where were you when all of this was going on? Oh yeah, I forgot, out fucking another bitch!"

"I know you're pissed at me but that shit you pulled today was disrespectful as fuck!"

"Well, who knows about disrespect better than you?" Belinda shot back with sarcasm.

"I don't want you to see that nigga no more and his ass better stay the fuck away from my kids!" Rufus demanded.

"Look at you making demands," Belinda teased and giggled. "Ordering me to stay away from a friend, but you can't stay away from Taryn and all of your other hoes."

"They don't mean shit to me. I love you."

"You have a very unique way of showing your love for me."

"I'm sorry. I know you're hurting. Just come home. I miss you. I miss the kids," Rufus begged. "I love you."

"Do you?" Belinda wanted to believe Rufus desperately.

"Yes, I do," Rufus pulled Belinda into his arms and gazed into her eyes. "I love you. That's all that matters. Will you please come home? I don't want to lose you, especially to that nigga."

"Nothing is going on," Belinda insisted. "I want to believe and trust you but Taryn—"

"Fuck Taryn! I love you and our family!"

"I need to ask you something!"

"Anything, baby."

"Why did you marry me? Was it because you love me or was it because of Macal?"

Rufus thought this was a very odd question. "What do you mean?"

"Macal was an 'unexpected gift'," Belinda reminded him. "After I told you I was pregnant, we went straight to the courthouse to get married. Taryn always accused me of stealing you from her and using the pregnancy to trap you. Do you ever feel that way?"

"Of course not. Don't let Taryn's bitterness get to you. What Taryn and I had is in the past. It's done. It's over. I married you because I love you and want to spend the rest of my life with you."

"If I move back home, will you promise to be faithful and never humiliate our family again?"

"Yes, I promise."

Belinda still wasn't sure.

Rufus gently caressed the beautiful face he fell in love with. "Baby, I promise."

"Okay, I'll move back home." Belinda kissed him. "I love you so much."

"I love you too."

Rufus and Belinda reunited and started making out on the couch like teenagers while Doris, Macal and Tylisha looked on with disappointment.

"Wake up, baby!" A beautiful, naked woman woke Macal up with a kiss.

"Sorry, baby. How long was I out?" Macal asked with a yawn.

"About three hours," Crystal answered.

Fallon was spending the week with Naomi in Columbus. What a better way to spend the week alone than with a fresh piece of ass. She may not have very good taste in perfume, and was tacky as fuck, but her pussy and head game made up for it. The best thing about waking up refreshed was that Macal had a hard-on.

"Now that me and my friend are wide awake—"

"Oh, I'm way ahead of you." Crystal climbed into the bed and shoved the dick in her mouth. She sucked on it for a little over a minute when Macal's phone rang. She took the dick out of her mouth and said, "I'll let you get that."

"You good, baby. They can wait." Macal grabbed the phone. He saw it was Lolette and pressed ignore. "Just keep sucking."

"Yes, Daddy."

Chapter 26

"Fuck!" Lolette yelled in frustration when Macal didn't answer his phone. She knew Fallon wasn't holding him up because she was out of town. "Where the fuck can his black ass be? That nigga was supposed to be here two hours ago!"

Lolette was pacing back and forth, wondering where the fuck Macal could be. Eventually, all that pacing made her hungry. Since she wasn't in the mood to cook and needed to get out of the house to clear her head, Lolette threw on some black jeans, a lime green shirt and some white tennis shoes, and headed out to find something to eat.

She drove around until she saw a Burger King. Lolette went inside and, lucky for her, there was only one person in line. When the person in front of her left, Lolette walked up to the counter.

"Welcome to Burger King. May I take your order?" The cashier greeted her.

"Yes, I would like a large number two and a Sprite," Lolette placed her order.

"Yes ma'am, that'll be $6.95."

Lolette made her payment via debit card and the cashier gave her the receipt.

The cashier came back with Lolette's tray of food. "Here's your order and you have a nice day."

"Thanks, you too," Lolette said.

She looked around to find a seat and found a booth near the window. She sat down and started eating her food. Lolette was really hungry because she consumed the meal in less than three minutes flat. As she was sipping on her drink, she looked across the street where an apartment complex was located. Something caught her attention. A burgundy Maserati was in the parking lot. Only one person she knew had a car like that in their collection. *Macal*!

"What the fuck," Lolette whispered. She remembered she was in public. *Is that why his ass stood me up? Oh hell to the motherfucking no!* "I know his black ass better not be over there!" Lolette hissed with jealous rage and stormed out of Burger King.

She hopped in her car and high tailed it across the street. She parked next to the Maserati and reached the door. She started banging on the door and wouldn't stop until someone answered.

It took a minute or two but the door finally opened. It was an attractive light-skinned woman with green eyes and long, curly, dark brown hair. Lolette knew she found the right apartment because the hoe was wearing one of Macal's t-shirts. Lolette had to agree with Fallon on one thing. This hoe had absolutely no taste whatsoever. Her terrible smelling, cheap ass perfume was strong as hell. Lolette would've thrown up all over the stank ass bitch but she was too pissed.

"Who are you supposed to be?" The bitch asked smugly.

"I'm looking for my man, bitch!" Lolette snapped.

"Excuse me?" The woman stayed cool and collected. "But if you got to look for your man, chances are, you ain't got one. Now, if you don't mind, I have some more fucking to do."

The woman was about to slam the door in Lolette's face but she caught it and pushed the woman, knocking her down on the floor on her ass to let herself in the apartment. "No the fuck you don't, bitch!"

The woman didn't say anything back. She bounced back up off the floor and made her point by backhanding Lolette in the face as hard as she could. Lolette charged for the woman and the ladies ended up wrestling on the floor, screaming at each other. Lolette tried to choke the woman, but she swatted her hands away and punched Lolette in the face. They continued to exchange blows until Macal came out of nowhere, wearing nothing but his boxers to separate them.

"Lolette! Crystal! Break it up!" Macal ordered. "Both of you calm the fuck down and act like y'all got some fucking sense! Lolette, what the fuck are you doing here?"

Did this nigga just ask me? "Waiting for your ass, nigga! I've been waiting on your ass for hours! Then, I went to get something to eat and I look across the street to find out that you stood me up to fuck this tacky, stank hoe!"

"Bitch, I got your tacky stank hoe!" Crystal tried to lunge for Lolette but Macal held her back.

"That's enough! Lolette, get your ass out of here right now, and I mean that shit!" Macal commanded.

"But Macal—"

"Right motherfucking now! I'll be over there when I get there!"

Lolette rolled her eyes and stomped out the door without saying another word, and slammed the door behind her hard enough to make the building shake.

Macal turned to Crystal and said, "Now, where were we?"

Crystal took off the t-shirt and stretched out on the floor, spread eagle. "We were right here!"

Lolette soaked her aching body in the bath tub with the bubbles from her eucalyptus bath oil. Also, she needed to scrub any trace of that disgusting scent of Crystal's off her body. When she felt completely healed, energized and cleansed, she climbed out of the tub and put on her bath robe. She looked in the bathroom mirror and saw a small bruise on her cheek.

"That bitch! That fucking bitch!" Lolette was pissed. First, Macal stands her up. Then that bitch bruises her beautiful face, and now that nigga had the nerve to shoo her away so he could go right back to fucking that stank thot.

Lolette washed her face and applied ointment on the bruised area. "The balls on that motherfucker! When his ass gets here, I'm getting in that ass! I don't play that shit!"

Right at that very moment the doorbell rang. "There goes that lying ass nigga, right motherfucking now!" Lolette stormed out of the bathroom and headed straight for the front door to give Macal a piece of her mind. She swung the door open and there he was. Lolette was all prepared to give him a well-deserved cussin' out. "Look nigga! You got some fuck—"

Macal pulled Lolette into his arms and shut her up with a rough kiss, and closed the door behind him. He took off her robe and threw her on the couch. He took off his clothes in rapid speed and pounced on top of her like a hungry lion. He forced her legs apart and shoved his dick deep inside her. He knew a good dick down was all Lolette needed to calm her down and stay compliant.

"Ah!" Lolette moaned.

"You gonna behave?" Macal grunted as he variously pumped in and out her pussy.

"Yes."

"You gonna act right?"

"Yes!"

Lolette was busting fat nuts all over Macal's dick. Her pussy was like a drug to him. He couldn't get enough. His phone rang but he couldn't turn away. The pussy was too good.

The aroma and sounds of wild, forbidden fucking filled the room. Lolette was loving the dick. She loved it so much she forgot she was pissed at him and the reason why. Macal pulled his dick out of Lolette's pussy and pulled her head toward his groin. She grabbed his dick and stuffed it in her mouth. She sucked on the dick hard like it was a popsicle. She wanted his cream bad and she was determined to get it. His dick erupted in her mouth and she swallowed every drop.

Lolette laid back on the couch in all of her sweaty nakedness. She looked over at Macal who had a panic look on his face while staring at his phone.

"Oh shit! That was Fallon!" Macal played the voicemail she left:

Hey Macal! It's me, Fallon. I called to let you know that I'm on my way home. I know I said I'll be back tomorrow, but I think Aunt Naomi had a date and wanted some private time. Anyway, I can't wait to see you. Love you! Bye!

"I gotta go!" Macal started throwing on his clothes.

Lolette stood up on her feet. "Wait a minute!"

Macal gave her a quick kiss. "I had fun, and keep it tight for me." He bolted out the door, leaving Lolette naked and alone with a sore, cum-dripping pussy.

"Macal, I'm home!" Fallon announced as she walked into house with her luggage. "Where is that husband of mine? Macal! Macal!" She kept calling out as she made her way up the stairs and into the bedroom. "Oh, he's in the shower," Fallon concluded when she heard the water running in the bathroom. She started unpacking her bags and placed them in her walk-in closet when she was finished. She turned around and smiled at Macal's perfect nude body. "Hey baby, I missed you so much."

"I missed you too, baby," Macal said. He pulled Fallon into his arms and stuck his tongue in her mouth. "Now strip and get in that bed so I can show you how much I missed you."

Fallon giggled and started shedding her clothing as she made her way to the bed.

Chapter 27

Sam quietly entered Thuy's office and found her at her desk, focused on her computer screen. "Hey, baby girl!" He spoke to get Thuy's attention.

Thuy looked up and saw her big cousin standing before her. "Sam! How are you doing?" She cheered and jumped out of her seat to rush over to give Sam a big hug, almost knocking him down. "What brings you here?" She asked and offered Sam a seat and sat back in her chair.

"I'm here for three reasons. First, I'm thinking about this endorsement deal that was proposed to me and I want you to check it out." Sam handed Thuy a folder and she placed it on her desk.

"Of course. I'll look into it right away." "Good! Good! The second reason. Remember my homeboy Devin?"

"That clown you graduated from high school with?"

"That's him." San confirmed. "He's getting married this weekend and he asked me to be his best man."

"He finally found somebody crazy enough to marry him, huh?" Thuy teased.

"Pretty much." Sam said and the two laughed. "He's calmed down a bit since high school. He's still a fool but his playing days ended the second he laid eyes on Robyn."

"Well tell him congratulations for me. What's the third reason?"

"I'm moving back to Atlanta." Sam announced.

Thuy was filled with excitement. "That's great! When are you moving?"

"I'm trying to make the move no later than—"

"Thuy!" Tori busted in the office out of nowhere.

Not this bullshit! Thuy rolled her eyes and asked as if she gave a fuck. "What the hell do you want? Can't you see I'm busy with a client?"

"Shit, Sam ain't nobody!" Tori dismissed. "No offense." She half apologized to Sam.

"None taken, my dear." Sam accepted with a straight face.

Tori then turned her attention back to Thuy. “Anyway, Daddy’s house needs to be renovated and rewired, and he needs somewhere to stay until the job is done.”

“Thanks for the update and enjoy your houseguest.” Thuy said.

“Uh, no. He’s staying with you.” Tori dropped the bombshell.

Is this bitch crazy! “The hell he is! He can stay with you. Considering how close you two are.”

“Because Jett will be getting out soon and there’ll be no room at my house, so you’ll have to take him in.” Tori explained.

“I ain’t got no room in my house for his deadbeat ass!” Thuy replied with contempt.

“Look you got one more time to—”

“I’m not dealing with this shit!” Thuy cut off Tori’s threat. “And you can spare the tired ass speech about how it’s all my fault our daddy went to prison because I testified against him when he almost beat my momma to death and knocked my best friend Bryn out in the process. You can spare me the tired ass sob story about how it’s all my fault your cruel bitter ass bitch of a momma fell asleep at the wheel because she was so exhausted from working three jobs to keep y’all afloat after daddy went to prison. You can also spare me how it’s all my fault Jett became a petty criminal and small time drug dealer in order to help y’all survive after y’all momma died. Besides, his ass had sticky fingers long before daddy set one foot inside a prison cell.”

Tori just shook her head. “You just can’t let shit go.”

“Wow! Finally, me and your momma have something in common.” Thuy said with sarcasm.

“She had trouble dealing with you and your momma.” Tori defended her.

“Nobody told her ass to stay with daddy after she found out about us.” Thuy shrugged.

“She stayed because she loved daddy and did everything she could to make their marriage work. Jett and I saw how hard it was for her to deal with that shit.”

“Whatever.” Thuy rolled her eyes at Tori’s justifiable bullshit.

"It's time for you to stop being bitter and petty. Jett and I were just kids. It's so fucking pathetic that you're still pissed about some harmless childhood pranks."

"A few?" Thuy scoffed. "One of those harmless childhood pranks almost got me killed! Remember when y'all tricked me into going into the neighbor's yard with the two pit bulls and they almost ate me alive?"

"But you didn't get killed! Now get the fuck over it!"

That did it for Thuy. The bitch couldn't even apologize. All she did was make excuses and expect Thuy to financially support a family that never gave two fucks about her. "Get your ass out of my motherfucking office! Now!" Thuy hissed with venom like she wanted to kill somebody.

The evil expression on Thuy's face scared Tori. All she could do was what her baby half-sister ordered and get the fuck out of her office.

Sam felt awful for his baby cousin. Seeing her shake with anger and frustration was all he could bare. He walked over to her and held her to try to calm her down. "You okay, Thuy?"

"I'll be alright." Thuy tried to convince herself. "You're lucky, Sam. Even though Uncle Sam and Aunt Sharde, rest in peace, didn't work out they were one hundred percent there for you. They squashed whatever beef they had between them for you."

"Yeah. Momma and dad were a mess." Sam chuckled. His parents reminded him of Bennie and Vera from Harlem Nights. "I miss how they used to go back and forth. It was all in fun and love. If you ask me, it was better that way. A marriage based on a one night stand was destined to fail."

"Not necessarily." Thuy said. "Good things can come from one night stands."

"Yeah, I mean, look at me."

"Trust me. I'd rather be a one night stand baby than an outside baby." Thuy joked but was dead ass serious. Sometimes she wondered what her childhood and life in general would've been like if the circumstances of her conception were different.

"Come on, Thuy. You know Aunt Isla didn't know Olson was married, right?" Thuy nodded and let Sam continue. "As far as Olson and them goes, don't let their misplaced feelings fuck you up. You are amazing. That's their loss for missing out because of their selfishness and immaturity. Also, look who you have in your corner. Aunt Isla, your friends, dad, me and pretty soon…" He rubbed Thuy's stomach. "He or she will be here to meet their terrific momma."

Thuy managed to crack a smile at Sam's look on the bright side speech. "My birthday is around the corner. Will you be in town?"

"Of course, baby girl." Sam answered. "Now, let's go to Aunt Isla's house and eat some of her good ass cooking."

They laughed.

Chapter 28

The day was May 2nd— the anniversary of Macal and Tylisha's mother's death. Every year the family gathered around Belinda's grave to update her on the positive things in their lives and to reminisce about their time with her.

"Here's your plate." Fallon placed Macal's breakfast in front of him on the table.

"Thanks baby," Macal said.

"How are you feeling?"

"I'm all over the place." He sighed. "Had nightmares all night."

"About that day?" Fallon guessed.

"Yeah." Macal nodded. "If only! If only!" Macal stopped himself so he wouldn't fall apart. "Tylisha is on the way with the kids and we'll pick up Grandma Doris and head for the gravesite."

"I'm sorry, baby. I wish there was something I could do." Fallon felt helpless not being able to do anything to help heal Macal's pain.

"You've done plenty and I appreciate it." Macal held Fallon's hand and kissed it.

"Trust me, I know how painful this is for you. During my visit back home, I stopped by momma's grave. Me and Aunt Naomi miss her so much. You would've loved her."

They started eating their meal.

"If she was half as amazing as her daughter, I'm sure I would have," Macal said.

He and Fallon finished their meal and Macal put the dishes into the dishwasher. The doorbell rang and Fallon answered the door.

"Hi, guys," Fallon greeted them.

"Hey, Fallon," Tylisha returned and hugged Fallon.

"Hi, kids." Fallon gave the kids a group hug and noticed Ayla holding a piece of paper. "What y'all got there?"

Ayla gave the paper to Fallon. It was a drawing of Ayla and Welton giving a plate of cookies to an angel wearing a t-shirt with the words, Best Grandma Ever. “We drew this picture for grandma,” Ayla said.

“This is so pretty,” Fallon replied.

Macal came up behind Fallon and grabbed the picture so he could take a look. “Yes, it is baby girl.” His eyes started to water as he took a seat on the couch and covered his face with his hands, while still holding the drawing.

Ayla walked over to Macal and slowly took the drawing out of his hand. She kissed him on the cheek and said, “It’s okay to be sad, Uncle Macal.”

Fallon turned to face Welton and Ayla and said, “Kids, why don’t you go into the game room and we’ll call you when it’s time to go? Your mommy and I need to talk to Uncle Macal.”

“Okay, Aunt Fallon,” Welton and Ayla said, and they went on their way.

When the kids were out of sight, Tylisha sat on one side of Macal, and Fallon sat on the other. The ladies put their arms around him.

“That drawing really got to me,” Macal said as he dried his tears. “Momma loved drawings.”

“I remember,” Tylisha said. “She kept every single one of them.”

“For real?” Fallon asked.

“Yep,” Macal replied. “She cherished every picture we drew for her. There was one I did for her baby shower when she was pregnant with Tylisha. It was her with a pregnant belly, a little girl inside and me kissing the belly.”

“I saw that one in Grandma Doris’ dresser drawer. It was cute,” Tylisha said.

“Remember our school plays? She would help us rehearse our lines,” Macal said to Tylisha.

Tylisha nodded. “She was the best. She loved games. She taught us how to play different kinds of card games, like poker. She taught us how to play Chess. She was a Chess Grandmaster.

“Oh, that’s why I could never beat you,” Fallon said to Macal, and playfully hit him on his arm. “You hustled me!”

"Hustled you?" Tylisha asked, wondering what Fallon was talking about.

Fallon laughed and began to tell Tylisha the story. "You already know Macal and I met at a charity event I was taking pictures for. He wanted me to join him for dinner the next day, and I was like 'no'. They were playing Chess in the next room. He asked me if I played. Aunt Naomi's ex-boyfriend taught me. The bet was, if he won, I'd accept his dinner invitation and the rest is history. Tylisha, he beat me bad." She turned to Macal and poked him repeatedly in the stomach. "You hustler, you."

"Aw, it turned out alright in the end." Macal pulled Fallon into a kiss.

"Uh huh." Fallon responded.

"Maybe I should tell Enzo the real reason why he has a problem beating me at Chess," Tylisha said.

"How are things between you two?" Fallon asked.

"Great," Tylisha answered. "We all went to Amery's recital the other day. That boy can sing. The kids got along right off the bat and Ligia and Vax are pretty cool. We had a great time."

"That's good," Macal said.

"Enzo is going to stop by here after we come back. Is that cool?" Tylisha asked Macal.

"Of course."

"I would've invited him to join us, but I kind of want to do this alone for the time being. You know."

"We understand," Macal and Fallon assured her.

"Plus, he promised Amery that he'd take him and his friends to a comic book fair today."

"Gotcha," Fallon said.

"Grandma Doris should be ready by now." Macal got off the couch and called out for the kids. "Kids, it's time to go."

"Coming," Welton and Ayla were heard as they made their way downstairs.

Macal hugged the two most important women in his life and expressed his deep gratitude, "Thanks."

"Anytime baby," Fallon said.

"We're in this together," Tylisha said.

The kids showed up and Macal announced, "Alright everybody, let's move out."

Chapter 29

The day was May 2nd— Thuy's birthday. So far, Thuy's special day was going great. First, Bryn and Vida took her out to breakfast at Golden Corral and now they were on their way to *Bloomingdales* at Lenox Square. They rode around in Bryn's black BMW SUV. Thuy was in the backseat with Bryn, leaving Vida in the front. They were all dancing to *It's Your Birthday* by Uncle Luke.

"Go, Thuy! It's your birthday! Go, Thuy! It's your birthday!" Bryn and Vida sang to the record with Thuy twerking in her seat.

"Y'all are a trip!" Thuy laughed. "Thanks for taking me out to breakfast."

"Anytime, I can't wait for this party," Bryn said.

"It's gonna be off the chain," Vida added.

"Thirty-five is feeling great," Thuy told them. "Y'all know y'all gonna have to be turnt up for me too, right?"

"Why?" Bryn asked.

"You know I can't drink in my delicate condition." Thuy rubbed her pregnant belly. "I hope I can find an outfit to kind of hide it."

"Don't worry. We got you," Bryn promised as he and parked the vehicle.

"And you're going to have a good time tonight," Vida said as they exited the vehicle, and started walking into the mall.

"Yeah, don't let a little thing like being pregnant stop you," Bryn said.

They walked into Bloomingdales to shop for their party outfits.

"Aw, hell! The baby ain't even here yet and I'm already being a bad influence," Thuy joked. "Teaching him how to get crunk or teaching her how to twerk." The trio chuckled, and all of the sudden Thuy got serious. "I hope this birthday turns out okay."

"Of course it will," Bryn assured her.

"Bryn's right, what are you worried about?" Vida asked.

"You guys are right," Thuy said. "I just hope this birthday doesn't turn out to be a disaster like my eleventh one."

May 2, 1993

It was the night of the father-daughter dance which happened to fall on Thuy's birthday. Thuy had her heart set on going to the dance with her father, Olson. Even if it meant sharing the moment with her wicked, big half-sister Tori. Unfortunately, Olson couldn't make it because he caught the flu and had to stay in bed all day. Miraculously, at the last minute, Thuy's Uncle Sam, Sr. was able to come in town and take her to the dance.

Sam, Sr. picked Thuy up in his brand new, candy apple red, four door Mitsubishi. Thuy had her hair in curls and was wearing a baby blue dress. Sam, Sr. had on his black tux and a baby blue tie.

"Thanks Uncle Sam for taking me to the father-daughter dance. You know you didn't have to take me," Thuy said.

"Baby girl, it's no bother," Sam, Sr. told her. "It's my pleasure."

"But, you live so far away."

"I don't live too far," Sam, Sr. corrected her. "Anything for my baby sister's little girl. You are growing into a beautiful, lovely young lady. Happy eleventh birthday." He leaned over and kissed Thuy on the cheek.

"Thanks, Uncle Sam," Thuy blushed.

Thuy and Sam, Sr. were listening to the radio, enjoying the sounds of Gin and Juice by Snoop Doggy Dogg. Next came a news report. "This just in, a bizarre freak accident near Fat Bugs bar claimed the life of wife and mother of two, Belinda Kilborn. Witnesses said she stumbled out of the bar, heavily inebriated when—"

Sam, Sr. turned to anther station. "What a tragic story. That family must be devastated. Especially those kids."

Thuy nodded in agreement.

Sam, Sr. found a parking space at the civic center. "Here we are." He got out of the car and walked around to open the door for Thuy. "After you, my lady."

"Thank you," Thuy said and exited the car.

Sam, Sr. offered Thuy his arm and the two went inside. "You are a beautiful princess. Tonight is your night," he said as he led Thuy to the dance floor.

They danced to Isn't She Lovely by Stevie Wonder.

"This is fun!" Thuy exclaimed with joy.

"Let's go to our table," Sam, Sr. said, and the two found their table to take their seats.

"How's school going?" Sam, Sr. asked.

"Great! I made all A's on my report card." Thuy answered proudly.

"Good girl! Congratulations."

"Sam showed me this car magazine earlier this week and—" Thuy stopped in mid-sentence, hoping that her eyes were playing tricks on her.

"What's wrong, baby girl? Cat got your tongue?"

Thuy pointed towards the dance floor at an obviously healthy Olson, dancing with Tori. "Daddy said he was sick."

That motherfucker! Sam, Sr. thought. He was going to comfort Thuy but she was already marching towards them. When they saw her, Olson looked like he saw a ghost and Tori had a taunting smirk on her face.

"Hey, Thuy! What are you doing here?" Olson managed to say. He had no idea Thuy would be there. He thought he was safe from being busted.

"I was about to ask you the same thing," Thuy said with disappointment. "You told me you were sick."

"Yeah, sick of you and your hoe ass momma, bitch!" Tori spewed out in hate.

"Listen, Thuy, Mycha thought it was best, because Tori didn't want—"

Thuy walked off because she didn't need to see and hear anymore. The message was crystal clear. She didn't matter. Never have and never will. Thuy ran out of there as fast as she could.

Sam, Sr. calmly got in Olson's face and said, "Your punk ass better be lucky we're in a room filled with sweet young ladies." He then glanced at Tori and corrected himself. "Well, most of them."

Sam, Sr. ran outside to look for Thuy. He found her sitting on the hood of his car crying. Thuy saw Sam, Sr. and jumped into his arms and continued to cry. "It's okay, baby, I'm here," he said.

"Why do they hate me?" Thuy sobbed. "I didn't do anything wrong."

"I know, baby," Sam, Sr. said and opened the door for Thuy. "We should get going." Sam, Sr. took his place in the driver's seat and took off.

He drove for quite a while before Thuy realized it wasn't the way back home. "This isn't the way home. Where are we going?" She asked.

"It's a surprise," Sam Sr. said. Thankfully, he and Isla predicted something like this would happen when it came to a nigga like Olson, so Sam, Sr. came up with a little insurance policy and Isla gave her stamp of approval. They parked at Philips Arena where the Atlanta Hawks were playing the Chicago Bulls. The promotional posters showed Michael Jordan and Dominique Wilkins.

Thuy's face lit up like fireworks and she literally jumped out of the car. She ran into her uncle's arms, jumping up and down like she won the lottery. "You're taking me to see the Bulls versus Hawks game?"

Sam Sr. nodded, with a smile.

"I get to see MJ and Dominique battle it out! This is great, but how are we gonna get tickets? The game is probably sold out." She wondered.

"Right here, baby girl!" Sam Jr. came up from behind Thuy and waved three tickets in her face.

Thuy turned around to hug her cousin. "Sam! Hey!" Thuy took a better look at the tickets and noticed they were courtside seats. "These seats are perfect! How did y'all pull this off?"

"Always have a backup plan," Sam Sr. advised.

Thuy hugged her uncle and cousin. "Thanks! I love you guys!"

Unfortunately, that wasn't the first and it wouldn't be the last time Olson would disappoint Thuy. Sometimes she wondered if she didn't have her loved ones in her corner, how she would have survived her drama-filled childhood.

"Thuy, how do you like this one?" Vida asked. She was wearing a lime green, floral, lace patchwork V-neck romper with a black belt. The outfit hugged her curves nicely and complimented her deep honey complexion.

"Girl, it's off the chain!" Thuy complimented.

"Thanks. And I have the perfect black shoes to wear with this too. All I need is a matching purse and I'll be all set."

"Thuy come over here!" Bryn called out.

Thuy searched for Bryn and found him near the men's dress shirts. "Yes, Bryn?"

"I'm trying to figure out what shirt to wear with my navy blue slacks. Should I go with light blue or gray?" Bryn waited on Thuy's suggestion.

Both shirts looked nice but the gray one did a better job matching Bryn's semi-brown skin, jet black mini-afro and neatly trimmed goatee. He was a sexy ass man. He could have any woman he wanted. If he was straight. "I'd go with the gray."

"Thanks. What are you going to wear?"

"I don't know. It needs to be something that's off the chain. Able to hide the belly and..." Thuy faced Vida's direction and saw the perfect outfit. "I think I found it!"

Thuy rushed over to the rack with Bryn right behind her. It was a one-shoulder, black jumpsuit. "What do you think?" She asked her friends.

"Perfect!" They answered.

"You should wear that black hat you bought during our trip to Paris," Vida suggested.

"That would go great with this outfit," Thuy agreed. "I can also wear my not too low black heels and my new black clutch purse."

"There you go," Vida said.

"Great, then it's all settled. Y'all finished?" Thuy asked.

"Yep," Bryn said.

"Definitely," Vida said.

"Alright, let's go," Thuy said.

Chapter 30

The Kilborn family arrived at the cemetery. It didn't take long for them to find the correct tombstone. They had paid too many visits to forget. Out of all these years Belinda's death was still unreal to her loved ones.

Doris was the first to walk up to the tombstone to pay her respects. "Hey, baby girl! This is your momma. I finally moved to a retirement village. It's wonderful. Gladys says hi." She placed a bouquet of hand-picked flowers on Belinda's grave. "She picked these flowers from her garden just for you. I told her how much you loved playing in the garden when you were a little girl." Doris stepped out of the way.

Tylisha and the kids were up next. "Hey, momma, this is your baby girl, Tylisha. Things are going great and your grandbabies are getting big."

Ayla placed the drawing on top of the flowers. "Welton and I made you this, grandma."

"I know how much you loved drawings," Tylisha said. "The business is doing great and I started dating again. You remember Xavion from Grandma Doris' neighborhood? He's a nice guy. I met his son Amery. He's a sweet, handsome boy and a great singer." Tylisha pulled out her phone and searched for a video. "At his recital, he sang one of your favorites." She played the video of Amery singing *Soon as I Get Home* by Babyface.

Everyone let the sounds of Amery's singing take over and touch their hearts and souls. They imagined Belinda enjoying this young man bringing one of her favorite songs to life.

The song ended and it was Macal and Fallon's turn. "Hey, momma! This is your baby boy, Macal. This here is your daughter-in-law, Fallon. That's right, your little boy is a married man now. I wish y'all could've met. Y'all would've loved each other. I tried a few of your recipes from your cookbook. I think I did a pretty good job, right guys?" Macal turned to the family for confirmation.

"Oh yeah," Tylisha agreed.

"Sure," Welton said.

"Great, Uncle Macal," Ayla said.

"Off the chain," Fallon said.

"You hooked it up," Tylisha said.

"An 'A' for effort," Doris said.

Macal caught on to them blurting out random compliments. "They're just being nice. You know I'm not an expert in the kitchen, but I do alright. That didn't stop you from making me help out in the kitchen." Macal let out a chuckle when a funny memory popped into his head. "One time, I jacked up the spaghetti and you and Tylisha were just laughing at me."

Tylisha whispered to the kids and Fallon, "Your genius uncle and husband turned the spaghetti sauce yellow."

"I thought it was seasoning, not food coloring!" Macal defended himself and everybody busted out laughing.

"Yellow spaghetti?" Welton responded weirdly.

"Eww! Uncle Macal!" Ayla exclaimed with disgust.

Macal shook his head. "Look at that, momma, just clowning me. Y'all still ate it!"

"It was actually pretty good," Tylisha confessed.

Everybody continued to laugh at Macal's mistake turned specialty. Macal waited until the laughter stopped to bid Belinda's gravesite goodbye. "We love you, momma. We miss you. Until our paths cross again." He blew a kiss at the tombstone. "Goodbye, momma."

Back at the Kilborn house, the family was enjoying Macal's accidental specialty— yellow spaghetti. The kids were skeptical at first but a little convincing from Tylisha made them give the strange dish a try. To their surprise, it was great. They even asked for seconds.

"See kids, that wasn't so bad," Macal said as he and Fallon gathered the dishes to put in the dishwasher.

"No, it wasn't, Uncle Macal," Welton said.

"What do you think of my yellow spaghetti now, baby girl?" Macal asked Ayla.

"That was yummy, Uncle Macal," Ayla answered with a big smile.

Someone knocked on the door and Macal opened it to find Enzo on the other side. "Enzo, what's up?" Macal greeted him.

"Hey, Macal." Enzo walked in the house and went over to give his woman a kiss on the cheek. "Hey, sweetheart."

"Hi," Tylisha blushed.

"Hi, Mr. Enzo," Welton and Ayla greeted him.

"Hey kids."

"How's Amery?" Welton asked Enzo.

"He's good. He told me to tell y'all hello."

Doris walked over to Enzo and poked him in his chest with her index finger. "I got a bone to pick with you, Xavion."

"Why, Mrs. Blair?" Enzo asked.

"All this time you've been in town and you didn't drop by to see me." Doris always liked Enzo. He was a sweet little boy. His parents were a nice and loving couple. Obviously, the apple didn't fall far from the tree.

"Aw, I'm sorry about that," Enzo said with regret mixed with charm.

"Uh huh, just don't let it happen again," Doris said and pulled Enzo into a hug and kissed him on the cheek. "Seriously, I'm proud of the fine young man you've become."

"Yes, ma'am."

"Tell your folks I said hi."

"Hi, Miss Lolette," Welton and Ayla greeted her. This was a shock because no one heard her come in.

"This is a surprise," Macal commented, maintaining his cool. He'd been working overtime to keep Lolette calm since the Crystal incident.

"I invited her," Fallon said, and motioned for everyone to gather around her in the living room. "I have big news and I want everyone here to share the moment. I told Aunt Naomi this morning."

Tylisha turned to the kids, "Y'all go upstairs—"

"Oh no, Tylisha, they need to hear this too," Fallon insisted.

"Alright." Now Tylisha was in total suspense about what the news could possibly be.

"What's the big news, baby?" Macal asked.

Fallon began to answer. "I found out this news yesterday. It's big news. It was very unexpected. What I'm trying to say is that...uh..." The news was so big she had trouble getting the words out.

"She's pregnant!" Doris blurted out for Fallon.

She caught Fallon completely by surprise. Doris was absolutely right. "How did you know?" Fallon asked her.

"Girl, do you know how long I've been living? I can tell when a woman is trying to drop the baby bomb, and your aunt told me," Doris confessed.

"Boy, can you keep a secret," Fallon said to Doris.

Macal was in disbelief. He asked Fallon again to be sure. "We're having a baby?"

"Yes," Fallon confirmed.

"Wow! We're having a baby!" Macal cheered with excitement, and lifted Fallon off the floor and gave her a deep kiss.

"Congratulations," Doris said.

"I second it," Enzo said.

"I'm going to be an aunty!" Tylisha cheered and gave the happy couple a group hug.

"Yay! Aunt Fallon!" Ayla cheered.

"Congratulations!" Welton cheered. "We're gonna have a cousin to play with!"

"Another great-grandbaby!" Doris said.

Lolette was horribly stunned by the news. This was not good. Not good at all. Tons of thoughts and concerns flooded her mind. She walked over to Fallon and put on one of her best fake ass bitch performances. "This is an amazing surprise. Congratulations, girl!" Lolette smiled and pulled Fallon into a loving embrace.

"Thanks, Lolette," Fallon said with glow. "I want you there every step of the way with me."

"Of course." Lolette couldn't take this shit no more and decided to call it a night. "I have an early assignment in the morning. I'll call you tomorrow."

"Aright, goodnight," Fallon said.

"Goodnight," Lolette said as Fallon walked her out and closed the door behind her.

That bitch ain't fooling nobody! Tylisha thought.

Chapter 31

The Platinum Palace nightclub was packed for Thuy's birthday party. Her family, friends, employees, business partners and clients were there to share the moment. Ambrosia had to be in Los Angeles the next day so she dropped by to give her gift and birthday wishes. The party was jumping and the owner, Anthony, made sure the DJ played all of Thuy's favorite songs she could think of. The song that was playing was *Make 'Em Say Uhh* by Master P.

The virgin daiquiris and sparkling cider helped Thuy fill the void and the food was excellent. It was nice. Being close to her man Jeromy. Enjoying her birthday with her loved ones. Not to mention having a baby on the way. Life was good. Then, it was time to cut the birthday cake. The words on the cake read: *Happy Birthday Thuy! Thanks for giving the world thirty-five years of fabulous grace!*

Anthony appeared on stage with the microphone and made the announcement. "Alright, let's gather around for the cutting of the birthday cake for the most beautiful and best sports agent on the planet— Thuy Ellis!"

Everyone gave a round of applause as Thuy prepared to cut the cake. Anthony started to sing Happy Birthday. His voice had the power to make women drop their panties. Thuy cut the cake when Anthony ended the song.

"Thanks everybody for making this the best birthday ever!" Thuy took a bite out of the cake. "Good cake. Try it, baby." Thuy fed a piece to Jeromy.

"Tasty!" Jeromy agreed and cut himself a slice. "Happy Birthday, baby," he said with a kiss. He checked out Thuy's body from head to toe. To the naked eye, it was hard to notice her pregnant belly. She hid it very well. "You're looking real sexy tonight!"

"Thank you," Thuy blushed and made her way through the crowd to mingle.

Thuy surfed through the crowd hugging people when she saw her mother and stepfather. "Hey, momma! Hey, Greg! Thanks for coming!" Thuy gave them a hug.

"We would never miss your birthday, baby," Isla said.

"How was your vacation?" Thuy asked. The week prior, she sent them on an all-expense luxurious trip to St. Thomas.

"Great," Greg answered. "You know you didn't have to send us on a trip."

"Come on, Greg, after everything you did for me and momma? Y'all have been there for me through thick and thin. It's the least I could do. You guys deserve it," Thuy insisted.

"Alright, let me borrow my baby," Isla said, pulling Thuy to the side and found a vacant couch for the ladies to sit. "How's everything with my baby and grandbaby?"

"Everything is great," Thuy said with all smiles. "We find out the gender the day after tomorrow. I can't wait!" All of the sudden, Thuy's joy turned to worry. "I want to be a mother, but I'm nervous. What if I mess up? What if I turn out to become a terrible mother?"

"Girl, stop that! You're gonna do fine," Isla assured her. "There's no such thing as the perfect mother, but you're gonna be a great mother. You know why?"

Thuy shook her head.

"Because you're a great woman."

"Aw, thanks," Thuy said.

"She's right," Sam said.

"Sam!" Thuy hopped out of her seat and hugged him.

"Happy birthday, baby girl."

Isla looked at her nephew up and down like he had lost his damn mind, saying with an attitude, "I don't get a hug, little boy?"

"Aunt Isla, you know I ain't forgetting you," Sam said and hugged Isla.

"Alright, how's your big headed daddy?"

"He's good. He couldn't make it because Natalie caught the flu."

Sam, Sr. and Natalie had been married for five years.

"She's treating my brother right?" Isla asked.

"From what I've seen, yes."

"Did you find a house here yet?"

"Still looking."

"Hi, Thuy!" Sophia came up and greeted her with Tony in tow.

"Tony! Sophia!" Thuy acknowledged and hugged them. "Y'all made it!"

"Happy birthday, sweetheart!" Tony said.

"Ditto!" Sophia added.

Tony turned to Sam and shook his hand. "SamIAm! Long time, no see!"

"Hey, Tony!" Sam said.

Tony turned to Isla and switched on the charm. "And the one whose radiant beauty lights up every room she enters and turns everything she touches into diamonds." He grabbed Isla's hand and kissed it.

Isla smiled and blushed through Tony's flirting. "Hello, Tony. Greg is over there." She pointed at the bar where Greg was drinking a beer.

"Oh, I always follow the look but don't touch rule," Tony said.

"Right."

"You can't stop a man from dreaming and looking," Tony said with confidence as he and Sophia excused themselves.

"He's never gonna give up, is he?" Bryn asked.

"And you know this, man!" Thuy answered in her Smokey from Friday's voice, and everybody laughed.

"Hey, Sam, I heard you were moving back here. Congratulations!" Vida said.

"Thanks," Sam replied.

"Are you going to stop racing?" Bryn asked.

"Hell to the motherfucking no!" Sam realized he had dropped the F-bomb and looked around to see if Isla was still around. "Oh good! She's gone! As I was saying. Hell to the motherfucking no, I ain't going nowhere! I'm SamIAm!" He declared.

"Speaking of all these life changes, when are you going to settle down?" Thuy asked.

"I tell you, little cuz, I don't know." Sam shrugged. "Sometimes I wonder if there's a woman out there for me."

"I feel you, Sam," Vida said. "My love life has been one disaster after another. These days my life is just work and home."

"That sounds just like me," Sam said in agreement.

"Excuse me, ladies and gentlemen. Thuy, will you be so kind and come up here with me please?" Jeromy spoke in the microphone on stage, motioning for Thuy to join him.

"Okay," Thuy said as she made her way on stage. She joined Jeromy and asked him, "Baby, what is this about?"

"It's time to open your presents, but first, there's something I need to get off my chest."

"You have my full attention."

The crowd grew silent and Jeromy began to recite his well-rehearsed speech. "Thuy, ever since you came into my life, everything has been wonderful and magical. You're beautiful, intelligent, giving and compassionate; all the things a man could ever ask for in a woman. And now, we're starting a family together, starting with our unborn child. Thuy, I love you and I want to spend the rest of my life with you." Jeromy pulled a small jewelry box out of his pocket. He opened the box to reveal a platinum five carat diamond ring. "Thuy Ellis, will you marry me?"

"Oh, Jeromy! I love you so much!"

Everyone in the club stood silent, waiting for Thuy's answer.

"Of course, I'll marry you!" She answered and the crowd cheered and applauded.

Jeromy put the beautiful, fat rock on Thuy's finger and the newly engaged couple sealed the deal with a deep, passionate kiss.

Jeromy then said, "I feel like the luckiest man in the world. You mean so muc—"

An older man rolled up on Jeromy and *pow*! He punched Jeromy in the face, blackening his eye. Somehow he managed to keep his balance. Security rushed on stage to hold the intruder back.

"You fucking bastard!" The intruder yelled. He tried to get another piece of Jeromy but security's grip was too strong.

Thuy screamed in terror and tried to run over to stop the confrontation, but Bryn and Vida was holding her back.

"Thuy, you're pregnant! Get back!" Vida warned with concern.

"What's going on?" Bryn asked the intruder.

"This bastard ruined my little girl's life!" The intruder accused.

"What are you talking about?" Vida asked.

While still being restrained, the intruder started to explain himself. "This perverted bastard took my eighteen-year-old daughter's virginity and got her pregnant. Then his punk ass forced her to get an abortion!"

Where did I hear this shit before? Bryn thought.

"That abortion caused her to not be able to have any more children! She went insane and had to be committed! Thanks to this nasty, bitch ass nigga!" The intruder tried to lunge for Jeromy again but security escorted him out as he continued to rant and rave. "Let me go! I'll tear his ass apart! You filthy bastard! You ruined my baby's life! You fucking bastard!"

The crowd had the exact same expression on their faces, like *what the hell*. Thuy was as still as a statue. She was too overwhelmed with total humiliation to speak or move.

"What a delusional weirdo that guy was." Jeromy tried to play it off, oblivious to Thuy's highly pissed off demeanor. He grabbed her by the hand and said, "Let's get back to the party."

Jeromy's hand touching her made Thuy's skin crawl. She quickly snatched her hand away. "I'm going home! Bryn! Vida! Get my presents and bring them to my house!" Thuy commanded with anger and stomped off stage like a madwoman.

Jeromy felt insulted. It was bad enough an old ass nigga punched him in public, and now Thuy was walking out on him. Now he was pissed. "I know you ain't believing that crazy, old nigga!"

Thuy didn't say anything. She walked out of the club and into the parking lot with Jeromy hot on her tail, feeding her bullshit stories.

"Come on, Thuy! You know it's probably some lying bitch trying to milk me by dragging her punk ass daddy into this!"

Thuy found Bryn and Vida loading her presents in Bryn's SUV. Thuy opened the door to the backseat and was about to climb in when Jeromy grabbed her arm to stop her.

"Wait, Thuy! You gotta listen to me!"

"Nigga, I ain't gotta do shit but stay black and die!" Thuy finally found her voice. "You made a motherfucking fool out of me again!"

"They're lying!" Jeromy lied.

"Just leave me the fuck alone!" Thuy yelled and climbed in the car and slammed the door.

Jeromy banged on the door and begged, "Come on, Thuy! Listen to me!"

Bryn got in Jeormy's face because his friend was hurting, and he wanted him to stop banging on his shit. "You heard her! Leave her the fuck alone!"

"You stay your faggot ass out of this!" Jeromy yelled.

Bryn saw Jeromy's left eye was the one that was blackened a moment ago and mustered up the hardest sucker punch to Jeromy's right eye, causing him to fall flat on his ass. "Now your eyes match!" Bryn taunted him, and walked around to climb in the driver's seat.

Vida stepped over Jeromy like he was a pile of shit she didn't want to step in and mess up her shoes, and climbed in the passenger seat.

"Bye, nigga!" Bryn yelled out the window. He pressed his foot hard on the gas pedal to take off.

Jeromy lifted himself off the ground and dusted himself off. He sighed heavily and let out a big laugh. "She'll be back! That dumb bitch always does!"

The drive home was dead silent. Thuy's brain was trying to figure out how in the fuck her birthday went from sugar to shit in the blink of an eye. Not even a second after becoming an engaged woman, her fiancé gets punched in the face by his side chick's father. The whole thing was fucked up. Thuy didn't know what to do. She just wanted to crawl into bed and forget this night ever happened.

The trio walked into the house and Thuy collapsed on the couch.

"We put all of your presents in the corner," Bryn said.

"Thanks, Bryn, I'll open them later," Thuy replied with no emotion.

"I'm sorry, Thuy." Bryn gave her a hug. "I'll see you tomorrow."

"Goodnight, Bryn."

"Bye, Vida. Take care of her," he said and left.

"Do you need anything, Thuy?" Vida asked.

"No." She sighed. "I just want to get out of these clothes and go to bed." She then got off the couch and headed for her room.

"See you in the morning."

"Goodnight." Thuy closed her bedroom door behind her. She took off her hat and threw it across the room like a Frisbee. She kicked off her shoes and took off her clothes. She went into her dresser drawer and slipped into an oversized black Pittsburgh Steelers Stairway to Seven t-shirt and a pair of black pajama bottoms.

Then, she climbed into bed, and out of nowhere started bawling. She couldn't hold the shit in any longer. She had to get it out. All the feelings. All the hurt. All the humiliation. Oh, the humiliation she endured in front of all those people on her special night was too much to fucking handle.

Thuy continued to sob uncontrollably. She then felt arms covering her and rocking her back and forth like a baby. Thuy knew it was Vida because of the smell of her favorite perfume— Hypnotic Poison.

"Why me? Why fucking me!" Thuy cried in Vida's arms.

"It's okay, Thuy," Vida tried to comfort her best friend.

"Why does love have to be so motherfucking complicated?"

"Do you believe Jeromy?"

Thuy honestly didn't know what to believe. All she had to go on was Jeromy's history and that poor man's anger. "I don't know."

She shook her head. "That man was so convincing. Didn't you see the anger and pain in his eyes?"

Vida nodded in agreement.

"Nobody can fake that shit. Nobody! What the fuck am I gonna do?"

"Thuy, don't think about that right now. This stress is not good for you and the baby. You just rest, and then tomorrow you can look at things a bit more clearly."

"Might as well. I mean, what else could go wrong?" Thuy shrugged.

The ladies continued to lay in bed, and then the doorbell rang.

"I'll get it," Vida said and left the room to answer the door.

Thuy snuggled in bed, trying to get comfortable.

Vida came back in the room with a perplexed look on her face. "Uh, Thuy... you might want to come downstairs."

Thuy sat up in the bed, wondering what the problem was. "Why?"

"Remember about a moment ago when you rhetorically asked what else could go wrong?"

Thuy heard two familiar voices downstairs she wished she hadn't heard. She jumped out of bed and dashed downstairs with lightning speed. Vida was impressed by how Thuy could move like that with a pregnant belly. Thuy made it downstairs to find her sperm donor and Tori in her living room, moving in his luggage.

"There you go, daddy. Here's the last of it," Tori said to Olson.

"Thanks, baby girl." Olson said and gave Tori a hug and kiss on the cheek goodbye.

Thuy couldn't believe this shit. "What the fuck is going on here? No, I got a better question. What the fuck are y'all doing in my house?" Thuy wanted answers and she wanted them now.

"You know daddy needs a place to stay," Tori reminded her.

"That is not my motherfucking problem!" Thuy replied rudely. "He can stay with you, Jett and your kids like one big happy family that y'all made crystal clear that I was never a wanted member of."

"That's enough!" Tori snapped. "Now he's staying here! Quit being a hateful and bitter bitch and start acting like you got some fucking sense!"

I know this bitch didn't just go there! "Get the fuck out of my house right now!"

"That's exactly what the fuck I'm about to do!" Tori said and proceeded to walk out the door.

"Don't forget to take daddy with you!" Thuy yelled, but Tori had already closed the door behind her.

Vida was right. Things had definitely gotten worse. Thuy was stuck with Olson in her house. The estranged father and daughter were staring at each other, not knowing what to say to break the ice.

"This is a very nice house," Olson complimented.

"Thanks," Thuy replied dryly.

"I wish you would treat Jett and Tori with respect."

"I'm going to bed. I'm tired," Thuy said and walked off in a huff. His ass could've at least said the words 'thanks for letting me stay here' and maybe Thuy would've at least thought about making an attempt to warm up to this, but he had to open up with that bullshit. That deadbeat motherfucker can forget it!

Vida didn't know what to say except, "Hello, Mr. Lager. Goodbye, Mr. Lager." And followed Thuy into her room.

The ladies went back to Thuy's bedroom and she slammed the door behind her. "Fuck! Fuck! Fuck!" She screamed at the top of her lungs, not giving a fuck if Olson heard her.

"Shit, girl! What you gonna do?" Vida asked.

"I don't know but I need to think of something because his ass ain't staying here. Believe that shit!"

"This is a big house. You can easily avoid him."

"Maybe, but I still want his ass gone, ASAP!" Thuy stood her ground. She then let out a sarcastic laugh. "What a perfect end to a perfectly fucked up birthday."

Chapter 32

May 2, 1993

"What you doing this weekend?" Macal asked a girl he met at school named Sabrina on the cordless phone. He was sitting in the living room, not paying attention to what was on TV while Tylisha was in the kitchen doing her homework.

"We're supposed to be going out of town to visit my grandma," Sabrina answered.

"Really? Where does your grandma stay?"

"Tallahassee."

"I wanted to see if you wanted to go to the movies with me, but you have other plans," Macal replied with disappointment.

Tylisha looked over at her teenage brother and rolled her eyes. At the age of seven, she knew when it came to girls, Macal was full of shit.

"Aw, I'm sorry," Sabrina sounded apologetic.

"It's okay, baby girl. Maybe some other time we can get together—" Macal's macking was interrupted by loud banging at the door. "Sabrina, I got to check something out. I'll talk to you later. Bye!" He hung up without waiting on a reply to answer the door. Shit! It was Taryn!

"Where the fuck your daddy at?" Taryn asked with an attitude.

Of course, Macal knew his father was taking a nap in the bedroom, but for obvious reasons, he wouldn't tell her hoe ass. Good thing Belinda was at Doris' house, or it would've gotten real ugly up in here. Macal didn't know what to say to the home wrecking bitch. All that came out was, "Well...I...well..."

Taryn rolled her eyes with annoyance. "Oh, never mind! Just get the fuck out of my way!" She pushed Macal out of the way, knocking him against the grandfather clock, causing his arm excruciating pain. Taryn let herself in the house and went straight upstairs to find Rufus.

Damn that hoe is strong! Macal thought. He rubbed his arm and took a seat on the couch. "Fucking bitch," he mumbled in pain.

Tylisha knew Macal was hurt. She stopped doing her homework and walked over to check on him. "You okay, Macal?" She asked.

"I'm cool, Tylisha. Don't worry about me, just get back to your homework," Macal instructed her.

"Okay," Tylisha said. She moved Macal's hand away from the area of his arm where he felt the pain. She kissed the area and said with a big smile, "There, all better!"

Tylisha's innocence touched Macal. That kiss really did make the pain go away. "Thanks, baby girl," he said and gave his baby sister a big hug and kissed her on the forehead. "You're a lifesaver."

"You welcome."

Boom! The door slam startled Macal and Tylisha. Taryn's pissed off yelling started to echo throughout the house. "Nigga, we need to talk!"

"Woman, what the fuck are you doing in my house?" Rufus yelled.

"It's been two motherfucking months and you ain't left that bitch yet!" Taryn went through with the abortion in order to hold up her end of the bargain, and now it was Rufus' turn.

"Don't be barging in my motherfucking house with my kids here!" Rufus was beyond pissed. Things were getting better between him and Belinda, and she was sticking with her commitment to cut back on the drinking. The last thing he needed was a bitch who didn't know her place fucking it up.

"Nigga, fuck those kids!" Taryn snapped. "As far as I'm concerned, those little bastards shouldn't have been born in the first motherfucking place!" In her mind, those kids, Macal in particular were the reason Rufus dumped her for Belinda. She wanted to reclaim what was hers, and fuck whoever stood in the way.

Whap! Rufus slapped the shit out of Taryn and she fell hard on the floor. "Bitch, don't you ever talk about my kids like that again!" He pulled her by her long, straight, off-black hair and yanked her off the floor. "Keep my kids out your motherfucking mouth and get the fuck out my house!" He hissed with venom in her face, and threw her towards the door.

Taryn caught her balance and tasted the blood in her mouth. She was beyond livid. This bastard manipulated her into killing their baby, and now he put his hands on her. Taryn was not going out like that. She was not letting Rufus get away with playing her like a sucka. "Nigga, you made a big mistake. First, you tricked me, and now you put your fucking hands on me!" She opened the door, getting ready to leave. "I'm calling the cops on your ass, motherfucker!" Taryn headed straight downstairs and found the phone on the living room couch.

She picked it up and Rufus caught her before she was able to dial the number. "Put the phone down right now!" He ordered.

"Make me, nigga!" Taryn bluffed.

Rufus ran over to Taryn and snatched the phone out of her hand, and threw it on the couch. He carried her out of the living room over his shoulder with her kicking and screaming.

"You fucking with the wrong one! Having me kill our baby! Your ass played me! Who the fuck do you think you are?"

Macal and Tylisha were left in the living room, appalled by what they just heard and witnessed. Something told Macal to go upstairs and investigate. He quietly tiptoed up the stairs to his parents' room. The door was slightly cracked but he was still able to get a terrific view of everything that was going on.

"Baby, please don't call the police. I'm sorry," Rufus apologized. He wasn't trying to go to jail behind this bitch, so he had to sweet talk his way out of this. "I didn't mean it."

"I'm getting tired of this shit," Taryn cried with hurt in her heart.

Rufus pulled Taryn into his arms to comfort her. "You got to give me more time." It was a fucked up thing to do, but Rufus had to get that pregnancy terminated. He may not had been the world's greatest husband, but he promised himself he would never bring a bastard, outside baby into this world, and he didn't give a fuck what he had to do to keep that promise. He owed Belinda that much.

"I waited long enough," Taryn replied with her head down in shame.

Rufus lifted her head up and looked into her tear-filled eyes. "You believe in me, don't you?"

"I want to so bad," Taryn said as she dried her tears.

"You can trust me." He placed a kiss on Taryn's lips. "Do you trust me?"

"Oh, Rufus—"

"Please. Say you trust me." Rufus kissed her again.

"Yes, I do," Taryn answered.

Rufus continued to kiss Taryn and laid her down on the bed, undressing her.

"That bastard!" Macal whispered to himself. He was old enough to know what was going to happen next. Rufus was getting undressed while Taryn positioned herself on the bed on all fours, with her ass in the air.

The sight of Taryn's nude body made Macal's dick rock hard. It was very disturbing, getting a hard-on from the woman who made his mother's life a living hell, and who was the cause of turmoil in his family, but it couldn't be helped. Taryn was a beautiful, sexy woman. Her dark brown bedroom eyes matched her beautiful face. Her chestnut skin made her body even sexier. Her melon titties bounced up and down with Rufus pounding her pussy from the back was all Macal could take. Watching Rufus tear up the pussy and holding that big, juicy ass for dear life made Macal sick and jealous. This man was betraying his beloved mother in their house and in their bed, but at the same time he wanted to know what that pussy felt like on his dick. Macal was squeezing his dick through his shorts, getting turned on by Taryn moaning with pleasure and taking the dick like a champ. Yes, Macal hated her but he couldn't help but lust for her.

Rufus took his dick out of Taryn and she spread her legs apart, exposing her neatly trimmed, dripping wet pussy. Macal almost fainted. She's got a pussy that's pretty! He thought. She took one of her hands and started rubbing her clit and used her other hand to put Rufus' dick in her mouth. Taryn's dick sucking skills impressed

Macal. She sucked on it like she was setting a world record. When it was Rufus' turn to give Taryn oral, Macal regained his composure and wanted to go straight to his room to jack off, hoping it would get his mind off wanting to fuck the shit out of his father's mistress.

He turned around and bumped into Tylisha. "How long have you been standing there?" He asked, hoping Tylisha didn't see what Rufus and Taryn were doing, let alone what he was doing.

"Just now," Tylisha answered.

Macal sighed with relief and pulled Tylisha by her hand, and went back downstairs. "I thought I told you to do your homework."

"My homework is finished. Now I want to help you," Tylisha said.

"Tylisha you need to stay out of this," Macal said. This was one fucked up situation. Finding out his father was even a bigger trifling nigga than he thought. He was up there fucking his main hoe in the bed he shared with his mother, and wishing that was him up there tearing up Taryn's walls instead. Macal didn't know what to do. He glanced at the phone and...

"Good morning sleepy head." Fallon woke Macal up to stop his tossing and turning.

"Good morning, baby," Macal yawned and kissed Fallon.

"You're not going to work today?"

"No, I'm staying in today," Macal answered. "What time is your doctor's appointment?"

"1:30."

"I'm there."

"Are you sure?" Fallon asked with concern. "It looked like you were having a nightmare."

"You're half right," Macal confessed. "I was dreaming about that day again."

"Your mother's accident?"

"Yeah," Macal said and let Fallon snuggle in his arms. "That bastard put her through so much. I hated him for what he did to momma. What he put our family through, how he crushed her spirit until she was reduced to nothing. If only I hadn't...Oh, never mind."

Macal shook the memory out of his mind. The guilt he felt still haunted him. In fact, he never told a soul about his forbidden desires for Taryn. Those thoughts were too shameful to share with another person.

"Baby, the accident wasn't your fault." Fallon held Macal's hand for comfort. "I know you loved your mother and wanted to protect her."

Macal rubbed Fallon's stomach and said, "I hope I turn out to be a great father."

"I know you will," Fallon returned.

"Trust me, I'll be a better father than that bastard ever was," Macal said with bitterness.

This particular conversation caused Fallon to have a whole different perspective. "May I ask you something?"

"Sure."

"Do you think Rufus loved you and Tylisha?"

Macal didn't know how to answer that question, but he gave it his best shot. "I'll put it this way. His mouth said yes, but his actions said something else. To be honest, I don't know. Maybe we were in his heart, but who the fuck knows."

Fallon nodded. "I know he wasn't faithful to your mother, but how was he towards you and Tylisha?"

"When he wasn't embarrassing us with his fucking around, I'll admit he was a great provider and protector," Macal answered, trying to find some of Rufus' good attributes. "He did love us in his own way, I guess. I never really understood that man." He sighed.

"Look at it this way, at least you and Tylisha knew who your father was, and he was in your lives and actually wanted to be there," Fallon said, hoping Macal could look at the bright side.

"Have you ever thought about looking for your father?"

Looking for her biological father was something Fallon never really considered. "I don't know, Macal. I really don't. I don't know if I even want to see his face right now. Not like I know what it looks like." Fallon paused and expressed her second thought about finding her father. "On the other hand, I have so many questions that need to be answered. Why did he leave? Why didn't he want me? Do I have other siblings out there? Did he ever think about me? I have more, but those are the main ones."

"It's his loss, baby," Macal said and held Fallon tighter. "It's his loss."

Fallon felt warm, special and protected in Macal's arms. "I'm so lucky and happy to have you in my life."

Macal kissed Fallon and said, "The feeling is mutual."

Chapter 33

Vida was sitting at Thuy's desk in her home office, grading papers. It was the perfect place to keep Olson out of her hair. Thuy wasn't home yet. For the past two days Vida had been doing her best to keep the peace. In other words, helping Thuy avoid Olson as much as possible.

Vida's iPhone started vibrating on the desk. She glanced at the caller ID and saw it was Bryn. She turned on her Bluetooth and answered the call. "What's up, Bryn?"

"Hey, Vida, is Thuy there?"

"No, she's at Jeromy's, but she'll be back soon. She might be slow about it. You know she's trying to avoid her sperm donor like the plague."

"Right! Right!" Bryn replied with a nod. "She's gonna believe him and take him back, isn't she?" He was referring to Jeromy.

"Looks like it," Vida replied with disappointment. "You know he surprised her at the doctor's appointment."

"I know. They're having a boy."

"Bryn, I know you didn't call me to have a Jeromy is a nothing but a no good bitch ass, fuck nigga bitching session. You asked if Thuy was home for a reason and something tells me you wanted to talk to me without her around."

"You got me, but before I start, promise to keep this conversation between us?"

"Okay."

"And don't trip, and keep an open mind," Bryn added another condition.

"What's on your mind?"

"I need you to promise me you won't trip and that you'll keep an open mind." Bryn needed confirmation before he went any further.

Vida sighed and said, "Alright, I promise I won't trip and I'll keep an open mind. Now spit it out already!"

"Yes, ma'am," Bryn teased at Vida's demanding response. "At

Thuy's party, that guy barged in making those accusations had me thinking. I heard something similar to what he was talking about before."

"Which was?"

"Forcing a woman to get an abortion. I knew I heard something like that before, and then it hit me. I know exactly where I heard that scenario."

"Where?"

"Onya."

"Onya?"

"Yes, Onya," Bryn repeated. "You remember her story?"

"Of course, she fell in love with a rich celebrity who had a pregnant girlfriend. He made her get an abortion. He was supposed to pay her off but never did. She threatened to tell his girlfriend and he beat her up." As Vida summarized Onya's story, she quickly figured out what Bryn was driving at. "Wait a minute. You're not suggesting that—"

"Jeromy was the dude and he killed Onya? Yes, the fuck I am," Bryn confirmed.

"But—"

"Remember your promises," Bryn reminded her.

Vida took a deep breath and kept her cool. It wasn't easy because this was some wild and crazy shit. "Okay, how did you come up with this conclusion?"

"You recall my suspicion about him volunteering at the center?"

"Yeah."

Bryn went on to explain his theory. "Well, I had good reason to be suspicious. Oh, I'm about to let it all hang out, balls and all."

"Proceed."

Bryn began to draw out the timeline. "Onya starts coming to the center. Then Jeromy starts volunteering at the center. All of the sudden, Onya stops coming to the center. Then a little bit after Onya's murder, Jeromy stops volunteering."

Vida's eyes stretched wider than saucer plates. "You're right. That is eerie."

"Exactly," Bryn continued. "Jeromy must've somehow found out Onya reached out to Thuy. He starts volunteering at the center to make sure it was her."

"Then when she threatened to tell Thuy, he beats her up to scare her away and he kept volunteering to make sure she never came back." Vida guessed, coming up with a theory of her own. "Marcus' party. Jeromy was nowhere to be found until after Thuy showed up."

What the fuck! "You're absolutely right, Vida. That was the day before Onya was killed. Thuy stopped by her house to check on her and found her all bruised up. Thuy tried to convince Onya to drop the charges. When Onya refused, Thuy told her to think about it and call her the next day with her decision. Jeromy must've followed Thuy and overheard their conversation. The next day he used the money he owed her as bait to lure her away and kill her so she wouldn't press charges or tell Thuy. Yes, that motherfucker killed her."

"And once Onya was dead, he didn't need to volunteer at the center anymore," Vida finished, but there was one little problem she needed to address. "Bryn, I'll admit this is a very wild coincidence. I'm not saying you're right or wrong. However, I am leaning towards right, but you do realize you can't go to Thuy with an accusation like this without any proof."

"Oh, I'm one step ahead of you, Vida, my dear," Bryn said. "You remember Smedvick?"

"That older white guy you had an on-off thing with in college?"

"That's him," he answered. "His sister, Joanna is a private investigator. I called Smedvick and he gave me her number. She's now on the case."

"How's she doing?"

"She's looking through the surveillance tapes from the party to see if she can get a clear shot of the man," Bryn said. "She wants to find him and compare his daughter's story to Onya's story. I noticed the father didn't mention anything about reneging on paying the daughter off. That part needs to be verified in order to link Jeromy."

Vida was impressed with Bryn's thoroughness. "For Thuy's sake, I hope you're wrong about this."

"I hope so too, Vida. I hope so too."

Thuy felt like she was driving on a rainbow. She and Jeromy found out that they were having a boy and they worked things out. She decided to believe him and let the birthday party incident go. Once again, they had their post exam quickie and this time they almost got caught, but they made up for it back at his house. During the drive home, she came up with an idea to get Olson out of her house.

Thuy called Vida to let her know she was on the way.

"Hey, girl," Vida greeted her. "What's up?"

"I'm good. I'm on the way. What's our houseguest up to?" Thuy asked sarcastically.

"He's in the living room watching westerns."

"Sorry for leaving you alone with him."

"It's cool. I've been in your office the whole time, grading papers and catching up on some work. Besides, I don't think he even knows I'm in the house." She joked.

"Listen, I have an idea on how to get rid of our unwanted houseguest."

"Really? What is it?"

"You'll find out when the time comes," Thuy said. "All I'll say is the idea is kind of childish, but hey, I'm desperate and it's the only idea I came up with."

"Well, you got to do what you got to do."

"Exactly, I'll see you in a bit. Bye."

The call ended and Thuy called the only person she knew who could get her out of this mess. "Hey, baby," Isla greeted her.

"Hey, momma."

"How are you and my future grandson?" She asked.

"We are good." Thuy sighed and cut to the chase. "Momma, I need you to come over to my house. I have a problem and only you can help me."

"I'll be right over." Anytime Thuy called for help, no matter how big or little the problem, Isla would spring into action like a superhero. "What's the problem, baby?"

"You'll know when you get here."

"Alright, I'm on my way. Bye, Thuy."

"Bye, momma."

Thuy arrived at her home and prepared herself to duck and dodge Olson before opening the door. When she entered the house, there was Olson. "Hey Thuy." He greeted her.

"Hey," Thuy returned without making any eye contact.

"Thuy, we need to talk."

"About?" Thuy replied coldly.

"All this tension and your attitude."

Thuy rolled her eyes and said, "I'm going to my room to change clothes." And went straight upstairs.

Vida saw Thuy from her guestroom and followed her into her bedroom. "What's this plan of yours?" She asked.

"You'll find out soon enough." She quickly changed into a pair of sweatpants, a t-shirt and a pair of thick black socks on her feet. "I am so ready for him to get the fuck out of my house." The doorbell rang and a smile appeared on her face. "Right on time."

Thuy rushed downstairs to answer the door. "Thuy, will you listen to me?"

Thuy ignored Olson's demands and opened the door. "Hey, momma!" She greeted Isla and gave her a big hug.

"Hey, baby!" Isla returned and entered the house.

"Hi, Mrs. Dawson," Vida greeted her.

"Hi, Vida." Isla hugged her.

"Oh, hell no!" Olson complained. Over the years his feelings towards Isla grew more bitter and hostile.

"My house. I can invite anybody I want," Thuy said to Olson.

"Hi, Olson," Isla greeted him with fake enthusiasm.

"Isla," Olson replied in a monotone.

Oh yeah! This is a problem! Isla took a seat on the couch. "What's going on here?"

"Tori moved him in here, without my permission, of course, because he's getting some work done to his house and she didn't have any room with Jett being home," Thuy explained and took a seat next to Isla.

"I'm sorry, baby," Isla said with sympathy, and rubbed Thuy's back.

"How was that trip I sent you and Greg on?" Thuy asked Isla.

"It was great," Isla said with glow. "First we—"

"You're sending her on trips!" Olson lashed out with jealously. He thought it was fucked up that Thuy spent her money on her bitter bitch mother, her chump bitch nigga stepfather and her friends like it was going out of style, but wouldn't throw not one fucking penny at him, Tori and Jett.

"Yes, I did. After all, she is my mother who has been there for me no matter what. Unlike some people," Thuy hinted at Olson.

"Thuy, you don't understand the kind of pressure I was under," Olson defended himself.

"And what pressure was that?" Isla wanted to hear this load of bullshit. "Running away from your responsibilities? Allowing your wife and kids to mistreat my baby and not make her feel welcomed in the family. The last time I checked, you were the one who caused this drama by lying about being single and not wanting to face the consequences."

Vida was just sitting there like all she was missing was some popcorn, watching the family drama go down.

"I'm sorry about all of that, okay? Mycha and I were having problems. It couldn't be helped. I paid for my mistakes, so drop it!" Olson yelled.

Thuy didn't like how the word mistake was used and needed to check her sperm donor. "Find a different way to say that. Considering that I'm the result of that mistake."

Isla pulled Thuy in her arms and kissed her forehead. "Thuy, you're not a mistake, baby. I wouldn't trade you for anything in the world. Yes, your deadbeat daddy was too busy kissing his real family's asses to care anything about you, but we made it through."

"Bitch, keep my family out your mouth!" Olson threatened.

Isla was unfazed. "You want another prison sentence?" Her retort shut Olson up real quick. Five years was enough.

"I wish you had at least half as much protective passion for me like you have for your real family," Thuy said to Olson with sadness. "That would've come in handy when I was beaten like a dog and almost raped. Instead, I got a shut the fuck up snap and a front row seat to you beating the hell out of my momma." She turned to Isla and replied, "Sorry." Referring to her profanity usage.

"Understood." Isla said.

Olson was starting to feel like less than rotting shit. He needed to explain himself. "Thuy, I know you spent your entire life walking around thinking I didn't give a shit about you, and that's not true. Mycha, Jett and Tori didn't hate you. They just needed time to accept you and it was very difficult for them. Trust me when I say I did the best I could for you."

Hearing Olson use the words, 'trust me' made Thuy want to throw up. She took a good look at Olson and asked, "Did you really do the best you could for me?"

"Yes, I really did," Olson replied with sincerity and regret.

Thuy covered her mouth and let out a giggle. She turned to Isla and Vida. "Y'all heard that?" She pointed at Olson's direction. "He did the best he could for me." Thuy then came up with an idea to drive her point home and turned her attention back to Olson. "Okay, since you did the best you could for me then you should be able to answer some of these questions. For starters, what was my personal best sprint time in the 100-meters in high school?"

Olson struggled to answer and confessed with disappointment, "I don't know."

"11.29 seconds in high school and 12.05 seconds in college," Isla answered.

"How many Chess tournaments have I won in my lifetime?" Thuy asked.

"You played Chess?" Olson answered a question with a question.

"Fifteen out of twenty," Isla answered.

"What's my favorite movie of all time?" Thuy asked.

"I don't know," Olson answered.

"Mommie Dearest," Isla answered.

Thuy shook her head and asked another question. "In order, who are my top three favorite soap opera villains?"

"I'll go ahead and put you out your misery Olson," Isla said. "Sheila Carter, Stefano DiMera and Sami Brady."

Thuy said, "Alright, how about two easy ones? Easy question number one: When is my birthday?"

Olson began to stutter. "Uh...uh..."

"It was two days ago, you dumb ass nigga!" Isla blurted out the answer with disgust. "She turned thirty-five. What a fucking shame, you didn't get that one with all those unopened presents over there in the corner." Isla pointed at the pile of presents, causing Olson to shake his head.

"Here's your last question, and it has two parts. How many months am I pregnant, and what's the gender of your grandchild?" Thuy asked.

"Six months and you're having a boy." *Please let me be right!* Olson hoped and prayed on the inside.

"Lucky guess," Thuy replied. "You said you did the best you could for me, but you couldn't answer any of those questions. I'm your child and you couldn't answer any of those questions about me. Why is that? I tell you if that was the best you could do for me then your best sucks big time."

Olson threw his hands up in defeat. "Fuck this shit!" He got out of his seat went straight upstairs.

"What's he about to do?" Vida asked.

"What he does best. Walks out when things get tough," Isla answered. She was proven to be right when Olson came back downstairs with his luggage and stormed out the house and slammed the door. "See."

"Thanks, momma," Thuy said to Isla and hugged her.

"Anytime baby," Isla replied. "This is your home. Nobody should be uncomfortable in their home."

Vida shook her head at Thuy. "You're right Thuy, your idea was childish. Calling your mommy to fight your battles for you? Really?" She teased.

"Hey, it worked," Thuy replied with no shame, and addressed something else to Vida. "And look at you, sitting there like you was watching a movie. I was about to ask you did you need some popcorn."

"Hey, good quality TV is hard to find these days," Vida defended her nosiness and everybody laughed.

"The balls on that nigga!" Isla was beyond disgusted. After all these years Olson was still hurting and disappointing Thuy. She wasn't sweating it though, because she had some very interesting information stored in her brain for safe keeping and cracked a smile. "You know, I can tear apart his whole fairytale delusions anytime I want to."

"How?" Thuy asked.

"What do you have on him?" Vida asked.

"Not him, but some people very close to him." Isla let out a little evil laugh. "All in due time my girls. Let's just say it's a small world after all and it's good to know people in high places."

"Okay," Thuy said. "Now I think it's time for me to finally open these presents and send out the thank you cards."

Chapter 34

Thuy, Vida and Bryn were in the *Lullaby Deluxe* shopping for the baby. Thuy was looking through a layout book for the nursery. "What do you think of this one?" Thuy asked Vida and Bryn for their opinion of the blue layout with little elephants dressed as athletes.

"I like that one," Bryn said.

"Me too. It's cute," Vida said.

"Alright, I'll go with this one." Thuy showed the sales associate her selection and gave her back the book.

"That layout is very popular! Excellent choice!" The sales associate said.

"I can see why."

The sales associate printed out a form and handed it to Thuy. "Here you are. All you have to do is fill this out and we'll set up an appointment for you."

"Thank you."

The sales associate went on to assist another customer.

"This is so exciting!" She cheered. "Thanks you guys for coming with me," she said to her lifelong pals.

"Anytime! Anytime!" Vida said.

"Have y'all come up with baby names yet?" Bryn asked.

"We're still working on it," Thuy answered. "So far we came up with Arnold, Jeremy, Orlando and Day'zon."

"I'm feeling Day'zon," Bryn said.

"Day'zon is different," Vida said with a nod.

"Day'zon," Thuy said and gave the form back to the sales associate when she came back to check on her. "Day'zon! Day'zon! Day'zon," She kept repeating.

The sales associate came back with a copy of the form to give to Thuy. "Here you are ma'am, your appointment date is circled on the bottom."

"This is perfect, thanks."

"Anytime."

"Let's look at the toys," Bryn suggested, and they walked over to the toy section.

"I don't know how many toys I bought so far," Thuy said.

"Kids can never have too many toys," Vida said.

"That's true. It won't hurt to browse." Thuy shrugged.

The toy section had a massive selection, from stuffed animals to bath toys to read-along books. They even had musical night lights. Thuy's toy browsing was interrupted by her ringing phone. She dug inside her handbag to answer the call, and a smile appeared on her face when she saw it was Jeromy calling.

"Hey baby! What's—"

"Oooh, baby! I like that!" *What the fuck?! Is that a female's voice I hear?*

"Oh, you do, baby?" That was definitely Jeromy's voice Thuy was hearing then.

"Yes," the unknown woman moaned.

Thuy came to the conclusion that Jeromy had butt dialed her by mistake. There was no question. She was going to do what any woman would do in this type of situation. She pressed mute on her phone and continued to listen to her fiancé and father of her unborn child with another woman.

"Shit! You sexy as fuck!" Jeromy moaned. "I can't wait to get you home and fuck the shit out your ass!"

The last comment made Thuy thirty-eight(it's slang) hot. Jeromy was about to take some random hoe back to his house so he could fuck her in the bed that they shared and where they created their unborn child. Oh hell to the motherfucking no!

"That nigga..." Thuy spun around with full force causing her to bump into a woman carrying two stuffed animals and a few yellow baby outfits. She ended up dropping them on the floor. "Oh shit! I'm sorry about that. Let me help you." Thuy apologized and helped the woman pick up her things.

"That's okay. It wasn't your fault," the woman said with a friendly smile.

"Yes, it was. I wasn't watching where I was going." Thuy insisted and handed the woman her items.

"It's okay. Thank you."

"You got everything?" Thuy asked.

The woman double checked to make sure. "Yes, I got everything. Thanks."

"Okay, goodnight."

Before Thuy turned around to leave, the woman stopped her. "Hey wait! I love your outfit!"

Thuy was wearing a lavender shirt with purple capri pants, with golden flats that matched her golden handbag. "Oh, thanks, I ordered this on the Roses and Diamonds website. They have great maternity clothes."

"Aww, I'll have to try them when I start showing." The woman tapped on her flat stomach.

"How far along are you?"

"About two months."

"I can't wait for this boy to come on out." Thuy rubbed her stomach.

"You're having a boy? Congratulations!"

"Thanks, the name is Thuy, and yours?" She extended her hand.

"Fallon." She shook Thuy's hand.

"Nice to meet you, Fallon. I'll see you around."

"Thanks, you too."

Suddenly a strange feeling came over Thuy. Somehow she felt connected to Fallon. She didn't quite understand why she felt like this towards someone she had never met in her life. The minor exchange almost made Thuy forget about why she needed to go to Jeromy's house, ASAP.

She found Bryn and Vida near the greeting cards. "Bryn! Vida! We need to go to Jeromy's house right now!"

"Why?" Vida asked.

"The nigga butt dialed me and I overheard him telling one of his hoes that he was taking her back to his house to fuck!" Thuy explained, trying to conceal her anger.

"Why in the fuck are we still standing around here looking all cute? Let's get our black asses over there right now and fuck his ass up!" Bryn rallied the troops and literally ran out of the store, jumping in Vida's off-white Jaguar, and they headed straight to Jeromy's house, hoping to beat him home by taking every shortcut they could think of.

Chapter 35

After Fallon made her purchases she decided to pay Macal a surprise visit at his office. He was working late and she was horny. Fallon's pregnancy was putting her libido into overdrive. During the drive, her mind drifted to the woman who bumped into her at the store. There was something about her that drew Fallon in— her beauty, grace and edge. Just her, in general. What caught Fallon's eye was Thuy's strength that she wished she possessed. It would've come in great use during her childhood and her adult life before Macal. There was also something else Fallon couldn't shake about Thuy. Even though she was a complete stranger, Fallon felt close to her, like they shared some sort of connection.

Fallon entered the building and headed straight for Macal's office. The building was pretty vacant and quiet as she walked up the stairs and down the halls of the third floor. All of the sudden, the building wasn't quiet anymore. Fallon started to hear voices as she made her way towards Macal's office. The voices were getting louder as she walked down the hall. By then Fallon realized the voices weren't people having a conversation. It was people fucking. She didn't pay the lovebirds any mind until she noticed the closer she was to Macal's door, the louder the moaning. She stopped walking for a moment to concentrate more on her hearing.

"Oh, shit, baby! Work that shit!"

"Baby! I'm cumming!"

"That's right! Cum for daddy!"

"Oh no! It can't be!" Fallon knew exactly who those voices belonged to.

Fallon slowly crept towards Macal's office door and slightly cracked it open, and her eyes widened with horror. She was absolutely right. Those moans belonged to Macal and Lolette. What she was seeing couldn't be true. Her husband with his pants down and his bare ass flexing hard with her best friend clinging onto his back for dear life with her legs wrapped around his torso and her little orange thong wrapped around her left ankle.

The look of satisfaction on Lolette's face made Fallon sick to her stomach. Watching her take in every rough thrust Macal could dish out deep in her pussy was difficult for Fallon to watch, but she remained silent and stayed.

"Oh shit! Fuck me harder!" Lolette screamed.

"You got some good pussy, baby!" Macal grunted and pumped harder.

"Yeah, baby! Fuck this pussy harder!"

"You got it, baby!" Macal breathed heavily and grabbed Lolette's ass tightly. He picked up the pace, trying to make her pussy sore, and she loved every minute.

Fallon's mouth hung opened. Lolette was cumming and tightening her pussy muscles all over the forbidden dick. She kept her grip onto Macal and let him fuck her as hard and as nasty as he wanted. She glanced over at the door and saw Fallon's face turn pale with disbelief, with her mouth still hanging open. Their eyes met, and in one motion Lolette blew Fallon a kiss, winked and threw up her middle finger.

What a shameless bitch! Being cheated on was nothing new to Fallon, but this was the worst. Not because the side bitch was her now ex-best friend, but more because the dirty little thot didn't even care about getting caught. In fact, if Fallon didn't know any better, getting caught actually turned the nasty hoe on even more.

Fallon lightly pushed the door open to let herself in the office. She took little baby steps and started whimpering. She tried to speak in full sentences but couldn't. All that came out of her mouth was whimpering. Macal heard the sounds, looked over his shoulder and there was Fallon, shaken up, trying to form words.

"Oh shit! Fallon!" Macal dropped Lolette on the floor and pulled up his pants. Fallon was already out the door. "Baby! I can explain!" He yelled and ran out of his office. He saw Fallon running towards the stairway and chased after her.

"Baby, come back!" Macal kept calling for her but Fallon's only goal was to get as far away from the filthy scene as possible.

She almost made it down to the first floor, but she missed a step, tumbled down the rest of the way and hit her head on the railing. She ended up lying at the bottom of the first floor.

"Fallon!" Macal called out as he ran down the stairs. "Fallon! Where are you? Fallon!" He stopped when he saw someone lying on the ground. He leaned over the railing to see who it was. To his horror it was Fallon lying unconscious. "Oh shit! Fallon!" Macal ran straight to her and held her gently, pleading, "Baby! Wake up! Baby! Wake up!" He pulled out his phone to call 911.

"911 emergency?"

"Help me! My wife fell down the stairs at my building; the Kilborn Firm! She's pregnant! She's unconscious!" Macal was hysterical.

"Is she breathing?" The operator asked.

Macal leaned in close to check Fallon's breathing and answered, "Yes she's breathing."

"Help is on the way. Stay with her until we get there," the operator instructed.

"Okay." Macal hung up the phone and switched his attention back over to Fallon with tears in his eyes. "Fallon, I'm sorry, baby! I love you, baby! Baby, please be alright! Please!"

Chapter 36

"I win again!" Tylisha cheered after another win against Enzo in Chess. Tylisha and the kids were having game night with Enzo and Amery at his home.

"Yay! Team Mommy!" Ayla cheered and gave Tylisha a high five.

"You got me again!" Enzo moaned and groaned, and Welton and Amery joined in.

"Now boys, it's not cute to be sore losers," Tylisha teased.

"Yes, ma'am," Enzo said, giving Tylisha a kiss.

"Tylisha, did you really decorate Mark Kelly's house?" Amery asked with excitement.

"Yes, Amery, I did," Tylisha answered.

"And Jackie Trace, and Angel Spencer?"

"Sure did."

"It must be fun working with celebrities."

"Nah, about the same." Tylisha replied unenthusiastically. "Always remember, celebrities are like everyone else. Except everyone knows who they are."

"Gotcha."

"Now you remember that when you make the big time."

"You really think I can?" Amery asked.

"Yes, boy, you have an amazing voice."

"Momma's right, Amery. You can blow," Welton said.

"Thanks, Welton."

"You're a better singer than Trey Songz," Ayla said.

"Thanks, baby girl!" Amery pulled Ayla into a big hug. "That means a lot! Those singing lessons from momma paid off."

Tylisha felt her phone vibrate in her pants pocket and pulled it out. She saw it was Macal calling and excused herself. "I'll be right back."

"Amery, don't you have a stepbrother going to the NFL?" Welton asked.

"Yeah, Sharmon Vax's youngest son," Amery answered.

"That boy can play," Enzo said.

Sharmon didn't join the family business like his big brother and sister, Vax Jr. and Quinn. All this talk about the future made Enzo want to drop a jewel on these three young minds.

"Amery, Welton and Ayla, I watch you guys with different interests, wanting to grow and blossom. I'm very proud of you guys. No matter what you want to do with your lives, always remember the two most important things— education, and always staying true to yourself."

"Yes, dad," Amery said.

"That's my boy," Enzo said.

"I'll remember, Enzo," Welton said.

"That's right, Welton, my man." Enzo turned to Ayla and said, "And I know you will, baby girl."

"I sure will, Enzo," Ayla said.

Tylisha slipped into Enzo's home office and answered the call. "Macal, what's up?"

"Tylisha! Come to Grady, now!" Macal sounded like he was in major panic.

"What's wrong?"

Macal sighed. "Fallon fell down the stairs in my building. She's unconscious in the emergency room."

"Shit!" Tylisha shook her head, hoping the worse didn't happen. "Alright, I'll be right there." She hung up.

Tylisha went back in the living room and pulled Enzo to the side. "I got to go. There's an emergency," she whispered.

"What's wrong?" Enzo asked with concern.

"Fallon fell down the stairs at Macal's building and had to be rushed to the hospital."

"What? I'm coming with you," he insisted.

"Thanks, baby."

They were all set to go when Tylisha remembered something very important. "Wait a minute. Who's gonna watch the kids? Grandma Doris and Gladys went to Atlantic City, and I don't know anybody else who can keep the kids for the night."

Enzo had an idea but wanted to make sure Tylisha was comfortable first. The suggestion he was about to make was highly taboo. "I know where the kids can stay, but only if it's okay with you."

Tylisha had a pretty good idea who Enzo was talking about. These were desperate times and she trusted his judgement. "It's fine, but we have to hurry."

"Okay."

"Baby, the movie is setup." Vax announced to Ligia, lying on the couch.

Ligia walked in with a bowl of popcorn in her loveliness. Her golden-bronze complexion and long, curly, light brown hair with a subtle touch of red, and gray eyes, topped off by her perfect size twelve, curvy body. "Thanks baby, and here's the popcorn." She placed the bowl on the table. She saw the TV screen and knew what Vax was trying to pull. "Really, Vax? *Friday*?"

"What's wrong with *Friday*? It's a classic." Vax said in his defense.

"Duh, I know that." Ligia took her place next to Vax. "I know what you trying to do. You trying to get in my drawers. Nigga, you ain't slick." She accused him playfully.

"Why would you think such a thing, my dear?" Vax did a terrible job trying to act all innocent.

"Anytime you pick the movie for Movie Night, you pick one we've seen over one hundred times. That way, in less than five minutes, you'll have me on my back with my thong to the side and my legs in the air." Ligia ran down the routine she always fell for and, why wouldn't she? The sex was great. Minus the neatly trimmed salt and pepper beard, Vax could pass for Morris Chestnut.

"You make it sound like a bad thing."

"That has nothing to do with it." *His ass better be lucky the dick is good!* "Now be good and watch the movie."

"Yes, beautiful wife of mine," Vax said with a kiss.

"Okay, handsome husband of mine."

"I'm still getting some pussy after this movie, right?" Vax asked for confirmation.

"Of course, darling," Ligia answered. "See, was that so hard? We're married now. You don't have to go through all this trouble. If you want to get between these thighs, all you have to do is ask." She teased.

"I'll remember that."

Vax and Ligia started watching the movie. Ligia made herself comfortable in Vax's arms. She knew him very well. Any minute now she'd feel his pleasure python getting hard and he'd grind up against her ass. She was right. Her thong became moist.

Ligia never pictured herself in a May-December marriage, but that's what her heart wanted. Vax's oldest child Quinn was only a month and some change younger than her and he was the grandfather of three boys and a girl. It didn't matter. Being with Vax was like a fairytale to Ligia. Plus, he treated Amery like his own, which was a plus in Ligia's book. She was also happy that her best friend Enzo, who happened to be her ex-husband and the father of her only child, finally found a good woman.

During the movie, right after the classic Smokey's *You Got Knocked The Fuck Out* scene, the doorbell rang.

"I'll get it!" Ligia kissed Vax and said. "Down, boy." She looked down and grabbed a handful of his dick. "That goes double for you." When she got off the couch, Vax gave her gorgeous ample ass a hard smack. Ligia giggled and answered the door.

"Hey, momma!" Amery greeted and hugged his mother.

"Amery, baby, what are you doing here?" Ligia asked. "I thought you were spending the night with your dad and Tylisha."

"Hi, Miss Ligia!" Welton and Ayla greeted her.

"Hey, Welton! Hey, Ayla!" Seeing the kids with their overnight bags made Ligia guess something serious happened and the kids needed to spend the night. "Amery, give them the two guestrooms next to your room, and make them feel welcome. I'm going to talk to your dad for a minute, okay?"

"Yes, momma," Amery said as Welton and Ayla followed him inside.

Enzo walked up to Ligia and she asked him, “Enzo, what’s going on?”

“Listen, Ligia, I know I said I was keeping Amery tonight, but something happened and we need you and Vax to keep the kids tonight,” he said.

“It’s cool. What’s the problem?”

Enzo sighed. “We have to go to Grady. Fallon fell down the stairs.”

“That’s terrible! Isn’t she pregnant?”

“Yes!”

Ligia shook her head. “I understand. Y’all go ahead. We got the kids. Keep me posted.”

“Sure thing,” Enzo said and hugged Ligia. “Thanks, Ligia. You’re a doll.”

“Anytime.”

Ligia went back in the house and found Vax on the couch.

“The kids are settled and Amery took them to the studio,” he informed.

“I’m sorry,” Ligia said.

“There’s no need to apologize. What’s going on with Enzo?”

“He and Tylisha had to go to Grady. Her sister-in-law fell down the stairs and she’s expecting.”

“Shit!” Vax said with sympathy. “I hope she and the baby are alright.”

“Me too.” Ligia sighed and joined Vax back on the couch. “Enzo said he’ll keep me posted. Sorry our kid-free night is over.”

“It’s okay, shit happens. There’ll be other nights, and our bedroom is always kid-free.” He commented suggestively.

“Right. Sometimes I wonder if you’re in your fifties or twenties.”

They laughed.

Chapter 37

"What's the plan, Thuy?" Vida asked during the drive to Jeromy's house.

"If I beat Jeromy home, I'm going to borrow a page from my grandmomma's playbook." Thuy tapped Bryn on the shoulder. "Bryn, I'm going to need to borrow your belt for this."

Thuy remembered a story Isla told her from her teenage years. Isla's best friend was spending the night at her house after a party. They came home two hours after curfew, and when they walked through the door, Isla's mother was waiting for them at the door, in the dark, with a surprise. When Isla told Thuy this story, she couldn't believe her grandmomma 'surprised' the best friend too. Isla said her mother was like James Evans from Good Times. She didn't care whose kid you were. If you stayed in her house, you got the exact same treatment as her own kids.

"Sure!" Bryn cheerfully obliged and took off his belt. "And you can keep it." Bryn handed the belt to Thuy.

She examined the black belt. It was long, thick and sturdy. Perfect for her plan. "Thanks, sweetheart."

"What if Jeromy and the girl are already at the house?" Vida asked.

"Then I'll improvise," Thuy answered. Then, her mind drifted back to Fallon. "It's interesting."

"Yeah, the nasty, no good nigga!" Bryn hissed with contempt.

"No, not that. That nigga will be dealt with. I'm talking about the woman at the store."

"What woman?"

"That woman I accidently bumped into back at the store. Y'all weren't around. She seemed like a nice person. The thing is, I never met the woman before in my life but I felt connected to her for some reason." She tried to explain the best she could.

"Really?" Vida responded.

"I heard about those type of encounters. You've never met the person, but you feel connected to them like you knew them in another life or something." Bryn felt what Thuy was saying.

"Exactly," Thuy said.

"We're here!" Vida announced and parked the car in front of Jeromy's house. "I don't see his car. It looks like we beat him here."

"Good! Vida, I want you to park a block over, and when I give the signal, come back here and pick me up." Thuy instructed, and opened the car door to get out.

"Alright, but what's the signal?"

"You'll know when it happens." Thuy replied with a smirk, and closed the door behind her.

Bryn and Vida stayed in the car and watched Thuy enter the house. Vida proceeded to drive a block over and parked the car. "How's Joanna doing?" She asked.

"Still hard at work, but making progress," Bryn answered.

"She needs to hurry up. We need to get Thuy away from that scumbag." Vida said anxiously.

Bryn looked over at Vida to give her the crazy eye. "Scumbag, Vida? Really? The correct term is no good, bitch ass, fuck nigga."

Vida returned the crazy eye and teased, "Oh, yes, sir. Thanks for correcting my English."

Thuy sat in the pitch black living room on the couch, wide awake, gripping the belt tightly. She was completely silent. She needed to see for herself if Jeromy was trifling enough to bring a bitch up in here to fuck in their bed. She patiently waited for Jeromy and his thot for the evening to walk through the door. The wait felt like a lifetime, but it was only fifteen minutes.

Thuy clearly heard Jeromy and the hoe giggling and making out, outside the door. She got up from the couch carefully to not make any noise. She walked four paces towards the door and positioned herself so they couldn't see her when the door opened.

Jeromy opened the door and the two walked in the house in total lustful bliss. "Damn girl! You suck a mean dick!" Hearing him compliment the hoe's head game made Thuy sick, but she had to remain quiet or the plan won't work.

"Do I?" The mystery thot blushed. "You sure your baby momma ain't coming by, or suspect anything?"

"Don't worry about her?" Jeromy assured and grabbed her ass. "That gullible bitch believes anything I tell her. That baby probably ain't mine anyway."

Thuy couldn't hold back anymore. She took the belt and started swinging. *Pop! Whap! Pop! Whap!*

"Ouch!" The hoe shrieked in pain, trying to shield herself from the blows with her arms.

"What the fuck! Aw!" Jeromy yelled in pain. The room was too dark to see the assailant. *Pop! Whap!* "What the fuck is that!" Jeromy scrambled around for the light switch while still feeling the blows to his back. "Shit!" Jeromy still struggled to find the light switch.

"Gullible bitch, huh!" Thuy yelled and gave Jeromy's body another strike with the belt. "Baby ain't yours, huh?" She yelled and gave him another lash.

Out of nowhere, the lights came on which made Thuy stop the beating. Jeromy looked up and saw Thuy's face of fury as she maintained her grip on the belt. The two looked over to see his bitch by the light switch, which solved the mystery on how the lights came on. Thuy took a good look at the hoe and was appalled. *This bitch ain't even cute!* Thuy guessed Jeromy paid more attention to the big titties, small waist and fat ass than her ugly ass rat face.

"Thuy, what the fuck are you doing here?" Jeromy had the nerve to ask.

Thuy used the belt to answer Jeromy's stupid ass question, and went back to tearing his ass up. "Whooping motherfucking ass and taking motherfucking names!" She screamed, and kept whopping his ass with the belt.

"Thuy, stop!" Jeromy pleaded.

"Stop what?" Thuy hit him again. "Stop what, nigga?" She hit him again. "What?"

It wasn't easy, but Jeromy managed to grab Thuy's wrist to stop her. "Look, calm the fuck down! I don't know what the fuck you heard!" He tried to run game but to no avail.

"Oh, nigga, I know what the fuck I heard from you and this ugly ass hoe!" Thuy pointed at the thot.

Thuy's insults made the hoe feel some type of way. She marched towards her with authority. "Bitch, who the fuck you calling an ugly—"

Thuy let the belt do the talking and went back into beastmode with the belt, whooping the hoe. *Pop! Whap! Pop!*

Dumb, ugly ass, ghetto thot! Jeromy thought. At least he wasn't stupid enough to insult an enraged person with a weapon. He felt no need to stop Thuy from beating her ass.

Thuy stopped suddenly to catch her breath. She saw her battered up victims and said, "Fuck this shit! I'm out!" She brushed past them and slammed the door behind her. She saw Vida's car parked in front of the house and hopped in the backseat. The three friends sat in silence for three seconds before they all busted out laughing.

"Damn, Thuy! You must've fucked them up bad!" Bryn laughed as Vida drove off.

Thuy responded modestly, "Well... yeah!" The laughter started back and Thuy gave Bryn his belt back. "Here's your belt. It was strong as hell. All that ass whooping I did and it didn't wear, tear or break in half."

"Alligator belt, heavy duty," Bryn said and put his belt back on.

Beating two nasty motherfuckers at the same time made Thuy work up an appetite. "Me and Day'zon are hungry. Let's go to IHOP." She suggested.

"I'm down," Bryn said.

"Let's go," Vida said and headed for the nearest IHOP.

On the way to IHOP, the trio kept laughing at Jeromy and his ugly, ghetto ass thot's beat down. On the inside, Thuy was hurt and broken down by the whole thing, but she kept laughing on the outside. She felt like she had to laugh to keep from crying.

Chapter 38

Macal was sitting in the waiting room, fidgeting like a crackhead going through withdrawal. “Please let her and the baby be okay!” He mumbled to himself. He couldn’t believe he got caught. He was so careful. Then again, he was careful all the other times he was caught with his dick in a woman, other than the woman he was committed to. This time, his marriage and unborn child’s life was on the line. He didn’t know what was going to happen when Fallon woke up. Whatever she said or did, Macal had no choice but to man up and take it.

“Macal!” He looked up when he heard Tylisha’s voice to see her and Enzo were coming his way. She hugged Macal and asked, “How is she?”

“She is still unconscious. The doctor is with her.” Macal sighed and said, “This is all my fault.”

“No, it’s not. It was an accident,” Tylisha tried to comfort Macal.

“You don’t understand, Tylisha. She dropped by the office and saw everything. She knows,” Macal confessed.

Fuck! Tylisha screamed on the inside. She wished Fallon wasn’t in this predicament, but at least now she knew what kind of woman Lolette really was. “Oh I see.” Tylisha simply responded. She and Enzo took their seats. “That’s why she ran away and started running down the stairs and fell?” Macal slowly nodded. “There’s no use beating yourself up over this. Let’s deal with one problem at a time. First, let’s hope Fallon and the baby pull through, and we’ll go from there.”

“Thanks, Tylisha.” Macal was expecting a vicious cuss-out from Tylisha, but instead she took the understanding and calm approach.

“Don’t worry, Macal, y’all will get through this,” Enzo said.

“Thanks Enzo,” he responded.

Enzo got out of his seat and pulled out his phone. “I’m gonna call Amery real quick. I’ll check on Welton and Ayla for you.” He kissed Tylisha.

“Thanks, baby,” she said.

Enzo stepped outside to make the call.

Macal, out of nowhere, said, “Go ahead.”

“Go ahead and what?” Tylisha asked.

“Go in on me. I know you want to,” Macal said with defeat in his voice.

Tylisha hugged her brother and kissed his forehead. “Macal, now is not the time for that. The focus right now is the well-being of Fallon and the baby. I know you love them and it’s hurting you that they are in this situation. It’s going to take time, but with hard work you can fix this.”

The doctor walked into the waiting room, looking for Macal. “Mr. Kilborn?”

Macal jumped out of his seat and walked over to the doctor with Tylisha in tow. “Yes, doctor?”

“She’s awake and will make a full, speed recovery.” The doctor informed him.

“Thank, you,” Macal said with relief.

The doctor prepared himself to deliver the rest of the news. “But we weren’t able to save the baby.”

“Oh no!” Macal covered his face to hide his shame and guilt as his eyes started to water.

“She’s been asking for you,” the doctor told Macal.

Macal wiped the tears with the back of his hand. “Really? I can see her?”

“Yes, you can.” The doctor led him to Fallon’s room and Tylisha followed him. Enzo followed suit after finishing his phone call.

Macal braced himself for Fallon’s anger and entered the room. “Fallon,” he called out nervously, and slowly walked towards her.

“Macal,” Fallon weakly uttered.

Macal broke down and started pleading for forgiveness. “Fallon, baby! This is all my fault! I’m so sorry, baby! Please forgive me! I didn’t mean to hurt you!”

“I know and I forgive you,” Fallon said and rubbed Macal’s hand.

Macal wasn’t expecting this reaction at all. “What?” He wasn’t sure if he heard her right.

“Macal, I love you. Yes, I’m hurt, but I want to make this marriage work. You are my life. I’m not losing you,” Fallon said. She leaped into his arms and placed a kiss on his lips.

Macal was in disbelief. Did Fallon remember what she walked in on at his office? “What went down at the office—”

“Shh.” Fallon placed her index finger on Macal’s lips to stop him from talking. “I don’t want to discuss that ever again.”

Macal shook his head. “The miscarriage. Oh, baby! It’s all my fault you lost the baby!”

“Macal, I tripped. I shouldn’t have been running down the stairs like that. It was an accident,” Fallon said.

Macal held Fallon in his arms, thankful for her forgiveness and unconditional love he felt he didn’t deserve. “I love you, baby, and I’m going to spend the rest of my life making it up to you.”

“I love you too, baby,” Fallon said.

Tylisha and Enzo stood there having trouble believing what the fuck they were witnessing. Tylisha pulled her phone out and sent Enzo a text.

Tylisha: DO YOU SEE THIS SHIT!?

Enzo felt his phone vibrate in his hand and answered the message.

Enzo: YES! I fell like I’m in the fucking Twilight Zone!

Tylisha: Oh no baby!! The Twilight Zone is more normal than this! Something’s up!

Enzo: Exactly!

“What are you two lovebirds over there whispering about?” Fallon teased Tylisha and Enzo.

"Happy that you're still with us." Tylisha walked over to hug Fallon.

"I'm not going anywhere," Fallon said with a smile. "I have my husband and my family. When I get out of here, Macal and I are going to try to get me pregnant again." She giggled.

"You are a true fighter," Enzo said and gave Fallon a peck on the cheek.

"Thanks, Enzo," Fallon said.

Everybody was deep in conversation, ignoring the door open and close. They assumed it was a member of the hospital staff. They were wrong. The visitor turned out to be the last person they expected to see.

"Oh, Fallon! I'm sorry about all of this!" Lolette said, trying to disguise her delight.

Fallon went from zero to one hundred at the speed of light by the sight of Lolette's face. "What the fuck are you doing here?"

Lolette stuck with her fake act. "I'm your friend. I was worried about you."

"Your hoe, thot ass have a sick, fucked up way of showing it!" Fallon yelled with anger. "Everybody tried to tell me you weren't about shit, bitch!"

Lolette let out a chuckle which was pissing Fallon off further. "You're gonna listen to those haters! You know a chick like me got a lot of them!"

"Oh, I believe it," Tylisha replied with sarcasm.

"I was a fucking fool to think you were a friend who gave a damn about me! I should've known better after what you did to your own sister!" Fallon yelled.

The mentioning of her sister struck a nerve, but Lolette couldn't let it show. "Relax, Fallon, girl. Don't get so upset. All I did was get a great fuck." Now, for the counter-attack. "It's not like I killed anybody."

Lolette's last statement made Fallon snap. She let out a vicious growl and jumped out of the bed to go straight for Lolette's throat, but Macal, Tylisha and Enzo restrained her and pulled her back in the bed.

"Fallon, calm down and relax. You need to take it easy. Don't let her stress you out." Tylisha tried to reason with Fallon.

"Lolette, I think you better to leave," Enzo said, trying to be nice.

"I'm not going anywhere!" Lolette didn't back down. "Not until Fallon and I see eye to eye about some things!"

"Bitch, we ain't got shit to see eye to eye about!" Fallon snapped.

"I think we do. Now that everything is out in the open. Well not everything," Lolette implied.

"Lolette, will you please leave this room," Tylisha tried to calmly diffuse the situation.

"Please leave, Lolette! You're making things worse!" Macal demanded.

Lolette was taken aback. "You want me to leave, Macal? Really?"

"Lolette, we said leave this room right now." Tylisha said calmly.

Ignoring Tylisha, Lolette resumed her slick taunting. "Why you over there trying to front, Macal? You wasn't saying that shit when you were making me bust all those fat nuts all over your big ole chocolate donkey dick!"

Fallon was about to leap again, but Tylisha caught her in time. "Fallon, remember you're in this hospital bed. You gotta calm down and relax." *But I'm not in the bed and my ass don't gotta relax and calm down!* With her final thought Tylisha punched Lolette dead in her nose. "Bitch, didn't we say get the fuck out of here!" Tylisha yelled after delivering the sucker punch.

"You crazy, bitch!" Lolette yelled and charged for Tylisha.

Tylisha stopped Lolette dead in her tracks by slapping her across the face, knocking her on the floor. Tylisha pounced on top of her and punched her. Tylisha been wanted to whoop that ass. She punched Lolette repeatedly in the face and chest. Lolette pulled Tylisha's hair and the ladies started rolling around the floor, exchanging blows.

Enzo and Macal tried to break them up. “Tylisha stop it,” Enzo said, trying to pull Tylisha off Lolette.

“You a hoe and you know you a hoe!” Tylisha yelled in Lolette’s face, and put her hands around her neck, trying to choke her, and kneed her in the stomach. Enzo pulled Tylisha off Lolette and carried her out of the room. “Enzo, let me go! Let me kick her ass! Let me kick her ass! Enzo, let me kick her ass!”

Macal carried Lolette as she struggled to try to get a piece of Tylisha. Security rushed over to stop the altercation but Macal assured him there was no need. “We go it!”

“Let that bitch go, Macal!” Tylisha screamed in anger as Enzo carried her out of the hospital and into the parking lot. “I ain’t done beating her ass!”

Macal let go of Lolette when Tylisha and Enzo were completely out of sight. “Lolette, get your ass out of here, now!” He demanded.

Lolette wasn’t through yet. “But—”

“Right now and I’m not fucking playing with you!” He shouted.

“I know your ass better call me. I know that much!” Lolette said and walked away.

Macal shook his head and went back in the room to check on Fallon. “I’m sorry, baby. I know I’ve been saying that a lot.” He took his seat next to Fallon.

“Good thing Tylisha was here to kick that sleazy hoe’s ass for the both of us,” Fallon joked. “Baby, can you get me some water?”

“Sure,” Macal said. He kissed Fallon and took his leave.

With the room all to herself, Fallon found her handbag and pulled her phone out. She clicked on the photo gallery, looking through the photo albums and found the one she was looking for. The photo album contained pictures of Macal in compromising positions with different women. Pictures of him with Lolette before their wedding day, and more occasions afterwards. The tacky hoe with the fucked up smelling perfume, now known as Crystal, and her fight with Lolette. As she was looking through the pictures, Fallon said to herself. “I’m not losing you, Macal! I won’t!”

Chapter 39

"That bitch had her motherfucking nerve! Showing her fucking hoe face at that hospital!" Tylisha ranted and raved all the way back to Enzo's house, and she didn't stop. Enzo didn't say a word while Tylisha's angry ranting went on after entering the house. "The way she disrespected Fallon like that! I can't believe her ass! If I see that bitch again, I'm gonna stomp that hoe! I know one motherfucking thing, Macal better stay the fuck away from that nasty ass thot!"

There's only one way to put an end to this! Enzo thought.

"If his ass used his brain to think instead of his dick, he'd be bett—"

Enzo pulled Tylisha in his arms and stuck his tongue deep in her mouth. He kissed her with rough passion, calming her down. "We're not at the hospital anymore, baby. We're home."

Tylisha blushed and took a seat on the couch. "I guess I got a little carried away, huh?"

"You think?" Enzo joked and sat beside her. "I know this is a fucked up situation, but there is a bright side."

"Really, what's that?"

"Now the whole dirty truth is out and Fallon finally sees Lolette for who she really is."

Tylisha felt deeply sorry for Fallon. "Fallon must be very devastated. She really thought Lolette was her friend. The pain in her eyes was heartbreaking."

"Towards Lolette, but not Macal," Enzo corrected her.

"It still puzzles me. She automatically forgave him. Like the whole thing never happened. All her anger was towards Lolette. Don't get me wrong, Fallon had every right to be pissed at her nasty, hoe ass, but why didn't she have any anger towards Macal?"

"Love is blind," Enzo concluded.

"Maybe."

"It's been a long, crazy, drama-filled night." Enzo gently rubbed Tylisha's face. "Time to put you to sleep."

"And how are you going to put me to sleep?" Tylisha asked with intrigue.

"With my dick," Enzo answered boldly.

"Really?" She blushed.

"Really!" Enzo lifted Tylisha off the couch and kissed her all the way upstairs and into his bedroom. "This is so much better carrying you upstairs than downstairs."

"Yes, it is," she giggled.

Enzo helped Tylisha get on her feet as he put her down. They helped each other undress, nice and slowly, admiring every inch of the other's body. Enzo couldn't wait to enjoy Tylisha's sexy body and Tylisha couldn't wait for Enzo's muscular body to press on top of her. Her eyes widened when she saw Enzo's thick, nine inch friend, making her pussy tingle with excitement. All of the sudden, reality settled in.

"Enzo, I'm a little nervous!" Tylisha confessed. "I haven't done this in a very— and I do mean a very— long time."

Enzo kissed her with love and tenderness, and said, "Relax, I'm a patient man." He kissed her again and rubbed her ass. He got on his knees, placed her left leg over his shoulder, and gripped her ass cheeks tight. He stuck out his tongue and explored her sweet box. Tylisha let out a moan and gripped the back of Enzo's head to maintain her balance. He licked all over her pussy lips before focusing on the clit.

"Aaah! Oooh!" Her leg trembled from the oral pleasure. "Oh fuck!"

Enzo had enough of the appetizer. It was time for the main course. He took Tylisha's leg off his shoulder, gasping for air. He stood up on his feet, tackled Tylisha and threw her on the bed where she landed flat on her back. He pounced on top of her and gave her a big, sloppy kiss while invading her pussy with his dick.

Damn! She's super tight! Enzo thought.

"Ahh!" Tylisha moaned and came.

Enzo found it unbelievable that she came the second he entered her. "It really has been a long time for you."

"Told you," she said breathlessly.

"That means we have the whole night to make up for it." He grinned.

"Making up—" Tylisha was cut off by Enzo's quick reflexes when he put both of her legs on his shoulders. With the dick still inside her, Enzo dug in deeper. "Ah!" She moaned.

The pussy felt good around his dick. He felt like he was in paradise. He savored her wet tightness with every stroke. Enzo held Tylisha tightly as he pushed his stroke game to the max. He fucked her like her pussy was a mine and his dick was a pickax. Enzo wasn't going to stop digging until he found gold.

Enzo pumped in and out of Tylisha like this was the last time he would ever get any pussy. "Shit, baby!" He grunted.

"Aw!" Tylisha came all over the dick, coating it with her juices. *Shit his ass can fuck!* Tylisha's pussy clinched and she squeezed Enzo's ass while she was having her next orgasm.

Tylisha's constant orgasms motivated Enzo to fuck her harder. "I love you, baby girl!" He moaned.

"I love you too!" Tylisha screamed and kissed Enzo. "Shit, you got some amazing dick, baby!" She managed to say.

"You think so, baby?"

"Yes!"

Enzo used his dick to wiggle around to find her spot and reached his goal. "You feel that amazing dick hitting your spot?"

"Oh shit, yeah!" Tylisha screamed.

"Now this amazing dick belongs to you!"

"Yes!"

Enzo climbed off of Tylisha and sat up on the bed. "Now, suck your amazing dick," he ordered.

"Yes, baby," Tylisha obliged.

She grabbed his dick and took it all in one gulp. She moved her head in a circular motion as she sucked. She made sure to make the dick nice and slimy. She loved tasting herself on his dick. After she sucked off every trace of her nectar, she stuffed his balls in her cheek like she was a squirrel. She tasted a little bit of her pussy residue while juggling the nuts with her tongue.

Tylisha was about to put the dick back in her mouth but Enzo snatched it away from her. “Alright, that’s enough of that. Now face down! Ass up!”

“Yes, sir!” Tylisha giggled and did as instructed.

Enzo positioned himself behind Tylisha and gave her ass a hard smack. “Look at all that ass jiggle!”

He roughly entered her pussy and spread her ass cheeks apart to get a perfect view of her making his dick wet and creamy as he screwed her with full aggression and making her scream, moan and cum. He leaned over Tylisha and whispered in her ear, “This my pussy, right?”

“Yes,” she moaned.

Enzo smacked and grabbed her ass. “This is my ass to smack and grab, right?”

“Yes!”

Enzo picked up the pace and thrusted harder. “You see what you do to me, girl?” He grunted. “I’m trying to be all professional with you looking all sexy and shit, making my dick hard.”

Enzo pulled his dick out of Tylisha and turned her around to put one of her titties in his mouth. “Can’t neglect these big, delicious titties.” He sucked on the titty and reentered the pussy.

“Yes baby,” Tylisha moaned.

Enzo pounded the pussy and moaned, “Shit, baby, I’m cumming!” He gave the pussy five hard pumps before exploding deep inside her. “Whoa!” He was winded. “See what you do to me, girl?”

“I see,” Tylisha said with satisfaction and glow. “Don’t worry, I’ll keep it up.”

“Please do.” Enzo wanted to confirm something with Tylisha to let her know his feelings are genuine. “Tylisha, I really meant what I said. I love you and I’m glad you’re back in my life.”

Tylisha was touched. “I love you too, Enzo and I need you to promise me something.”

“Anything.”

“I need you to promise to always love and cherish me, and you’ll never hurt me and my babies.”

Enzo wrapped his arms around Tylisha and looked into her eyes. "Baby, you don't have to worry about a thing. You and your children are safe with me and in my heart."

"And vice versa. I love you and Amery. You guys are dear to me. Also, I have a confession to make."

"What's that?"

"My mother was a Chess Grandmaster."

"That's very impressive and a great achievement." Enzo congratulated her. Then it dawned on him what Tylisha was really trying to say. "You naughty girl! You played me! I'm gonna tickle you!" He started tickling Tylisha.

"I'm sorry, baby!" Tylisha laughed hysterically.

"Oh no! Too late for apologies!" Enzo kept tickling her.

Tylisha caught her breath when Enzo finally stopped tickling her. "Okay! Okay!"

The two sat in silence until Tylisha started tickling Enzo. "Girl, cut it out!" Enzo laughed and Tylisha didn't let up. She saw Enzo's dick fully erect and stopped tickling him to jump on top of him, ready to ride.

Chapter 40

"How's my trade looking?" Thuy's client, Percy Loy, one of the best running backs in the league asked.

"The Seattle Seahawks, Tampa Bay Buccaneers and the Arizona Cardinals are interested," Thuy informed him.

"Good," Percy replied with a nod. "To be honest, I really don't want to leave the Miami Dolphins. That's the team that drafted me. I've spent all eleven years of my career with them, but they gotta do what they gotta do. I guess."

The Miami Dolphins drafted a new running back from the University of Alabama and he had a phenomenal rookie season. Since Percy's contract was up, he's gonna be traded with the exchange of three draft picks.

Percy was one of Thuy's favorite clients. He was humble, nice, family oriented, and most importantly, he kept his nose clean. Clients like him made her job a whole lot easier.

"Percy, it's going to be okay." Thuy said with sympathy. "You're a talented athlete who's destined for the Hall of Fame. I did reach out to the Carolina Panthers this morning, and I'm expecting a call back. We'll see how it goes."

Their meeting was interrupted by Jeromy busting in Thuy's office without the common courtesy of knocking first. He and Tori had that rude ass shit in common. "Thuy, we need to talk!"

Thuy rolled her eyes at Jeromy and placed her attention back to Percy. "That'll be all for now, Percy. We'll meet up for lunch tomorrow for further discussion."

"Thanks, Thuy. Have a nice day." Percy shook her hand and took his leave.

The second Percy closed the door behind him, Thuy went in on Jeromy in a hushed whisper. "What the fuck are you doing here?"

"I need to talk to you right now and I need you to understand where I'm coming from! I need you to hear me and right motherfucking now!"

Does this nigga know he's in no fucking position to be making demands? "This is how you do it by busting in my place of business like you ain't got no fucking sense?"

Jeromy started to play his game. "What was I supposed to do? You won't return my calls. You won't answer the door at your house. I'm not going to be ignored, Thuy!" He used the same tone of voice as Glenn Close's character in Fatal Attraction.

"Stealing movie lines is not going to get you out of this one."

"Look, I'm sorry."

"You're sorry?" Thuy scoffed. "What you sorry about? Bringing that hoe in our house to fuck her in our bed? Badmouthing me to the bitch? Telling her thot ass this baby ain't yours? What the fuck are you sorry about? By the way, if you're going to fuck around on me, at least pick a pretty hoe! I don't know what the fuck you were thinking! The rat faced, ghetto thot!"

Did this bitch refer to my house as our house? "Baby, it was a mistake. I was drunk. It'll never happen again. You said it yourself, that hoe was ugly as fuck. I must've been out of my mind." *She sure can suck and fuck though!* After Thuy left, he gave the ratchet hoe a good fuck and sent her ass on her way.

"Your ass said that shit the last time!" Thuy wasn't budging.

Jeromy anticipated this attitude, so he came up with a backup plan. He walked over to Thuy and grabbed her hand. "Baby, this time is different. Let me prove it to you. Let's go on a romantic getaway at the cabin."

"The cabin?" Thuy's face lit up. "I love the cabin."

"Remember our first night together?" Jeromy asked and pulled her into his arms.

"Yes, I do. Great times." Thuy blushed, flashing back to the first time they made love.

"This little vacation with just the two of us is exactly what we need to clear our minds and start over fresh," Jeromy suggested.

"I'm open to it but when will we be able to go?" Thuy asked. "You are going to New York to play the Yankees this week. Next week, I'm going to LA for a UCLA game, to check out this kid going into the NBA draft, and the week after that I'm helping Sam house hunt."

"That's also the week I go to Chicago to play the Cubs," Jeromy said. "What are you doing three weeks from now?"

"Nothing."

"Same here. There, it's all settled. Three weeks from now, we'll be at the cabin, away from everyone, enjoying each other." Jeromy kissed Thuy on the lips.

"Can't wait," Thuy said with a smile.

Jeromy left the office. As he made his way out of the dealership, he sent a quick text to one of his associates.

Jeromy: Be ready to get to work in three weeks.

Chapter 41

"Thank you so much for picking Amery up from school," Ligia said to Tylisha with deep gratitude. The ladies were sitting in Tylisha's living room while the kids were in Welton's room.

"It's no problem," Tylisha returned, handing Ligia a glass of wine.

"That meeting was too long." Ligia sighed and took a sip. "Vax is checking out a store in Miami, and you know Enzo is at a seminar in D.C."

"Yes, I can't wait until he gets back. Five days is too long." Tylisha took a big gulp of her wine. Ever since the first night Enzo put it on her, she couldn't get enough of the dick.

"I know the feeling. I know it's only two days, but still Vax needs to hurry up."

"Gotcha."

"How are things with Macal and Fallon?" Ligia asked.

"Things are great and that's what's bothering me," Tylisha said with concern.

"I know what you mean," Ligia agreed. "Enzo filled me and Vax in, Little Miss Hospital Brawler you." She teased.

"Hey, that bitch had it coming," Tylisha said unapologetically. "Did you know the hoe threw herself at Enzo before we went on our first date, and the bitch was talking slick shit about me?"

"And her ass is still walking around with teeth in her mouth?"

"Welton and Ayla were in the house."

"Understood." Ligia nodded. "So, this Lolette chick really rolled up in the hospital like everything was all good?"

"Yeah, just disrespecting and taunting Fallon. That shit was a problem. That bitch has no shame," Tylisha recalled with disgust. "Her ass didn't give two fucks about getting caught."

"Obviously, but something tells me she's not going away anytime soon," Ligia guessed.

"I hate to say it, but I think you are right." Tylisha sighed.

"From what you and Enzo told me about her, I almost guarantee it."

"Even so, as long as Macal learned his lesson and Lolette stays the fuck out of Macal and Fallon's lives, things will get back on track for them and stay there."

"Or Macal doesn't let Lolette back in," Ligia added.

"Let's hope he's not that stupid, but with him, you never know," Tylisha said with disappointment. Deep down she knew Macal had no discipline when it came to controlling his dick. She then saw a tattoo on the left side of Ligia's chest that read the name *Sasha* in cursive, with angel wings on both sides of the name with a halo on top. "What's with the tatt?"

Ligia glanced at her tattoo and answered. "That's my big sister's name. She passed away a month after the divorce was finalized."

"I'm sorry. What happened? If you don't mind me asking."

"It's okay. I'm good," Ligia sighed before explaining what happened to her beloved big sister. "Unbeknownst to me and the family, she was in an abusive marriage. I knew there was something I didn't like about that nigga, but I never suspected anything like this." Ligia shook her head and continued. "Sasha suffered in silence. She was ashamed and scared. I wished she would've talked to me. I would've understood. I would've tried to help her. She was scared she'd be judged for staying and didn't want to risk him coming after us. When she finally decided to leave, let's just say her husband was the *If I Can't Have You No One Will* type."

"That bastard better be under the prison!" Tylisha hissed.

"He is. For life."

"Good."

"Sasha was always there for me, and I couldn't even be there for her." Ligia's eyes started to water and Tylisha handed her a tissue.

"Ligia, that man was a monster and he is where he belongs. Don't let his actions make you feel guilty. You loved Sasha and she loved you."

"Thanks, Tylisha." Ligia wiped her tears and hugged Tylisha. "Enzo is a lucky man to have you in his life."

"He is a good man." Tylisha smiled.

"Yes, he is. Even though we were freshly divorced, he was my biggest supporter and helped me cope. He even accompanied me to the funeral. That man has a genuine heart." Ligia got off the couch and grabbed her purse. "Amery, it's time to go!"

"Yes, momma!" Amery was heard calling out.

Before she left, Ligia left Tylisha with some final words. "Enzo is my best friend and I love him. You take care of him." Ligia hugged Tylisha.

"I will."

Chapter 42

"Zoo Atlanta employee, Crystal Turner, was pushed into a cage with two rare poisonous pythons by an unknown assailant who locked the door. Fortunately, Ms. Turner was able to escape the cage safely with the help of a fellow coworker and tourist." The Channel 2 News reporter said.

Lolette laughed at the misfortune of her smelly ass adversary on the news and had a pretty good idea who the attacker was. "Sounds like somebody's not taking their meds." She turned off the TV and went into her bedroom. She grabbed her phone off the night stand where it was charging and saw Macal's text message. "I knew that nigga couldn't stay away."

Lolette was really feeling herself, despite being on Fallon's shit list, and taking a few punches from Tylisha. Lolette wasn't sweating that shit. A bitch like her never stayed down for long. She opened the message and her mouth stretched wide open at the picture of the delicious dick she loved and craved so much.

Macal: You miss this dick, baby?

Lolette slipped out of her dress and was completely nude. She didn't bother to wear a bra and panties underneath, today. She climbed on top of the bed and spread her legs open. She placed the phone between her legs and snapped the picture to send to Macal with a message.

Lolette: Do you miss this pussy?
Macal: You know I do. Bend that ass over for me baby!

Lolette placed the phone at the edge of the bed and set the timer for fifteen seconds. She positioned herself in front of the phone and bent over on all fours. She used her hands to spread her ass cheeks apart. She stayed in that position until the camera snapped the picture. She grabbed the phone and sent the picture with a message.

Lolette: How's this baby?

Macal: SEXY AS FUCK! I WISH I WAS DEEP IN THAT PUSSY RIGHT NOW! SHOW ME THOSE BIG BEAUTIFUL TITTIES!

Lolette blushed, squeezed her titts together and took another picture. She typed a message and pressed send.

Lolette: Put them in your mouth!

Macal: I will baby! You've been so good and patient. You deserve a reward.

Lolette: What kind of reward?

Macal: Have you ever been fucked in the back of a limo?

Lolette: No, but I would love to have that dick in my pussy in style!

Macl: Be prepared because three weeks from now I'm gonna tear that pussy up!

Lolette: Can't wait! Bye!

Macal: Bye!

Macal turned off his phone and got off the toilet in the bathroom. He put the phone in his pocket and washed his hands. *Why can't I stay the fuck away from her?* Things with Fallon had been great. Their marriage was back on track and the lovemaking was great, but he couldn't shake the drugs called Lolette and other women's pussies. He dried his hands and opened the door to find Fallon standing in the doorway, wearing nothing but a thong.

"Fallon, baby!" Macal was surprised. Good thing he wasn't actually talking to Lolette on the phone. Who knows what Fallon could've overheard?

"Did I surprise you?" She asked with boldness in her voice, and a strange look in her eyes.

Macal never saw this side of Fallon before. He didn't know whether to be concerned or turned on. Watching her prance around with her titties bouncing and ass jiggling in her burgundy two sizes to small thong was making it hard to concentrate on thinking, with his upstairs head anyway. His downstairs head was thinking just fine.

"Yes, baby, you did surprise me."

"I have a question."

Please don't let her suspect anything! Please don't let her suspect anything! "What's that, baby?" Macal kept his cool.

Fallon strutted towards him and tugged on his shirt, pulling him close to her. "Why are you still wearing clothes?"

"I see your point." Macal caught the hint and took off his clothes in a hurry.

Fallon took her place on the bed and laid on her back. Macal stood over her completley nude. She zeroed in on his yard stick and got in the spread eagle position. "Now!" She ripped her own thong off and threw it at Macal. "Take this pussy!" She ordered.

"You ain't said nothing but a word, baby!"

Chapter 43

Three Weeks Later

Thuy was in deep sleep after three rounds of mind-blowing sex. She was awakened by a kiss on the lips from Jeromy, like in Sleeping Beauty.

"You ready for our trip, baby?" He asked.

Thuy yawned and answered, "Yes, my bags are packed. I need to jump in the shower and freshen up. I needed that nap."

"Me and my dick took a lot out of you, huh?" Jeromy bragged.

"Boy, you are something else," she giggled and climbed out of bed.

"I'll start loading the car while you get ready."

"Alright." Thuy gave Jeromy a kiss and headed for the bathroom. Closing the door behind her.

Jeromy gathered Thuy's bags, took them outside and packed them in the trunk of his chrome Porsche. After he finished loading the car, Jeromy went back in the house and into the bedroom to grab his phone to make an important call. He checked on Thuy really quickly to make sure she was still in the shower. He walked down the hall and took a peek inside the nursery where Day'zon Malcolm Fuller would reside. The thought made Jeromy shiver. To him, the adorably decorated nursery was an eyesore that made his balls itch, and it was a reminder of why his plan was in the works. He shut the door so he'd no longer be subjected to that disgusting display.

"It'll all be over soon," Jeromy said to himself while making his way downstairs and into the living room. It was time to end this nightmare once and for all. He was sick and tired of being tied down and having a woman trap him. Just like all the others. Before making the call, he made sure he was facing the stairway in case Thuy happened to appear. Jeromy placed the call and waited for an answer. "Hello!" The caller greeted him.

"We're all set. She's in the shower getting ready right now. I'll text you when we leave the house," Jeromy said.

"Good! Good! We'll follow the path you gave us and wait for our queue."

"And you'll receive the payment when the job is done."

"Excellent!"

Jeromy heard the bedroom door open and close, and footsteps were coming downstairs. "She's coming. I gotta go." Jeromy hung up the phone.

"You look radiant and sexy, future mom!" Jeromy complimented and kissed Thuy. She was looking beautiful with her hair in a ponytail, wearing black leggings and a gold shirt, with white tennis shoes that had gold lining. Jeromy would admit that Thuy was a very attractive woman with great taste in fashion. She knew how to look fabulous and sexy with a stomach bigger than a beach ball.

"Are you ready to go, handsome, sexy, future dad?" She asked.

"Yes, I am, baby," he answered. "All the bags are packed in the trunk and the cabin is all set for our getaway."

"Sounds great!"

Jeromy opened the door to let Thuy out first. He locked the door and began phase one of the plan. "I'm hungry. You want to eat first before we go?"

"Great idea," Thuy said. "I'm craving steak."

"Outback Steakhouse it is."

"I'm gonna tear those wings up."

"Those wings are good." Jeromy agreed and opened the passenger door for Thuy.

Jeromy walked around the car and sent a quick text before taking his place in the driver's seat.

Jeromy: Phase 1 has started.

Jeromy made himself comfortable in the driver's seat and started the car. "Alright, let's hit the road."

"Let's," Thuy said and kissed Jeromy. The engaged couple and expecting parents were on their way. Thuy took comfort in the relaxing drive, unaware of what was in store for her and her unborn son.

"I came over as soon as I got your message. What's up Bryn?" Vida asked, making herself at home in Bryn's condo.

"Joanna is on her way with the information, and I might need some backup," Bryn said.

"Gotcha," Vida replied. "It's time to get rid of that disgusting nigga-prick!"

Very unique combination, but I'll accept! "Exactly," Bryn said.

There was a knock at the door and Bryn answered. He welcomed an attractive brunette who resembled Sandra Bullock into his home and helped her carry her files. "Hi, Joanna."

"Hey, Bryn."

He placed the files on the coffee table and everyone took their seats. "Joanna, this is me and Thuy's best friend, Vida. Vida, this is Joanna."

"Hello." The ladies exchanged greetings.

Vida studied Joanna's face for about five minutes until she realized she was staring too long. "Pardon me for staring, but you look exactly like—"

"I know; Sandra Bullock, right?" She guessed and Vida nodded. "I get that all the time."

"It's uncanny," Vida said in awe.

"It is, isn't it?" Bryn agreed and focused on the matter at hand. "What you got for us Joanna?"

Joanna dug through her files. "This is one of my toughest cases yet. It took longer than usual, but I wasn't going to stop until I found the gold."

"What did you find?" Vida asked.

Joanna prepared her clients for the worst before she began. "Before I get started, I need to caution you. Based on my discoveries, I've come to the conclusion that your friend is in serious trouble, and that's being nice about it. When I do my investigations, I start from the beginning, and when I'm through, you'll understand the reason behind my method. Observe." She gave a file to Bryn as Vida looked over his shoulder.

Bryn saw the first page and couldn't believe his eyes. "His mother was killed in front of him when he was six years old by his father?"

"Stepfather," Joanna corrected him. "You see, his mother was having an affair with a married, rich federal judge and Jeromy was the result."

Vida skimmed through the page. "She passed Jeormy off as the husband's son. He found out and killed her."

"What happened with the judge?" Bryn asked.

"He moved Jeromy into his mansion after the stepfather was sentenced to life. Apparently, he openly cheated on the wife and was very abusive towards her. Jeromy was treated like a king," Joanna said.

"Did the judge have any kids with the wife?" Vida asked.

"Nope, and the judge is very important in this story."

"How?" Bryn asked.

Joanna continued. "When Jeromy was in high school, he got a girl pregnant. He told her to get an abortion. She refused, and two days later, she was found dead."

"What did I tell you?" Bryn said to Vida.

"Yeah, pregnant chicks and mistresses tend to die around your guy." Joanna commented. "Like about a month before his prom, a girl he was cheating on his high school sweetheart with was found beaten to death. Not so coincidently about two days after she confronted the girlfriend revealing the affair."

Joanna gave Bryn another file to look through as she played narrator. "Then he goes to USC on a baseball scholarship. During one of his visits back at his hometown, San Francisco, he gets the high school sweetheart pregnant. He tells her to get an abortion. She refused and he dumps her. She then sues him for child support, and the last time anybody saw her was when she was on her way to meet up with Jeromy to try to work things out."

"She ends up dead, right?" Vida guessed.

"Drowned in the ocean when she slipped off a low level bridge," Joanna confirmed. "Only problem was that she was a swimming instructor who had been the captain of the high school swimming team for two years."

"That bastard pushed her," Bryn said.

"And somebody else held her down under the water," Vida added.

"I was almost hoping one of you would point that out." Joanna said and gave Vida a copy of a man's mug shot.

"Who's this?" Vida asked.

"Eric Knight," Joanna answered. "He was granted probation by a certain judge." She hinted.

"Jeromy's father?" Bryn guessed correctly. "He used Eric to clean up his son's messes."

"Bingo," Joanna said.

"How did you find this out?" Vida asked.

Joanna pulled out another file and handed it to her. "Read them and weep."

Vida flipped through the documents and ran across some divorce papers. "The judge's wife files for divorce." She came across another document. She had to read it again to be sure. "Am I reading this right?"

"Yes, you are," Joanna said. "She became a confidential informant of all these cases in order to turn her husband and stepson in. Payback for making her life a living hell, you know."

"Obviously, so how did Jeromy and his daddy get out of this?" Bryn had to know. No nigga could be this lucky.

"Next page, darlings," Joanna said.

Vida turned to the next page and there was the wife's death certificate. The cause of death was five shots to the head. "Oh, that's how."

"Now that we've covered his California life, let's move on to his Georgia life." Joanna pulled out another file and handed it to Bryn. "He gets signed with the Atlanta Braves, and things are pretty quiet until—"

"His last girlfriend before Thuy." Bryn finished. "Oh, hey Vida, does this sound familiar?" Bryn started paraphrasing the document. "He gets a stripper pregnant. He agrees to pay her off after getting the abortion. She does but he ends up stiffing her. She goes to the girlfriend's job and tells her everything. The girlfriend breaks up with him and the stripper ends up dead."

Joanna took the file back and flipped through the pages until she found what she was looking for, then gave the file back. "Take a look at who was Jeromy's father's Hospice caregiver back in San Francisco."

"Onya Hanks!" Bryn and Vida exclaimed.

"She transferred her job here two years after the father died. Obviously, Onya and Jeromy ran into each other. He recognized her, pursued and seduced her." Joanna guessed. "You were right, Bryn, about everything and those documents prove it."

"What did you find out about the guy who crashed Thuy's birthday party?" Bryn asked.

"Sim Boone and his daughter Alice." Joanna answered. "I took a good look at those tapes, and Jeromy is a great actor."

"How so?" Vida asked.

"He knows Sim alright," Joanna said. "Sim lived next door to his last girlfriend, and he was the custodian at the Braves practice facility. After Alice told Jeromy she was pregnant, he made her get an abortion—"

"He stiffed her too, right?" Bryn guessed.

"Not only that, he also got Sim fired," Joanna added.

"That cold blooded motherfucker!" Bryn lashed out. All the pain and suffering Jeromy brought into the lives of every single woman he ever came in contact with. It was going to end right motherfucking now on Bryn's watch. He was determined to make sure Thuy would not be added to Jeromy's long list of victims. "How's Alice doing?"

"Better," Joanna said. She then pulled out three mug shots and placed them on the table. "Also, Jeromy has been very, shall we say, charitable and friendly towards these three characters."

"Let's see here, assault and battery, drug possession, petty larceny, gun charges. This list is like the Energizer Bunny. It just keeps going and going." Bryn read the list. "We have to save Thuy, and quick! Vida, did she tell you where she was going?"

"Just some romantic getaway," Vida answered.

Bryn was racking his brain to try to figure out where Jeromy could've taken Thuy. "Wherever he's taking her, I know it's by car because the bastard is too arrogant to take the Greyhound, and there will be too many witnesses and security to go through an airport."

Joanna was highly impressed with Bryn and Vida's knowledge and crime solving skills. "If you guys are this good, why do you need me?" She joked.

"Because we like you and like throwing money away," Bryn teased.

"Charmed," Joanna replied with a smile. "If I may throw in my two cents. My guess is wherever Jeromy is taking Thuy, it has to be a place where she'll have her guard completley down. A place she loves dearly. Do you guys have any ideas?"

"The cabin? The cabin!" Vida thought out loud. "That's where Jeromy is taking Thuy. The cabin was where they spent their very first night together."

"That's right," Bryn said. "She talked about the cabin like a child would talk about Disney World."

"That's good. Do you know where the cabin is?" Joanna asked.

"I think so." Vida nodded.

"Normally, the words *I think so* are not very concrete in my book, but in cases like this, anything is worth a shot." Joanna pulled out her phone and dialed a number. "I'm calling for backup. Let's roll."

Chapter 44

After eating their delicious meal at Outback Steakhouse, Jeromy and Thuy were on their way to the cabin.

"That was good eating," Jeromy said.

"You can say that again," Thuy replied. "I can tell Day'zon loves to eat."

"Yes, he does."

"I can't wait until we get to the cabin."

"I feel you, baby." Jeromy made a left turn on Fuller Street. It was a long road filled with beautiful green trees on the sides.

The drive down the long, quiet road was tranquil and soothing. It was just them and the road. Out of nowhere, a black limousine was speeding down the road, flying past them like a bat out of hell. The limo was almost an inch away from running Jeromy and Thuy off the road.

"Whoa!" Thuy shrieked. "Did you see that shit, baby?"

"Yeah." Jeromy nodded. "A speeding limo. I hope they asses get there."

"I know, right?"

The drive continued until they came across a black van on the side of the road, where a man was looking under the hood.

"Damn! Somebody's stuck on the side of the road." Thuy said.

"Let me pull over and help them real quick"

"Alright."

Jeromy slowed down and pulled over behind the van. He stepped out of the car to offer his assistance.

Thuy was left alone in the car, waiting patiently for Jeromy to come back. She took a better look at the van. It looked somewhat familiar. She quickly dropped it, figuring it would come back to her eventually. She felt the baby kick a little bit and rubbed her belly. "Hey, little man. Can't wait to meet you. My little Day'zon. Mommy loves you." She said in a sweet, baby voice.

Thuy rubbed her belly, talking to her unborn son some more. She leaned back in her seat and heard two guns cocked in her ear.

She slowly turned her head to her right and saw two men with their guns in her face. "Get out the car, bitch!" one of the men growled.

Thuy trembled with fear. "Okay! Okay!" She whimpered. "I don't want any problems!"

"Bitch, shut the fuck up and get your ass out!" The other man shouted.

Still trembling, Thuy unbuckled her seatbelt and slowly opened the door. One of the men yanked her out the car. "Please don't hurt me!" She begged. "I'm pregnant!"

"We ain't blind, you stupid bitch!" The man hit Thuy hard across the face with his gun as the other guy was holding her arms tightly behind her back.

"Jeromy, help!" Thuy yelled.

The man hit her in the face with the gun, making her spit out blood. "Your man can't help you, bitch!" He screamed in her face. "Don't make us fuck up that pretty face of yours!"

Thuy saw Jeromy with a gun to his head by the man he was helping with the van. "Jeromy!" She screamed and her face was hit with the gun again.

"Scream again, bitch, and we'll blow his fucking head off!" The man holding the gun to Jeromy's head said.

"Baby, it's gonna be alright," Jeromy said, trying to be brave.

"Fuck this shit!" The man who was holding Thuy's arms back yelled, and threw her on the ground.

The two men aimed their guns at Thuy's stomach. "No! Please!" She begged for mercy.

The men fired two shots each in Thuy's abdomen. Her eyes rolled to the back of her head and her eyelids closed. The third man removed the unloaded gun away from Jeromy's head, and the other two men ran back to the van.

"Let's get the fuck out of here now!" Jeromy ordered and ran back to the Porsche. "Dump her shit outta my fucking trunk!" The three men ran to the trunk to carry out Jeromy's orders. They threw Thuy's bags out the trunk and onto the road. Jeromy climbed in the driver's seat and saw Thuy's purse in the passenger's seat. He saw the passenger's door was still opened. He knocked the purse out the car and closed the door. He took three envelopes out of the glove compartment and gave them to his co-conspirators. “You’ll get the rest when she and the baby have been reported dead, like we agreed.”

“Agreed,” one of the men said. “Let’s go.”

That nigga set me up! Thuy struggled to open her eyes when she heard Jeromy and his accomplices drive off. “Please God! Shield me and Day’zon.” She prayed.

Thuy was in terrible agony but she needed to push. She had to fight to stay alive and save her child. She struggled to stand up on her feet. She used her hands to apply pressure to her stomach to stop the bleeding. She started walking towards the road in big sloppy steps.

“I need to hang on! I need to! I have to!” Thuy told herself, struggling to make her way towards the road. “Day’zon! Momma’s here! She’s gonna save you! Momma’s got you!” She stopped for a brief moment to catch her breath and held her stomach tight. “If 50 Cent can survive nine bullets, I can at least survive four.”

Thuy stumbled towards the road where she saw bright red and blue lights flashing. They were police cars and an ambulance. “Help me! Somebody help me! Please help me!” She screamed.

One of the police cars came to a halt. Bryn and Vida jumped out and ran to Thuy’s aide. “Oh shit! Thuy!” Bryn yelled in horror.

Thuy collapsed in Bryn’s arms, covering him with her blood. “Two men forced me out the car. They pistol whipped me and shot me. Jeromy stopped to help someone with their van. He left with them.” She struggled to explain.

“Let’s get her inside,” the EMT said, and gently laid Thuy on the stretcher.

“Thuy, you hang on! You hang on!” Vida pleaded. The cops sealed off the area and Thuy was carried into the ambulance with Bryn and Vida right behind her.

Thuy didn’t expect to see anyone on the road, let alone her friends bringing an entourage of cops and EMTs. “How did y’all know I was in trouble?”

"Thuy, we're your brother and sister," Bryn answered. "We always have your back."

"Thanks you guys," Thuy said. She glanced out the window of the ambulance and saw some more police cars and three ambulances at a crash site. The completely totaled car was the black limo that sped past her and Jeromy earlier.

"Take this dick, baby!" Macal grunted as he roughly fucked Lolette in the backseat of a black limo with her legs in the air.

"Yeah!" Lolette screamed with pleasure. They weren't worried about the limo driver. The limo company Macal hired was used to these types of activities. Macal made sure Lolette busted one more nut before unloading his hot, backed up cum deep inside her pussy.

"Shit, girl! I missed that pussy," Macal breathed out with a smile and climbed off of Lolette.

"I needed that dick," Lolette sighed with relief and correctly readjusted her thong.

"You did, baby girl?"

"Uh huh! I missed you so much!"

Macal pulled Lolette in his arms and kissed her. "I missed you too. You know what else I miss?"

"What?"

Macal kissed her again and answered, "That warm pretty ass mouth of yours."

"I see," Lolette giggled and leaned over to suck Macal's dick. She gave the dick three sucks before getting up, because something didn't quite feel right to her.

"What's wrong, baby?" Macal noticed Lolette's sudden change in mood.

"Is it me, or is this limo going a little bit too fast?" She asked.

"I don't think so."

"Alright, maybe it's just me," Lolette said and went back to sucking.

Macal heard a text notification. He pulled out his phone and let Lolette keep sucking while replying to the message.

Tylisha: Hey, big bro!

Macal: Hey, baby sis! How was your date tonight?

Tylisha: What are you talking about?

Macal: Fallon said she was watching the kids for you while you and Enzo went out.

Tylisha: No, she's not. We're all at Vax and Ligia's house, celebrating his granddaughter's birthday.

Macal: Alright, have fun. Talk to you later.

Why would Fallon lie about babysitting the kids? That's not like her at all! Macal wondered.

Lolette picked her head up from Macal's lap and said, "Macal, I think this limo is going too fast."

"Shh!" Macal ignored and shushed Lolette. "I need to ask Fallon something."

When the limo turned on Fuller Street, the driver increased the speed, almost running a chrome Porsche off the road.

"Hey, slow the fuck down you stupid motherfucker! You almost hit that fucking car!" Lolette yelled at the driver.

Still ignoring Lolette, Macal called Fallon to see what the hell was going on. He waited for Fallon to answer the phone and *Shawty Is A Ten* by The Dream was playing in the limo. *Oh fuck! That's Fallon's ringtone!* Macal's milk chocolate skin turned pale.

"Macal, what's the problem?" Lolette asked.

Macal didn't answer back. He was putting two and two together. He faced the front seat and the limo came to a car jerking stop. The limo driver turned around to face Macal and Lolette, and the two screamed in bloody murder. "Fallon!"

"Surprise, bitches!" Fallon yelled with a big, sinister, scary smile and daggers in her eyes. She hit the gas pedal hard and resumed driving like a speed demon.

"Fallon, slow down!" Macal yelled.

"Macal, I loved you! How the fuck could you do this to me?" Fallon yelled with tears in her eyes.

"Baby, let me explain." Macal tried to reason with her.

"Let you explain!" Fallon let out a crazy, sinister laugh. "Let you explain! I heard and saw everything! Calling this hoe, slut bitch, baby! Nigga, don't you ever call me baby again!"

Lolette was terrified. "Fallon, please slow down!"

"Fuck you, bitch!" Fallon snapped with venom. "Smiling in my fucking face! Coming to my wedding as my Maid of Honor, smelling like the nasty little thot bitch in heat you are! Didn't even bother to wash Macal's scent off you!"

What the fuck? Macal was blown away. "You knew the whole time?"

"Yes, the fuck I did!" Fallon let her emotions equal her speed. "I know about all of your hoes! From this nasty two-faced bitch to the stinky-stank, cheap perfume wearing thot that beat her ass!" She confessed.

"You know about Crystal too?" Macal asked.

"Know about her? I know about her so much I introduced her to two friends." Fallon hinted.

"It was you? You were the one who pushed her in that cage!" This was news to Macal but not Lolette.

"They might not be the two pythons she's used to taking in her pussy, up her ass and in her mouth but hey, pretty close." Fallon shrugged.

"Fallon, please slow down! I'm sorry!" Macal begged. "It'll never happen again!"

"You're sorry? It'll never happen again? You said that I'm sorry it'll never happen again bullshit while I was laid up in that hospital! Now, you're here fucking this bitch! Out of all the bitches to keep on fucking around on me with, you pick the one who killed your fucking seed!" The angrier Fallon got the faster she drove.

"Fallon, you need to calm your crazy ass down!" Lolette yelled with authority. "Nobody told your ass to drop by the office and run down those fucking steps like a pathetic, crazy, delusional bitch!"

Being called crazy and a pathetic, crazy, delusional bitch triggered something in Fallon. She turned around to ask Lolette, "What did you say, bitch?"

Lolette boldly repeated, "I said, your crazy—"

Fallon took her hands off the steering wheel and started beating Lolette with her fists.

"Fallon! Stop it!" Macal tried to pull the ladies apart. He saw bright flashing lights from a big truck coming towards them and he yelled, "Oh shit! Look out!"

Fallon stopped beating on Lolette and grabbed the wheel to try to gain control. She tried to get out of the truck's way, but the limo skidded off the road, flipped over two times and hit a tree. The hard blow from the impact knocked all three of them out.

Chapter 45

Jeromy frantically barged into the Grady Hospital Emergency Room. He ran to the receptionist's desk and screamed, "Where is she? Where is my fiancée?"

"What's her name?" The receptionist asked.

"Thuy Ellis. I heard she was here. She's carrying my baby! Please! I need to know if she's okay!" Jeromy was really playing his part.

"The doctor is still with her." The receptionist informed him as she pointed to her right. "You can go through those doors where the family is waiting."

Thanks." Jeromy followed the receptionist's direction and walked through the doors. He searched for the waiting room and found Isla, Greg, Bryn and Vida.

"Jeromy!" Isla approached him with tears in her eyes.

"How is she, Isla?" Jeromy asked with concern.

"We still don't know," Isla answered.

"What about the baby?"

"They had to do an emergency c-section. Don't know the status."

"This is all my fault. I should've fought those bastards off!" Jeromy said with anger.

"Don't blame yourself Jeromy," Greg said.

"There goes the doctor." Vida pointed at the doctor coming their way.

The doctor approached the group and Isla was the first to start asking questions. "How is she? How's my baby and grandbaby?"

The doctor sighed heavily and gave the update. "I'm sorry. We did everything we could—"

Isla's emotions took over and she lost it. She fell to the floor, screaming. "No! No! Not my baby! Not my grandbaby! No!"

Greg and Bryn struggled to lift Isla off the ground. She couldn't stop screaming and crying, but they were able to carry her to a chair and sit her down.

"They can't be dead! They can't be!" Vida cried.

"I loved that girl!" Jeromy yelled in disbelief. "This shit can't be real! I have to see for myself!"

"Are you sure?" The doctor asked.

"Yes!" Jeromy nodded.

"I think it's best if y'all go in one at a time," the doctor advised.

"We understand," Greg said. Judging by Isla's emotional state, he made a suggestion. "Jeromy, you better go first."

"Okay," Jeromy said.

Jeromy followed the doctor to Thuy's room and opened the door. The EMTs rushed past them with a man on a stretcher. "Make way! Make way! Coming through! Limo crash victim! Male!"

"Gotta go! You can just go inside!" The doctor said to Jeromy and took off.

"Thanks." Jeormy entered Thuy's room and closed the door behind him. He slowly walked towards Thuy's motionless body. Her eyes were closed and she wasn't breathing at all.

"Good motherfucking riddance, you bitch! You and that little bastard are finally out of my life!" Jeromy cheered. He pulled out his phone and made a phone call.

"Hello," the caller greeted.

"It's done. They're both dead. Good work," Jeromy congratulated them.

"Thanks."

"In thirty minutes, meet me three blocks away from where you took care of Onya," Jeromy instructed.

"Alright."

"Bye."

Jeromy hung up the phone. "Let me get my fucking ring back." Jeromy grabbed Thuy's left hand and didn't see the ring on her finger. He wondered where it could be, because she never took it off. "Huh! Where the fuck is the ring?"

Thuy snatched her hand away from Jeromy's grasp, sat up in her bed and yelled at the bathroom door. "Did you get everything, gentlemen?"

"And then some," one of the two police officers said, coming out of the bathroom. He was holding a voice recorder and his partner was waving a pair of handcuffs.

They went over to a stunned Jeromy and started reading him his rights. "Jeromy Fuller, you are under arrest for the attempted murder of Thuy Ellis, the murder of Onya Hanks, the murder of Day'zon Fuller, conspiracy to commit murder and a plethora of other charges."

"Thuy, what the fuck is this!" *This bitch set me up!*

"Your plan only half worked," Thuy said as the doctor let everyone in the room.

The doctor walked over to Thuy's bed and carefully pulled the machines from under the bed. Everybody, including the doctor, was in on Thuy and the cops' plan to catch Jeromy. Bryn and Vida even changed out of their bloody clothes to not raise suspicion.

"You may have killed our baby, but I'm still standing, you lowdown, dirty motherfucker!"

Jeromy tried to talk his way out of his inevitable doom as the handcuffs were being slapped on him. "I don't know what you think you heard—"

"Get him the fuck out of my face!" Thuy ordered the cops.

"With pleasure, ma'am, and thanks for all your help," the cop said. "Alright, let's go." The cops led Jeromy out the room in handcuffs.

"I hope you drop the soap, you bitch ass, fuck nigga!" Vida yelled.

Bryn smiled at Vida and gave her a hug. "Oh, Vida, I'm so proud of you."

Isla walked over to Thuy and hugged her. "My baby! I'm so glad you're alright!"

"Thanks, momma," Thuy said. "Good thing Jeromy forgot everybody in this room was in the drama club in high school." Fortunately for Thuy, her doctor paid for his medical school tuition by being a bit player.

"How did you know about Jeromy?" Bryn asked.

Thuy went on to explain. "During the car jacking, I got suspicious when I was the only one who was getting dragged, pistol whipped and shot, and I wasn't the driver. After I was shot, I heard everything, of course. Also, Jeromy's genius friends didn't bother to wear masks. Those were the same guys that dropped by Jeromy's house the day after Onya's murder do discuss 'business'."

"They killed Onya and were there to collect their money business." Bryn said.

"Right. The final clue was the van. It was the same van that was parked in the driveway when they dropped by the house, and I saw that van creeping around Onya's neighborhood after I left her house the day before they killed her." She sighed and hugged her friends. "Thanks guys. Can you do me a favor?"

"Sure," Vida said.

Thuy pointed at the dresser drawer. "Go in that drawer and donate that engagement ring to charity."

"I'll do the honors," Bryn said, and took the ring out of the drawer.

Thuy looked down at her wrapped up stomach filled with stitches, and reality settled in. "My baby! My baby! My baby is gone!" She sobbed. "I was so stupid and dumb!"

"Don't do that to yourself, baby girl," Greg said. "Don't let that nigga get to you."

Thuy kept crying and everyone wrapped their arms around her for comfort. "It's okay, baby," Isla said, and kissed Thuy's forehead. "We got you. Always have! Always will!"

Oh shit! I feel like I got hit by a big ass truck! Macal woke up with a splitting headache and his body aching all over. He looked around at his strange surroundings and discovered he was in the hospital. He looked around for the button to call the nurse, but instead found someone lying in the bed next to him. It was a woman whose beautiful face had a couple of bruises like she had been pistol whipped, with long, jet black hair and glowing brown skin. "What the hell?"

The woman woke up. She turned over in her bed and saw a man lying in the bed next to her. He was handsome, tall, and muscular with milk chocolate skin. "What the hell?" She responded with a yawn.

"My thoughts exactly," Macal said.

"Who are you? What are you doing here?" The woman asked.

"Looks like they put me in your room by mistake," Macal concluded.

"Big ass mistake."

"Right." Since Macal was in this woman's space, he might as well be polite and introduce himself. "I'm Macal Kilborn?"

"Hey. Thuy Ellis. What are you in for?"

"Car accident." Macal didn't really want to go into the details. In fact he wasn't exactly sure of the details his-damn-self. "Driver lost control of the car. You?"

"Long story," Thuy sighed.

Macal looked around the hospital room and replied. "You know I got time, right?"

"Obviously," Thy replied with sarcasm, and the two shared a chuckle.

Sexy sarcasm. Macal thought.

"It's too fucking exhausting; pardon the expression," she apologized.

"I've heard and said worse."

Thuy then thought, *hey what the hell.* Even though this was a complete stranger, he was going to find out about her fucked up love life and the rest of her tale of woe, eventually. He might as well know right then from her. "But if you really wanna know, all you have to do is turn on the TV to any news or sports channel you wish."

"Alright," Macal said. He looked around for the remote but couldn't find it. "Trying to find the remote over here."

"Never mind. It's over here on my side." Thuy grabbed the remote and turned on the TV.

The TV was on the NBC channel and Thuy was right. There was Jeromy's mug shot and her picture on the news. She and Macal sat back and watched her humiliation on national news.

"Atlanta Braves pitcher, Jeromy Fuller has been arrested for hiring three men to gun down his pregnant fiancée, sports agent and Audi dealership owner, Thuy Ellis in a staged car jacking. She survived, but unfortunately, the child died. Jeromy Fuller will also be charged with the unsolved murders of Onya Hanks and—"

Thuy saw and heard enough, and turned the TV off.

That motherfucker! Macal thought. What kind of monster would do something like that to the woman carrying his child? "Thuy, I'm sorry. Have you seen the baby?" He didn't know why he asked that question.

Thuy shook her head. "I can't! It's too much! I wanted to be a mother so bad. I couldn't wait for my son to come into this world. Jeromy was an all around bastard, but I couldn't see it. I didn't wanna see it. All the lies, cheating and the secrets, but I kept taking him back, believing in him, his lies and bullshit promises. I don't know who the fuck that nigga was. How can I show my fucking face with all this shit out there?"

Macal couldn't stand to see this woman crumble before his eyes. He wanted to comfort her but he was stuck in his hospital bed. Thuy seemed like a sweet woman who didn't deserve to be dragged into this bullshit. "Thuy, I wish there was something I could do."

The doctor came in to check on Thuy and saw the mistake that was made. "Oh my goodness! You're awake," he said to Macal. "I'm sorry you were placed in the wrong room. Let's get you out of here." The doctor stuck his head out of the room and waved for a staff member to approach him. "Take this man out of here and into his correct room."

"Yes, sir," the staff said. A few minutes later, he came back with a wheelchair."

"Nice to meet you, Thuy. I wish it was under better circumstances," Macal said as he was being placed in the wheelchair.

"You too," Thuy returned. "Hey, Macal." He turned around to face Thuy. "Thanks for listening, and get well soon," she said.

"Anytime. Keep your head up," Macal said, and was wheeled out the room.

Left alone, Thuy turned on the TV and flipped through the channels. It seemed like every channel was talking about Thuy's shooting. There was only one way to make this stop. It was the oldest trick in the book to avoid situations such as this. Thuy changed the channel to the Boomerang channel. Luckily, they were playing a Looney Tunes marathon. As Thuy distracted herself with old school cartoons she grew up on, she replayed Macal's last words in her mind. *Keep your head up! Keep your head up!* "Easier said than done, Macal. Easier said than done."

Chapter 46

Six Months Later

Thuy was standing over a gravesite with a tombstone that read *Day'zon Malcolm Full*er. She placed a teddy bear dressed in a baby blue sailor suit on the grave. "I love you, baby boy. Momma is always with you." Thuy said with sadness in her heart, and let a single teardrop fall onto the grave.

The last six months had been very difficult for Thuy. Day'zon's funeral and Jeromy's trial, which ended with him being sentenced to life in prison, and the whole world got to see what a fool she was when ignoring all the signs, and unknowingly befriending her fiancé and baby daddy's side piece. Thuy felt like a joke. A big, fat, fucking joke. Everywhere she went she got the look of pity. All the stress caused her to lose all her baby weight and then some in less than a month.

Thuy left the cemetery and her next stop was Phipps Plaza. She hopped in her brand new powder blue Audi the company gave her as a gift, and drove to her destination. She arrived at Phipps Plaza and found a close parking space and parked the car.

"Hopefully I'll get through the day without being subjected to the dreaded, *that's her*, looks." Thuy hoped as she stepped out of the car.

Thuy walked through the mall to see what store she should check out. There was a large gathering near the food court and something told Thuy to be nosy. She approached the commotion and saw it was a book signing. She looked at the promotional poster to see who the author was and was stunned. It was Marsha Brinkley. The detective who was over Thuy's case against Levi. She aged a tad bit but was still beautiful with her still flawless light skin. She put on about twenty pounds, mostly in the right places. She grew her hair out. Her natural hair was down to her shoulders, all curled up.

Thuy got in line, not wanting to be rude by cutting in front of everybody. Thuy saw Marsha had written five books, grabbed all of them off the table and said, "Detective Brinkley? Do you remember me?"

Marsha was wearing her reading glasses, looked up and saw an adult version of her very first solo case as a detective. She could never forget Thuy and, of course, she was aware of what happened to her six months ago. "Thuy Ellis? 1996?"

"That's me," Thuy answered.

"Hey, girl! It's been a long time!" Marsha jumped out of her seat and hugged Thuy. "How you been?"

"Taking it one day at a time," Thuy said and paid Marsha for the books. "It ain't easy considering."

"I feel you," Marsha said and autographed the books. "You'll make it through." She gave the books back to Thuy. "Listen, I'm taking my break in five minutes. Let's meet up."

"Sure, I'll find us a seat."

"Okay."

Thuy left for a few moments to put the books in the trunk of her car. She reentered the mall and went to the food court. She bought a plate from a Jamaican restaurant and found a table. Marsha located Thuy and joined her with her wings and fries.

"How long have you been retired?" Thuy asked.

"About seven years," Marsha answered.

Thuy was still geeking out about the cop turned author. "This is unbelievable. You're an author now. When did you get into writing?"

"Actually, I started writing when I was eleven years old. I wrote short stories and poems. After high school, I joined the force, following my daddy and brother's footsteps," Marsha explained.

"Do you miss the force?"

Marsha had to think long and hard about her answer. "Yes and no. I loved making a difference and helping people. I hated that a couple of bad apples made it hard for the rest of us."

"What made you decide to retire?" Thuy took a bite out of her jerk chicken.

"My heart wasn't in it anymore." Marsha shrugged and ate a few of her fries. "Also, despite my credentials, tenure, reputation, family history in the profession, hard work and dedication, I realized I was never gonna be promoted to captain and commanding officer."

"Why not?"

"Two reasons, and I think you can guess what they were." Marsha hinted.

Black woman and a young one at that. Thuy answered to herself. "Oh."

"Yeah."

"Sorry to hear that."

"It's all good. Like the saying goes. When one door closes—"

"—another one opens." Thuy finished the saying.

"Life is good. I have my pension, retirement, 401k and benefits. I get to travel. I make money doing what I love, writing full time and being a motivational speaker."

"You're a motivational speaker?"

"Yes, I speak out against sexual violence and domestic abuse."

"That's wonderful. I don't know if you're interested, but I'm on the board of the Restart Project. We can use you to speak at some of our events."

"Y'all do some great things. I would be very interested."

"Thanks. The new library at the women's center has become a huge success."

"You're a very busy woman."

"I have to be. Working and keeping busy keeps my mind off of the incident." Thuy said, knowing Marsha knew what she was referring to.

"You survived. That's the difficult part. Now you can recover and heal," Marsha said with compassion.

"You gave me that same advice over twenty years ago." Then she said in defeat, "I'm calling it quits."

"Calling what quits?"

"Relationships and men," Thuy said in frustration. "I can't deal with the bullshit anymore. The lies, the cheating, secrets and hiring dumb ass niggas to try to kill me. Fuck this shit! I'm done!" Thuy took a deep breath and covered her face with her hands.

"You know who you sound like?"

Thuy uncovered her face and looked at Marsha.

"Me," Marsha answered her own question.

"How?"

"I said the exact same thing when I was twenty-eight years old. My husband had a baby on me with my cousin and left me for her. I promised myself no nigga was gonna hurt me again. Now, I'm in my late forties with an established life, but no one to share it with. All because I was scared to get hurt again," Marsha confessed with regret.

Her confession made Thuy think. "What are you saying?"

Marsha proceeded to drop a jewel on this young, beautiful, successful black woman who wanted to be loved but was tired of the hurt that stood before her. "What I'm saying is everybody has baggage, but be careful what you pack and carry with you. Think about it."

Chapter 47

Macal went into his office after a meeting and two conference calls. He plopped down on the couch, trying to get a minute to himself.

"Hello," Tylisha greeted him as she let herself in.

So much for that minute to myself. "Hey, baby girl," Macal said, while he took a seat behind his desk.

"I finished decorating your new penthouse, and the house is officially on the market."

"Great."

"I spoke to Naomi and she's gonna be in charge of Fallon's divorce settlement until she's released from Wadley Hospital."

Macal decided not to press charges against Fallon. He had to do some major convincing to get Lolette on board. What Macal didn't know was that Tylisha was the reason Lolette came around. She threatened to beat her ass again if she didn't cooperate. Due to Fallon's history of mental illness and being off her medication since her miscarriage, she was committed to a mental institution in Athens, Georgia.

"How is she?" Macal asked.

"Fine," Tylisha answered. "I brought the kids to see her. Ayla and Fallon were close." Tylisha picked up on Macal's distant attitude on the subject of Fallon. "So, you're just never going to see her, huh?"

"I'm not ready, Tylisha."

"Alright, when will you be ready?"

"Oh, I don't know, Tylisha, my dear. Maybe when I get over the fact that I ended up marrying a fucking undercover psycho who tried to kill me!" Macal lashed out in anger. After the accident and the truth about Fallon's mental state came out, Macal couldn't look at her the same way. He had no choice but to divorce her and give her a $20 million settlement.

"I believe the correct term is mentally ill," Tylisha corrected him. "You know she wasn't in her right mind when she pushed that girl in that cage and bribed that limo driver to switch places with her. She was taking her medication and going to her doctor. She had her issues under control until she lost the baby. That woman was devastated when she found out about you and Lolette, and you made plans to fuck the hoe again. No wonder she lost her fucking mind." She defended Fallon.

Macal couldn't believe his own sister was actually defending the woman who almost killed her brother. "Are you saying I deserve this shit?"

"No, I'm saying I've been the wife of an unfaithful man, constantly putting up with his bullshit. It could drive any woman over the edge." Tylisha sympathized. "And judging by your attitude, I can't imagine why Fallon never told you about her meds."

"Regardless what you or anybody else may think, I do care about Fallon. I just can't face her right now."

"So mailing divorce papers and a $20 million check is going to fix everything, huh? I know these past six months have been difficult, and even though I don't agree with how you handled this, the outcome might be for the best. Now you and Fallon can start over fresh, fix yourselves and move on."

Macal nodded in silence.

"What are you doing in three months?" Tylisha asked.

"Why?"

"You need a vacation," Tylisha suggested. "Enzo and I are taking the kids to New Orleans for a week."

"What's in New Orleans?"

"Enzo's parents," she answered. "They're having a party to celebrate their wedding anniversary."

"You're meeting the parents, huh?"

"Yes, I am," Tylisha said with glow, taking this big step in her and Enzo's relationship. "Why don't you come with us?"

"Why not?" Macal agreed nonchalantly. "You're still helping me pick out a car today, right?"

"Anything for you." Tylisha hugged Macal and was ready to leave. "I'll pick you up after my last appointment."

"Okay. Love you."

"Ditto."

Tylisha drove around with Macal in the passenger's seat, trying to find a car dealership. "Any particular car you're looking for?" She asked.

"Surprise me," Macal said.

"Alright." Tylisha drove down the road until she saw an Audi dealership. "How about this place?"

"Thuy's Audis," Macal read the sign. *I wonder if it's her.* He recalled Thuy from the hospital being a sports agent and owning an Audi dealership.

"You want to check it out?"

"Sure."

Tylisha turned into the dealership. The siblings walked into the showroom where Thuy was talking to one of the mechanics. *What perfect curves and all that ass!* Thuy was wearing a navy blue conservative dress with matching pumps, and a diamond jewelry set. The dress hugged her body like it was a second skin, and her double-D tits looked like they wanted to pop out.

"It's her." Macal mumbled.

"Who?"

"Do you remember the news report about Jeromy Fuller?"

"How can I forget?" Tylisha said. "He was all over the news. He was that baseball player who hired three men to kill his pregnant fiancée. She lived but the baby died."

"That's her," Macal whispered.

"You're kidding?"

"Dead ass."

"Isn't that the same chick whose room they accidently put you in at Grady?"

"Yep."

Macal and Tylisha approached Thuy, and he was the first to speak. "Hey, Thuy."

Thuy looked up and saw the guy who she met at the hospital coming her way, along with a woman who looked like she could be related to him. "It's you! Macal! The wrong hospital room guy! How are you?" Thuy greeted him.

"Maintaining," Macal said.

"What brings you here?"

"I was browsing for a car and my sister Tylisha here randomly picked this place." Macal then pointed to Tylisha.

"Why, thank you," Thuy said to Tylisha.

"Anytime," Tylisha said.

"Thuy Ellis, at your service. What type of car did you have in mind?"

"I don't know. Something reliable. Not too flashy but with a luxury appeal," Macal explained.

"I think I have the car for you." Thuy walked over to a dark gray sports car and presented its features.

"You have a great eye," Macal complimented. "I'll take it."

"Alright, I'll have Jade set you up and we'll draw up the paperwork in my office." Thuy signaled for Jade to set up the car. "If y'all would follow me please." She said to Macal and Tylisha as they followed her into her office, where Tylisha closed the door behind her.

"Here we are." Thuy offered the siblings a seat and she took her place at her desk. She printed out the paperwork and handed it to Macal. "Here's your paperwork, and when you're finished, Jade will take care of your transaction and give you the keys."

"Alright," Macal said and started filling out the paperwork.

Thuy took a better look at Tylisha and recognized her. "That's it."

"What?" Tylisha was wondering what Thuy was talking about.

"I remember you. You used to be married to Milton Dryer."

"Have we met?" Tylisha asked with confusion.

"Briefly, at Antonio Blanchi's birthday party. You remember Tony?"

"Milton's agent, Italian guy, big silly flirt, has a thing for black women. His daughter, Sophia is a doctor," Tylisha recalled.

"That's him," Thuy confirmed. "I spoke with Tony yesterday and he told me he had to drop Milton."

"He dropped Milton? Why?"

"He was kicked off his last three teams for breaking the rules, and his suspected drug issues."

"He's on drugs?" Macal asked.

"That's the word on the street," Thuy said.

"I'm sure that white hoe he threw me and our babies out for is taking care of him just fine." Tylisha dismissed.

"Oh, no. They're divorced," Thuy informed her.

"Huh?" Tylisha was really out of the loop.

"Oh, yes. She got the house and half his assets."

"I wonder what his coon, nigga father gotta say now," Tylisha scoffed.

"What do you mean?" Macal asked.

"He always told Milton to never marry black. Always marry white. Black bitches don't do nothing but lie on their backs and hold men back." Tylisha repeated her ex-father-in-law's self-hating bullshit logic verbatim.

"I know you lying," Macal said.

"I wish I was."

"Wasn't Milton's momma black?"

"Yes. You see, Milton's father was in the NBA and was engaged to the mayor's daughter who was white. He cheated on her with Milton's momma and she ended up pregnant with Milton's sister, Nikki. The fiancée found out and she left him. He married Milton's momma. They had Nikki and later on Milton. That man put that woman through hell. He had a career-ending injury and blamed his momma for his misfortunes; always saying that she trapped him."

"Did she stay with him?"

"Oh, no, she divorced his ass and remarried a congressman. Happy ever since. After Nikki graduated from high school, she went straight to the Air Force. She wanted to get as far away from that coon, nigga father of hers as possible." Tylisha said.

"Who could blame her?" Thuy commented in agreement.

"That man hated my guts," Tylisha said. "When Milton and I told him I was pregnant with Welton and we were getting married, his ass nearly fainted."

"Tony told me Milton's dad was a piece of work," Thuy said as Macal handed her the completed paperwork. "Thank you. Your copy will be mailed to you." Thuy copied the first page and handed it to Macal. "Take this to Jade and she'll process your payment and give you the keys."

"Thanks," Macal said, and the siblings walked out the office. "Isn't she something, Tylisha?" Macal said with admiration.

Oh no! "Macal, do you remember our little talk back in your office about starting over and fixing yourself first before jumping into another relationship?" Tylisha reminded him in a little kid's voice.

"I know, but there's something about her," Macal said, feeling like a schoolboy meeting the most popular girl in school, trying to figure out how to get close to her. "If only there was someway to get close to her to see what she's all about."

"Well, compared to her last dude, you'll probably be the equivalent to Prince Charming," Tylisha said with sarcasm.

"Aww, quit bragging, Tylisha. You're only saying that because I'm your brother," Macal replied with the same sarcasm as he went on to purchase his new car.

Chapter 48

Thuy was on her way to have dinner with Bryn and Vida. First, she stopped by Sam's house real quick to drop off some contracts. When she hugged him, she smelled some perfume on him. Hypnotic Poison to be exact. Vida's favorite perfume. Whoever Sam's new lady friend was, she had great taste.

Thuy arrived at the restaurant and went over to the reserved table where her friends were sitting. "Hey, guys," she greeted them.

"Thuy! We're so glad you came," Bryn said, giving her a hug.

"Since y'all begged, pleaded, and in a way dragged my ass out here, of course I showed up," Thuy said.

"That's because you needed to get out," Vida said, hugging Thuy.

During the hug, Thuy could've sworn she smelled traces of Armani Code cologne on Vida's dress. The thing was, Thuy bought Sam the exact same cologne for Christmas. Thuy broke the embrace and she took her seat.

"I know, right? All you do is work, go home, grab a bottle and lock yourself in your room." Bryn ran down Thuy's current routine.

"Well, it feels good to spend the entire day without the 'that's her' looks." Thuy faced forward and saw two white women staring at her, whispering to each other. The clincher was when one of them had the nerve to point. *Rude bitches!* Thuy rolled her eyes and got out of her seat. "I spoke too soon. Peace out, y'all."

"No, Thuy! Sit your black ass back down!" Bryn ordered with authority.

Thuy looked at Bryn up and down like he had lost his fucking mind. She slowly sat back down.

Bryn continued. "Look, Thuy, Jeromy and his band of idiot lowlifes are where they belong, and will be there for the rest of their lives. They can't hurt you anymore. Quit letting those motherfuckers dictate your life, and fuck what everybody gotta say. It's time to stop being a hermit and live your life."

"He's right, Thuy," Vida agreed.

"I'll stay," Thuy sighed.

"Like your ass had a choice," Bryn said on the sly as Thuy punched him in the arm. "Ouch!" Bryn rubbed his arm.

"Let's check out this menu," Vida said.

"Thuy!"

Thuy heard a familiar man's voice call her name. She took her eyes off the menu and saw it was Macal accompanied by Tylisha. "Macal! Tylisha! What brings y'all here?"

"Joyriding in the new car you suggested. I love it by the way, and now we stopped by to grab a bite to eat," Macal said.

"Here, you can join us." Thuy offered Macal and Tylisha a seat. "Ooops, where are my manners? These are my BFFs since childhood, Bryn and Vida. Bryn, Vida, this is Macal and his sister Tylisha. He's the wrong hospital room guy."

Everyone exchanged greetings and took their seats. During the meal they all made small talk, getting to know each other. Now, they were enjoying their drinks.

"This was nice. I'm glad you made me come out against my will." Thuy's joke made everyone laugh.

"Real talk, we need to come up with a way to raise this money," Vida said.

"What's the money for?" Macal asked.

"We're on the board of the Restart Project. We're trying to build a new women's shelter and do some expansion, among other things," Thuy explained.

"Isn't Ambrosia Jackson the founder?" Tylisha asked.

"Her and Bryn, here," Thuy answered.

"You're that Bryn?" Tylisha asked.

"Yes, I am," Bryn confirmed.

"You are an entertainment genius. I love your shows, plays and movies," Tylisha complimented.

"Thanks," Bryn said.

"Tylisha, did you by any chance decorate one of my actress's houses? Dee Bacon?" Bryn asked.

"That was me," Tylisha answered with a nod.

"I thought it was you," Bryn said. "I was talking to Ambrosia about what a great job you did. She wanted to hire you so bad. I just couldn't remember your name for nothing in the world. I'm gonna text her right now."

"Thanks, Bryn," Tylisha said with deep gratitude. "Decorating for Ambrosia Jackson. That's big time."

"Oh, and I need some work done to my condo too," Bryn said. "Decorating is not my thing. I know it sounds weird coming from a faggot."

"If only we met before my cousin Sam moved in his house." Thuy said to Tylisha. "SamIAm to be exact."

"SamIAm is your cousin?" Macal asked with amazement.

"Yes, and my client also," Thuy said.

"Two successful businesses under your belt, and part of an organization that helps women in need. You put Superwoman and Wonder Woman to shame," Macal said.

"Thanks," Thuy blushed.

"In fact, I'm going to make a donation to the Restart Project and tell my clients from my investment firm about your cause," Macal said.

"Me too," Tylisha said.

"That would be wonderful." Thuy dug in her purse in search of two business cards to give to Macal and Tylisha. "This is the bank that handles all the deposits and transactions for the organization."

Macal read the business card. "AGlobe Loans and Trust Bank is the bank you guys use?"

"Yes, why?" Thuy asked.

Macal pointed to Tylisha and said, "She's the bank president's girlfriend."

"You're dating Enzo?" Vida asked Tylisha.

"That's my boo," Tylisha blushed.

"So you're the chick Ligia and Vax were talking about," Thuy said.

"You know them too?" Tylisha asked.

Thuy nodded. "Ligia is on the board with us, and my momma and grandma used to work for Vax's family in some of their stores. Also, some of my clients endorse his business."

"This world is too small," Bryn said.

"Vax also graduated from high school with Ambrosia," Thuy said.

"Really?" Macal and Tylisha replied together.

"That's how Ligia got on the board," Thuy said. "Plus, she wanted to make a difference after what happened to her sister."

"Damn! We're about to close down the restaurant." Macal saw the employees getting ready to close. "I guess it's time for us to go."

"Goodnight, everyone, and nice seeing y'all again Macal and Tylisha." Thuy said, and left the table to go home.

"Thuy, wait." Macal got out of his seat to catch up with her.

"Yes, Macal?"

"I hope I don't sound like a thirsty nigga, but may I have your number so we can talk and text a little bit more?" Macal requested.

Thuy giggled and said, "One, you don't sound like a thirsty nigga and, two, you already have my number."

"I do?" Macal was baffled.

"Turn over that business card I gave you."

Macal turned the business card around and it had Thuy's cellphone and office number written on it.

"Nightie, night." Thuy winked and strutted out the door.

"Goodnight," Macal said, enjoying the view of Thuy's sexy, fat ass as she walked out the door.

Thuy felt Macal's eyes glued to her backside and switched harder to really give him something to look at.

"She's a smooth one." He admired Thuy's gangsta.

Run, Thuy! This nigga is a fucked up individual! Tylisha wanted to scream out the warning on the outside, but for some reason kept it bottled up on the inside.

Chapter 49

"This place is packed," Macal said as he, Tylisha, Enzo and the kids entered Vax and Ligia's house. The occasion was to celebrate Sharmon being drafted by the Atlanta Falcons.

"Yes, it is," Enzo said.

A lot of people came to the party. Sharmon's teammates from the University of Georgia, his big brother Vax Jr. and his daughter Lily, his big sister Quinn and her three boys Rex, Gatsby and Lucas. Welton and Ayla had run off to find Amery, and Macal, Tylisha and Enzo had caught up with Vax.

"Hey, Vax. How are you doing?" Tylisha asked.

"Good. So proud of my boy," Vax said with pride.

Ligia approached Vax and kissed him. "Hey, baby." She was the sore thumb in the entire house. Most of the guests were wearing either Atlanta Falcons, UGA or other sports gear. Ligia, on the other hand, was the only person decked out in a cute New Orleans Saints outfit. She turned to Macal, Tylisha and Enzo and greeted them. "Hey guys."

"Hello," they greeted dryly, obviously appalled at Ligia's attire.

"Sorry, I couldn't talk her out of it," Vax apologized and offered everyone a seat on the couch.

"Not so easy, is it Vax?" Enzo asked.

Ligia cut her eyes at Enzo and said, "Looks like somebody forgot how badly they were clowned every time they wore that Deion Sanders Atlanta Falcons jersey back at our high school in New Orleans."

"Oh, y'all was just hating because y'all asses were jealous." Everybody laughed at Enzo's comment. He then turned to Amery who was shaking his head at Ligia while supervising Vax's grandkids with Welton and Ayla's assistance. "And you got our son over there all embarrassed."

"He will be alright," Ligia said. "He knows at the end of the day, I'm momma and I ain't never gonna change."

"Still love you, momma!" Amery yelled out.

"See, that's my baby," Ligia said with a smile. "Love you too, baby!"

"You ride or die, I give you that," Vax said and let Ligia get comfortable in his arms.

"What in the world?" Macal approached one of the party guests. "You know we really need to stop meeting like this," he said with his deep, sexy panty-wetting voice behind Thuy.

She turned around and smiled. "Hey, Macal."

"What brings you to the party?"

"I'm Sharmon's agent."

"Really?"

"Yeah, I wasn't going to take on anymore clients for a while, but Vax and momma begged me until I caved," Thuy explained.

Macal checked out Thuy's outfit. She was wearing black shorts that showed off her shapely legs and made her ass look even more delicious, with a cut up Antonio Brown jersey. "Steelers fan, huh?"

"Yep," Thuy replied.

Macal led her to the couch to join everyone. "Nothing against the Steelers." Macal then whispered to Thuy, "Better than being a Saints fan."

"Nigga, I heard that!" Ligia objected.

"Some of y'all are okay!" Macal joked.

"Here's your drink, Thuy," Bryn said and handed Thuy her drink.

"Thanks," Thuy accepted and took a sip.

"That bar is well-stocked. Just the way I like it," Vida said. "Hey, Macal."

"What's up?" He greeted her, noting the coincidence that Thuy and her friends cheer for the same team by their outfits.

"Once again, thanks for representing Sharmon," Vax thanked Thuy with gratitude.

"Anytime, Vax, and don't you worry. Sharmon is in great hands," Thuy assured him.

"I know," Vax said. "You have your mother's intelligence and work ethic. How is she?"

"She and Greg are great."

"Bryn, thanks for that contact. Ambrosia is putting me to work and I'll be at your condo on Monday to take a look," Tylisha said.

"Good," Bryn responded.

"Vax, Thuy tells us you and Ambrosia graduated from high school together," Tylisha said.

"Yes, I graduated with Harley Mae," Vax confirmed with a nod.

"Wait a minute. Her name is Harley Mae?" Tylisha asked.

"Harley Mae Ambrosia Jackson. That's her full government," Vax said, and everyone laughed their asses off.

Macal Googled it real quick on his phone. "Yep, that's her real name alright."

"I'm one of the very few people she lets get away with busting her government out," Vax said.

"How did you and Ambrosia meet?" Bryn asked.

"She was my lab partner in chemistry class and she set me up with her best friend, Lily, who became my first wife, may she rest in peace." Vax explained.

Fuck it! Macal couldn't resist Thuy any longer so he grabbed her arm and said, "I need to steal you away for a moment."

He pulled Thuy away to find a private area. *This nigga is crazy!* She thought. Macal took a peek outside on the patio and saw it was vacant. He pulled Thuy outside and closed the door behind him. "Now we can be alone."

Thuy was stunned by Macal's boldness. "You just snatched my ass up like that because you wanted some alone time?"

"You go it," Macal said unapologetically. "It's nice and quiet out here."

"Yes, it is. How's the new car?" Thuy asked.

"Off the chain. I'm impressed with your knowledge about cars and your taste in them."

"I have Uncle Sam and SamIAm to thank. When I was growing up, I spent time in Uncle Sam's mechanic shop. It was so fun."

"I can imagine so."

"How's the investment firm?"

"Great. It has its moments, but nothing I can't handle."

"Right."

"I love what I do, and getting through the challenges makes it all rewarding." Macal wanted to check to see how Thuy was holding up. "How you been?"

"Taking it one day at a time." Thuy sighed. "Gotten used to the occasional 'that's her' looks. If I didn't have my support system, I don't know where I'd be."

"You're a brave woman," Macal said.

"I try to be." All the focus was on her, but Thuy never asked about Macal's recovery. How inconsiderate of her. "How was your recovery from the accident?"

"A couple of broken bones. My arm was in a cast for about a month."

"You seem to be in tip-top shape, and fine and sexy as hell." Thuy blushed in embarrassment for letting her inner thought come out. "Did I just say that out loud? My bad."

"No, you good," Macal said and held her hand. "Nothing wrong with saying how you think and feel. Like me saying you're beautiful, sexy, smooth and highly intoxicating. You have more attributes, but those were the ones that came to mind."

"Aww, thanks."

Macal suddenly threw caution out the window and pulled Thuy into an impromptu lip lock. Thuy wasn't thinking clearly so she went along with the flow. Macal was hard to resist. His big, strong hands were all over her body, making her super wet. Thuy's soft, full lips and her tasty mouth made Macal's dick rock hard. He grabbed a handful of her ass, further turning her on. The lustful make out session was crazy and out of character, but it felt so right and it felt so good.

Macal broke the kiss and looked deep in Thuy's eyes. "We're going out on our first date next weekend."

Nigga is you crazy? "That's how you ask a woman out on a date?"

"I didn't ask you out on a date. I told you that you're going on a date with me." He corrected and rubbed her cheek, and added with a victorious sneaky grin. "You see, my beauty, if I tell you instead of asking, you can't turn me down."

Thuy had to laugh because this nigga knew his shit. “You are so bold.”

“Oh, baby, you haven’t seen bold yet.”

Chapter 50

"Shit, Thuy! This house is looking like a fucking funeral home," Vida said, sitting in a chair in the living room filled with red roses, courtesy of Macal's week-long delivery binge up to the big date on this night.

"Macal has been sending me red roses all week here and at my office." Thuy said. "How in the world did he know these were my favorite?" Thuy wasn't used to this type of attention from a man before. She remembered telling Marsha she was done with men, but there was something about Macal she couldn't turn away. It was like he put a spell on her. To be honest, she kind of liked it.

"Are you ready for your big date tonight?" Vida asked.

"I'm as ready as I'm going to be," Thuy said nervously. "I know I said I was done with men after Jeromy, but there's something about Macal that wouldn't let me say no. I don't know what it is about him. He's different." Thuy took note of the sexy yellow dress Vida was wearing. "What do you have planned for tonight?"

"Going out," Vida answered.

"Oh, really? You've been very secretive about your mystery man. How come?" Thuy picked up on the changes in Vida. She had a gut feeling it had something to do with a man. Thuy was happy Vida was finally getting out there and taking chances. Vida's luck with men was a lot worse than Thuy's and that's saying something. Hopefully this mystery man was good to her. If not, Thuy would not hesitate to stomp that ass.

"It's hard to explain," Vida replied. "I want to make sure this is real first before I make it public. For now, we're just having fun. Plus, I'm not sure how everyone is going to react to our relationship."

"Vida, trust me, as long as this guy treats you right, we'll be happy for you."

Then, the doorbell rang.

“That’s Macal.” She opened the door and there was Macal in all his sexiness with his black slacks and black buttoned down shirt. “Hello.” She greeted him.

“Hey, baby,” Macal said, kissed Thuy on the cheek and gave her a bouquet of red roses. “Hi, Vida.”

“Hey, Macal. You’re gonna make us open a flower shop soon.” Vida joked, taking the bouquet from Thuy so she could put them in water.

“Trying to step my game up. This is a very special woman,” Macal said.

“Aww, go on, and I really mean that,” Thuy joked.

“Girl, you are silly, and very sexy, I might add.”

Thuy looked gorgeous in her strapless black dress with red rose prints and red pumps, topped off with a red clutch purse.

“Shall we?” He extended his hand.

“Let’s.” Thuy gave Macal her hand. He kissed it and she blushed.

“Have a good time,” Vida said.

“We will, and you enjoy your evening too,” Thuy responded.

“I will.” Vida closed the door behind the new couple.

“Nice.” Thuy commented on Grant Park’s set up for Movie Under the Stars. It was an event where people could bring their own food and drinks like a picnic and watch a movie on the screen, sort of like a drive-in.

“Between me and you, this is my first time coming here,” Macal said, and laid the blanket down on the grass.

“Same here,” Thuy said as she sat on the blanket, set up the wrapped up plates of food and poured the wine. “I’m glad we came. What’s playing?”

“It’s a double feature. Lady and the Tramp, and 101 Dalmatians.”

“Disney classics? Good. Good.”

“They’re showing Lady and the Tramp first, which is appropriate for our meal for tonight.”

“Which is?” Thuy unwrapped her plate to reveal the weirdest looking spaghetti she had ever seen. “Spaghetti with... Is that sauce yellow?”

Macal chuckled and shook his head. “Funny story. My momma was teaching me and Tylisha how to cook spaghetti. I was either eleven or twelve. When it was time to add seasoning to the sauce, I honestly thought I grabbed the right bottle but it turned out to be yellow food coloring instead.”

They laughed their asses off and started eating. “Good yellow spaghetti,” Thuy said.

“Thanks for liking my cooking,” Macal returned. His phone vibrated in his pocket, and he took it out to see who could possibly be interrupting him at a time like this. He saw who sent him a text message and was speechless at the sight of Lolette’s tits.

Lolette: SURPRISE! Did you miss me?

Macal: Where have you been?

Lolette: Recovering from the accident, working and traveling. It would’ve been nice if you had checked on me, but it’s all good. WYD?

Macal: Hanging out with Enzo and Vax.

Lolette: Okay.

Macal shoved the phone back in his pocket without a second thought and poured all his attention on the sexy cutie eating his accidental specialty like it was her last meal.

“Mmm! Mmm! Mmm! Your ass know how to cook, I’ll tell you that! Boy, you know how to cook! You hooked this shit up! Macal, boy, you can come cook at my house!” Thuy said between bites. “This yellow spaghetti is off the chain. You need to give me the recipe to this! You are full of surprises.”

“You have no idea.” The unknown female voice stopped Thuy’s eating. She glanced up at the woman standing over her and Macal.

“Lolette, it’s good to see you,” Macal said, trying to keep his cool after being caught in a boldfaced lie.

"Macal, darling, it's great to see you." Lolette flashed her seductive smile, playing her game. "I just passed by and thought I'd say hi. Enjoy your date. Toodles!"

"Bye," Macal said as Lolette strutted away.

"Who was that?" Thuy asked.

"Mutual acquaintance." Macal stretched the truth big time.

Thuy accepted and went on eating and sipping her wine. After Lady and the Tramp was over, there was a ten minute interlude before 101 Dalmatians started.

"I'm finally going to ask and I hope you don't take this the wrong way."

"What is it?" she asked.

"Your name, Thuy, how can I put this? It's not a bad name, don't get me wrong. In fact it's a beautiful name."

"I think I know what your question is," Thuy said.

"You do?"

"Yes. You're not the first person to wonder why a non-mixed black chick is walking around with an Asian name. Let me explain. My mother had a best friend she grew up with in the same neighborhood and graduated from high school with. Two months after graduation, she died in a car accident. My momma took it very hard. She vowed, if she ever had a daughter, she would honor her best friend and honorary sister's memory."

"What a story," Macal said. "Your mom's best friend's name was Thuy?"

"Yep. Her mom was Vietnamese and her dad was black. Her parents, Mr. and Mrs. Lappel, were like surrogate grandparents to me. They live in Tallahassee now."

Macal's phone rang and he rolled his eyes, assuming it was Lolette calling to bitch about him lying to her. His annoyance dropped when he saw it was Tylisha calling. "I have to take this. It's Tylisha."

"Okay," Thuy said with understanding.

"Hello," Macal answered the call.

"Uncle Macal!" Welton answered the phone sounding very upset.

"Welton, why do you have your momma's phone? What's wrong?"

"She's sick! She has food poisoning! She told me to call you. She's in the bathroom."

"I'll be right there." Macal hung up. "I'm sorry, but we have to go. Tylisha's sick!"

"Will she be alright?" Thuy asked with concern.

"I don't know. I need to stop by the store first to pick up some medicine for her."

He and Thuy quickly packed up everything and headed straight to Tylisha's aide.

Macal and Thuy arrived at Tylisha's house and Welton let them in. "Hey, Uncle Macal! Hey, Miss Thuy!" He agreed them.

"Hello," Thuy returned.

"Where's your mother?" Macal asked.

"In her room," Ayla answered.

Thuy followed Macal upstairs and into Tylisha's room. They found her lying in her bed, holding her stomach in pain.

"Hey, baby girl. What did you eat?" Macal asked.

"I ate some kind of stew." Tylisha weakly answered. "I'm throwing up shit I ate two weeks ago."

"Here's your medicine." Macal handed the bag to Tylisha.

"Thanks." Tylisha saw Thuy leaning on the door and said, "Hey, Thuy, I'm sorry for ruining your date."

"Don't worry about it. You just rest and get better. I'll check on the kids for you." Thuy offered.

"Thanks," Tylisha said as Thuy walked out the door. Macal helped her take her Pepto Bismol, causing her to whine in disgust. "This pink shit is fucking disgusting!"

"I know, but you need to get better," Macal said. He rocked Tylisha in his arms, singing their song *Just a Friend* by Biz Markie.

Tylisha let out a soft chuckle and fell asleep. Macal quietly walked out the room and closed the door.

"You're so sweet," Thuy said. Watching the love and care Macal had for his baby sister touched her heart.

"I try to be," Macal said as the two headed for the living room. "All part of being a big brother."

"You and Tylisha seem to be really close." Thuy said as the two sat on the couch.

"We are. That's my girl."

"Must be nice."

"What about your siblings?"

"Shit! I have an older brother and sister that would've let my ass die after eating that stew." Thuy was exaggerated, but not by much.

"Y'all don't get along, huh?" Macal guessed.

"They're cruel bitches. They take after their mother Mycha, Queen of the Cruel Bitches."

"Step-siblings?"

"Half-siblings," Thuy corrected. "You see, our dad cheated on Jett and Tori's mom with my mom."

"And you were the result?"

Thuy nodded. "Despite the fact that my mom was unaware of our father's marital status, they still held it against us."

"What about your dad? Didn't he look out for you?"

"Nigga, please!" Thuy scoffed with an eye roll. "If it wasn't for momma forcing him to pay child support, he would've pretended I never existed." She shook her head and made a very sad observation. "You know what's fucked up? My shooting made worldwide news. Millions of complete strangers all over the world who I've never met, cared enough about me to show their concern, support and offer condolences to my unborn son, Day'zon. Meanwhile, my sperm donor and half siblings live in the same city and I haven't heard a fucking peep out of them! The only time I hear from they asses is when they need money!"

"That is pretty fucked up," Macal said. "That must've been very painful for you." He pulled Thuy into his arms to comfort her and be the protector she desperately needed in her life. "Actually, with the kind of father I had, I wished he walked out and abandoned us."

"Why?"

Macal began to share his no-good daddy story. "Our parents died when we were young, and we had to stay with our Grandma

Doris. Our father cheated on our mother all through their marriage. The drama and humiliation he put us through, watching momma in tears, drinking her pain away, I wish she would've just left that bastard and found happiness with a man who loved and appreciated her. Even though he was fucking around, he wouldn't let momma go."

"You must've really loved your mom," Thuy said.

"Yes, I did. She was the best. She was beautiful, loving, warm and highly intelligent. She was everything you could ask for in a mother." Macal shook his head and sighed. "I don't think I'll ever get past her death. May 2nd, 1993 was the worst day of my life."

"Did you say May 2nd, 1993?"

"Yeah, that's the day momma died."

"Wow." Thuy took a deep breath and said, "I will have no problem remembering the day your mom died."

"Why not?"

"Your mom died on my eleventh birthday." She uncomfortably admitted and saw another connection. "We both went through life, and had scarring moments on the exact same day?" Thuy then told Macal how Olson betrayed her on her birthday. Then she remembered a detail. "Was your mom's name Belinda?"

"Yes," Macal answered. "How did you know?"

"When Uncle Sam was taking me to the father-daughter dance, we heard this news report on the radio about a woman named Belinda Kilborn who was a wife and mother of two, dying in some kind of accident. We didn't hear the whole thing, only that part." Thuy was blown away. "That was your mom we heard about."

Macal nodded.

"I'm so sorry."

"Me too."

He and Thuy laid in each others arms, comforting each other. Thuy saw the pain in Macal's eyes when he talked about his mother. This man was suffering on the inside. She wanted to be there for him, and hopefully somewhere down the line, he'd know he didn't have to go through this agony alone. At the same time, Macal wanted to give Thuy the love and protection she deserved and desperately needed, but was unfortunately denied by her father—the first man that was supposed to give it to her.

Chapter 51

"Aww, you made it!" Tylisha cheered and hugged Macal.

"Yep!" Macal said and placed his bag by the door, all ready for the week long trip to New Orleans. "Where's Enzo?"

"He's picking up the van to take us to the airport, and he has to pick up Amery," Tylisha answered. "Check on the kids for me."

"Alright." Macal headed upstairs.

Tylisha did a final check of all her bags. She heard knocking at the door. When she answered the door she wished she hadn't. There stood the 6'3", muscular, coffee-colored skinned, good looking adult version of Welton, who Tylisha hadn't seen or heard from in six years. "Milton!"

"Tylisha, baby, how have you been?" Milton asked with the charm Tylisha fell for time and time again, when she was younger. But now she was six years older and wiser which made her immune to whatever bullshit Milton was on.

"What the fuck are you doing here?" Was Tylisha's first question. "Wait a minute! I got a better question. How in the fuck did you find my house?"

"That's not important," Milton said.

"The hell you preach!" *Thuy was right. This nigga must be high on some shit!*

"I wanna see my kids!"

Tylisha let out a laugh. "Oh, now you remember you got kids. Where the fuck was this memory when you tossed us out on our asses and moved that white bitch and her brats in our places?"

"I'm sorry, but you didn't understand what was going on in our marriage." Milton tried to make excuses.

"You need to get outta here and miss me with that bullshit explaination."

"I want my family back."

"Good luck with that," Tylisha smugly responded. "I've moved on with a wonderful man. Ayla doesn't know who the fuck you are and Welton hates the fuck outta your guts."

Milton rolled his eyes and said with spite, "So you got random niggas around my kids and turning them against me? Dad told me you would pull this shit!"

Bringing up his coon ass nigga daddy was the deal breaker for Tylisha. "Nigga, get your black ass outta my house!"

"No! I'm gonna stop you from turning my kids against me!" Milton protested.

"Nigga, you did that all by yourself," Tylisha calmly retorted.

"And that nigga better stay the fuck away from my kids!"

Macal walked into the living room to update Tylisha. "The kids are all ready and—" He saw Milton and his blood began to boil. "What the fuck are you doing here?" He hissed at Milton.

"Macal, stay the fuck out of this!" Milton demanded.

"Nigga, this is my sister and her kids. I'm already in it, motherfucker!" Macal defended and stood by Tylisha. "What you need to do is walk your ass out that door!"

Milton turned around to leave and said, "I'll be back."

"Bring your motherfucking ass back here and see what happens!" Macal threatened and slammed the door behind him.

"Just what I need," Tylisha sighed.

"You all right, Tylisha?" Macal asked and rubbed Tylisha's shoulder.

"I'll be okay."

"Don't let him get to you."

There was another knock at the door and Tylisha answered.

"Hey, baby," Enzo greeted Tylisha with a kiss. "Hey, Macal."

"What's up?" Macal greeted.

"Where's Amery?" Tylisha asked.

"Waiting in the van," Enzo answered.

"Kids, let's go!" Tylisha called out from the bottom of the stairs.

"Coming, momma!" Welton and Ayla replied.

"Next stop, New Orleans!" Enzo cheered.

Macal entered his hotel suite in New Orleans and tipped the bellhop. After he left, Macal laid down on the bed to rest from the long flight. As he laid in bed in silence, Thuy popped into his mind. He pulled out his phone and gave her a call. "Hey, Thuy."

"Hey, Macal," Thuy greeted him. "What's up?"

"Tylisha dragged me to New Orleans with her, Enzo and the kids for a week. They're celebrating Enzo's parents' wedding anniversary."

"For real? I'm on my way to New Orleans."

This is my lucky day! "Stop bullshitting!"

"I'm serious. I'm about to board," Thuy said. "I have to meet with two clients from the New Orleans Saints. A player from the New Orleans Pelicans is looking for a new agent. Also, I'm trying to sign these beautiful fraternal twin sisters who are like the Venus and Serena of gymnastics. I really want to represent these girls. They are so sweet and smart. What hotel are you staying at?"

"Windsor Court Hotel," Macal answered. "That's where Enzo's parents are having their party. He booked the rooms here for convenience."

"I'll check it out. What room are you staying in?"

"Room 252. After you get settled in, come to my room. I'll tell the front desk to give you a keycard."

"Thanks and I'll see you later."

"Looking forward to it. Bye." A smile appeared on Macal's face. Tylisha was right. He needed this vacation, and because of Thuy Ellis, this was going to be the best vacation ever.

Chapter 52

"See, I told you momma and dad would like you," Enzo said to Tylisha, and kissed her. They came back from dinner at Enzo's parents' house and everyone was heading to their rooms.

"They were nice," Tylisha said. "I think, in a way, Grandma Doris broke the ice."

"True," Enzo agreed. "They never forgot Mrs. Blair."

"This hotel is great. Thanks for the suggestion, Enzo," Macal said.

"I thought y'all would like it," Enzo said.

"There is so much to do here. I don't know where to start," Welton said with excitement.

"We have to check this place out," Amery said.

"Kids, if you're going to venture off, stay together, remember your room number and always have your keycards with you at all times," Tylisha addressed.

"Yes, momma," Ayla replied.

"If you can't reach me, Enzo or Uncle Macal, ask one of the hotel workers for help," Tylisha added.

Everyone bid each other goodnight and went to their rooms. Macal entered his room and made himself comfortable on the bed when he heard a knock at the door. "Hey, baby! "He greeted her. "You made it!"

"Of course, I did," Lolette said and kissed Macal.

Macal slapped her hard on the ass, and directed her with bold, sexy authority, "Get that ass in here! We got some serious fucking to do!"

"This is very nice!" Thuy soaked in her luxurious surroundings when she and the bellhop entered her suite on the third floor.

"Is there anything else I can help you with ma'am?" The bellhop asked.

"That'll be all." Thuy dug in her purse and pulled out twenty dollars to give to the bellhop. "Here you go."

"Thanks," the bellhop said and took his leave.

Thuy sat on the bed in her suite and grabbed the room phone to call Macal's room. She waited for an answer but didn't get one. She then pulled out her phone and called Macal's cell. When she didn't get an answer, she left a message on his voicemail.

"Hey, Macal. This is Thuy. I made it to the hotel. That meeting was longer than I thought. I tried calling your room but didn't get an answer. I picked up the room key from the front desk like you said, and now I'm on my way to your room. See ya."

"Oh, shit!" Macal grunted as he was hitting Lolette's pussy from the back.

"Ah! Shit!" Lolette panted and was holding on to the edge of the bed for dear life, loving every minute of Macal pounding her pussy with her ass in the air.

Macal's room phone rang. He ignored it and kept making Lolette's pussy sore and creamy. Lolette made her ass clap and took the dick like a champ. Then, Macal's smartphone rang.

"You want to answer that?" Lolette asked between moans.

"Fuck that phone!" Macal breathed out, feeling Lolette's pussy tighten around his dick, not paying attention to his phone on the nightstand that had Thuy's picture flashing on the caller ID.

Thuy took the elevator down to the second floor where Macal's room was. She walked down the hall, trying to find Macal's room.

"Thuy, is that you?" Tylisha asked when she saw her walk by.

Thuy turned around and saw Tylisha and Enzo, arm and arm, dressed to kill. "Tylisha! Enzo! What's up?" Thuy pulled them into a group hug.

"What brings you here?" Tylisha asked.

"Didn't your brother tell you? I'm here on business this week," Thuy answered. "Actually, we kind of surprised each other. He told me about this hotel and I decided to check it out for myself. Where are the kids?"

"Playing laser tag," Enzo answered. "We're heading out to check out some of the clubs."

"I'm trying to find Macal's room," Thuy said. "I know it's on this floor."

"Oh, it's down the hall. Make a right and it's the very first door on the left." Tylisha pointed down the hall to the left, giving Thuy the directions.

"Thanks, and have fun."

"See ya."

Thuy followed the directions and headed straight for Macal's room in all smiles. The closer she got to the door, the happier she got. Thuy couldn't wait to see Macal's face and continue their blossoming courtship. She felt like a little girl on Christmas morning. She approached his door and pulled the keycard out of her purse. She slid the keycard in the slot to unlock the door. She opened the door and...

To Be Continued...
Addicted to the Drama 2
Coming Soon

Stay Connected with Us!

Text **LOCKDOWN** to 22828 to stay up-to-date with new releases, sneak peaks, contests and more…

Thank you!

Coming Soon from Lock Down Publications/Ca$h Presents

BOW DOWN TO MY GANGSTA

By **Ca$h & Jamaica**

TORN BETWEEN TWO

By **Coffee**

BLOOD OF A BOSS **IV**

By **Askari**

BRIDE OF A HUSTLA **III**

THE FETTI GIRLS **III**

By **Destiny Skai**

WHEN A GOOD GIRL GOES BAD **II**

By **Adrienne**

LOVE & CHASIN' PAPER **II**

By **Qay Crockett**

THE HEART OF A GANGSTA **II**

By **Jerry Jackson**

LOYAL TO THE GAME **IV**

By **T.J. & Jelissa**

A DOPEBOY'S PRAYER **II**

By **Eddie "Wolf" Lee**

TRUE SAVAGE **III**

By **Chris Green**

IF LOVING YOU IS WRONG… **II**

Jamila

By **Jelissa**

BLOODY COMMAS **II**

By **T.J. Edwards**

A DISTINGUISHED THUG STOLE MY HEART **II**

By **Meesha**

ADDICTIED TO THE DRAMA **II**

By **Jamila Mathis**

Available Now

(CLICK TO PURCHASE)

RESTRAINING ORDER **I & II**

By **CA$H & Coffee**

LOVE KNOWS NO BOUNDARIES **I II & III**

By **Coffee**

RAISED AS A GOON I, II & III

By **Ghost**

LAY IT DOWN **I & II**

LAST OF A DYING BREED

By **Jamaica**

LOYAL TO THE GAME

LOYAL TO THE GAME II

LOYAL TO THE GAME III

By **TJ & Jelissa**

BLOODY COMMAS

By **T.J. Edwards**

IF LOVING HIM IS WRONG…

By **Jelissa**

A DISTINGUISHED THUG STOLE MY HEART

By **Meesha**

PUSH IT TO THE LIMIT

By **Bre' Hayes**

BLOOD OF A BOSS **I II & III**

By **Askari**

THE STREETS BLEED MURDER **I, II & III**

THE HEART OF A GANGSTA

By **Jerry Jackson**

CUM FOR ME

CUM FOR ME 2

CUM FOR ME 3

An **LDP Erotica Collaboration**

BRIDE OF A HUSTLA **I & II**

THE FETTI GIRLS **I & II**

By **Destiny Skai**

WHEN A GOOD GIRL GOES BAD

By **Adrienne**

A GANGSTER'S REVENGE **I II III & IV**

THE BOSS MAN'S DAUGHTERS

THE BOSS MAN'S DAUGHTERS II

A SAVAGE LOVE **I & II**

BAE BELONGS TO ME

A HUSTLER'S DECEIT I, II

By **Aryanna**

A KINGPIN'S AMBITON

A KINGPIN'S AMBITION **II**

I MURDER FOR THE DOUGH

By **Ambitious**

TRUE SAVAGE

TRUE SAVAGE II

By **Chris Green**

A DOPEBOY'S PRAYER

By **Eddie "Wolf" Lee**

WHAT ABOUT US **I & II**

NEVER LOVE AGAIN

THUG ADDICTION

By **Kim Kaye**

THE KING CARTEL **I, II & III**

By **Frank Gresham**

THESE NIGGAS AIN'T LOYAL **I, II & III**

By **Nikki Tee**

GANGSTA SHYT **I II &III**

By **CATO**

THE ULTIMATE BETRAYAL

By **Phoenix**

BOSS'N UP **I & II**

By **Royal Nicole**

I LOVE YOU TO DEATH

By Destiny J

I RIDE FOR MY HITTA

I STILL RIDE FOR MY HITTA

By **Misty Holt**

LOVE & CHASIN' PAPER

By **Qay Crockett**

TO DIE IN VAIN

By **ASAD**

BOOKS BY LDP'S CEO, CA$H

(CLICK TO PURCHASE)

TRUST IN NO MAN

TRUST IN NO MAN 2

TRUST IN NO MAN 3

BONDED BY BLOOD

SHORTY GOT A THUG

THUGS CRY

THUGS CRY 2

THUGS CRY 3

TRUST NO BITCH

TRUST NO BITCH 2

TRUST NO BITCH 3

TIL MY CASKET DROPS

RESTRAINING ORDER

RESTRAINING ORDER 2

IN LOVE WITH A CONVICT

Coming Soon

BONDED BY BLOOD 2

BOW DOWN TO MY GANGSTA

www.ingramcontent.com/pod-product-compliance
Lightning Source LLC
Chambersburg PA
CBHW071109250626
47159CB00002B/658

* 9 7 8 1 9 4 8 8 7 8 0 0 5 *